THE CATHERINE-WHEEL

The door was open. She looked into the passage and it was empty – empty and dark. But there was a light at the end where the stair went down. She went along as far as the landing and looked over the stair. The door of the little room halfway down was open and someone was coming out. It was Jeremy. That is what she thought when she saw him. And then she wasn't sure. His hair was much longer, and he looked so ill. His hands were pressed hard against his side, the blood ran between his fingers. He came out of the room and looked up at her standing there. She knew that he was going to die. She screamed, and the scream waked her.

Also by the same author

The Watersplash
Miss Silver Comes to Stay
Out of the Past
The Gazebo
Miss Silver Intervenes

and available in Coronet Books

The Catherine-Wheel

Patricia Wentworth

CORONET BOOKS
Hodder Paperbacks Ltd., London

Copyright © 1951 Patricia Wentworth
First published 1951 by Hodder & Stoughton Ltd
Coronet edition 1973

Printed and bound in Great Britain for
Coronet Books, Hodder Paperbacks Ltd,
St. Paul's House, Warwick Lane,
London, E.C.4
By Hunt Barnard Printing Ltd,
Aylesbury, Bucks.

ISBN 0 340 16952 4

To those readers who have so kindly concerned themselves about Miss Silver's health.
Her occasional slight cough is merely a means of self-expression. It does not indicate any bronchial affection. She enjoys excellent health.

P. W.

Chapter 1

JANE HERON took a few graceful gliding steps and came slowly back round the circle of watching women. Clarissa Harlowe's dress show was in progress, and she was showing a dress called Sigh no More. There was not very much of it above the waist, just a few opalescent folds, but the skirt was new and rather exciting. There were almost more yards of stuff in it than you would have believed possible, all coming in slim and tight to the waist, but they would swirl like spray in the wind when you danced. Jane lifted her arms in a movement which she contrived to make perfectly natural and took a few floating waltz steps. The skirt flew out. A woman close to her drew in her breath with a gasp. Another said, 'Heavenly! But I mustn't – I really mustn't.' Mrs. Levington raised her rather harsh voice and called across the room to Mrs. Harlowe, 'I'll have it – but you mustn't sell a copy for three months.' She turned as soon as she had spoken and beckoned to Jane.

'Come here! I want to see how it fastens.'

Jane came with the graceful submissive air which was part of the job. Inwardly she was thinking that Mrs. Levington wouldn't get into the dress by at the very least four inches. She wasn't fat, but she was solid – rather high in the shoulder, rather square in the hip. Handsome, of course, if you liked them that way. Jane didn't.

It wasn't her business to mind who bought Clarissa Harlowe's dresses – they were out of her reach, and always would be. She was there because her really lovely figure added at least twenty-five per cent to the price.

Mrs. Harlowe came up, brisk, businesslike, smartly tailored.

'That will be quite all right, Mrs. Levington. You can have a fitting tomorrow at ten thirty. No, I'm afraid I can't

7

make it any other time – we are very busy.'

Indifference bordering on rudeness, that was her line – 'Take it or leave it – we can do better than you.' It was astonishing how it went down. It went down with Mrs. Levington now. She accepted her appointment quite meekly. Jane was dismissed.

The dressing-room was full of clothes and girls. One of them went out as Jane came in, a lovely blonde in a thin black afternoon dress made incredibly distinguished by its cut and some clever skirt drapery. Jane took off Sigh no More and hung it up carefully. She had a feeling that she would never look so nice in anything again. It was only her figure that was beautiful. Her face was too small, too colour-less. When she looked in the glass she would see a pair of good grey eyes and quite a lot of dark hair, and that was about all you could say for Jane Heron apart from her figure. No one had any fault to find with that. It was slim without being thin. Everything about it was just right. Jane thought a lot of it, and well she might, since it provided her with the roof over her head and her daily bread and butter. It was a good biddable figure, too, not the sort you had to pander to and placate. She knew girls who went in daily fear of their hip measurement, and who simply didn't dare to look at a potato or a pat of butter. There was no nonsense like that about Jane's figure. If she ate chocolate and suet pudding for a year she wouldn't put on an ounce. Jeremy had given her a box of chocolates last week.

She turned round from hanging up Sigh no More and began to put on her own clothes. The show was nearly over – she wouldn't have to go through again. She slipped into a dark skirt, pulled a jumper over her head, and put on her coat. Everyone was trying to dress at once. She had to stand on one leg at a time to change the shoes she had worn for her own dark ones. All the girls were dressing now, chattering nineteen to the dozen. She managed to get the glass for a moment while she pulled on the small dark turban which went with her suit, and there she was – Cinderella after the last stroke of twelve – no features, no bloom, no colour, except for the lipstick which brightened her mouth. It was too bright really, but you had to make up a bit extra for a

8

show. Jeremy would look sideways and say things about pillar-boxes. Well, let him – she didn't care.

She came out on to the street and found it icy cold. It was going to freeze quite hard. She exchanged good-nights with Gloria and Daphne and took her way to the end of the street. Sometimes Jeremy met her there, but he wouldn't tonight because of the show. There just wasn't any saying how long it would go on.

She turned the corner, and he loomed up out of a doorway. It was heartening when you had been feeling like Cinderella. He slipped his hand inside her arm, and she said, 'Oh, you shouldn't have come!'

Jeremy Taverner said, 'Don't be silly! How did it go?'

'Two of my things sold. That puts my stock up.'

'The usual frightful women?'

'They're not all frightful.'

'I don't know how you stand it.'

'Well, I don't see there's anything else I could do which I shouldn't hate a good deal worse.'

'As?'

'Serving in a shop – nursemaid – companion – '

'There are lots of jobs for women.'

'Darling, I'm not trained for any of them.'

He said in an angry voice, 'Don't call me darling!'

'Did I?'

'You did. I don't like it.'

She laughed easily.

'It doesn't mean anything – one does it all the time. It just slipped out.'

He said still more angrily, 'That's why!'

The hand inside her arm gripped her quite painfully. She said, 'Darling, you're pinching me!' Then, with a sudden change of voice and manner, 'Don't be a tiresome toad, because I want to talk to you – I really do.'

In spite of being called a tiresome toad in the sort of voice which makes an intimate and flattering term of it, Jeremy remained angry.

'I don't see why you weren't trained for anything. Girls ought to be.'

'Yes, darling, but I wasn't. My mother married a more

9

or less penniless parson with his head in the clouds, and they never thought about it. They never had any time to think about anything, because the parish was much too big and poor. And they died when I was fifteen, and my grandfather took me in and sent me to the sort of school where they concentrate on your manners and don't bother about sordid things like earning your living.'

'Which grandfather?' said Jeremy in a different voice.

'Oh, the Taverner one – mother's father – your grandfather's brother – old Jeremiah Taverner's eighth child and sixth son. I know the whole lot off by heart. The eldest was Jeremiah after his father, and then there were Matthew, Mark, Luke, John, Acts, and the two girls, Mary and Joanna. Your grandfather was John, and mine was Acts. And if we hadn't met by accident six months ago at the dullest party on earth we shouldn't have known we existed. I mean you wouldn't have known I did, and I wouldn't have known you did.' She came up close, so that her shoulder rubbed against his arm. 'You know, the other six probably all left descendants too, and I expect most of them will have seen the Advertisement and answered it. I do wonder what they're like – don't you?'

Jeremy said, 'It must have been a whale of a family row.'

'Oh, I don't know – people drift away –'

'Not to that extent. My grandfather used to talk about his twin, Joanna, but I don't think he ever saw her. He was clever, you know – took scholarships, and got into one of these research laboratories. That's how my father came to be a doctor. He was killed in nineteen-eighteen. My mother married again and went to Australia, leaving me with the old boy. So we were both brought up by our grandfathers – Hi! There's your bus!'

They ran for it, and managed to scramble on, but it wasn't possible to go on talking. Jane was lucky, because the bus passed the end of her road. When they got off they had only to cross the street and go about a third of the way along Milton Crescent to No. 20.

She let herself in with her key and took Jeremy up three flights of stairs to the attic floor. There were two attics which had once been maids' bedrooms, and there was a boxroom and a bathroom. Jane had both the attics, and alluded to them as 'my flat'. The back one was the sitting-room. With the light switched on and the curtains drawn it always gave her a thrill, because it wasn't in the least what you would expect. There was an old walnut bureau, and two Queen Anne chairs with seats of Chinese brocade. A walnut mirror surmounted by a golden eagle hung above the bureau. There was a very good Persian rug, and a comfortable sofa heaped with many-coloured cushions. The oddly named Mr. Acts Taverner had, in fact, started life as a purveyor of second-hand furniture and finished up by achieving the kind of antique shop which provides its owner with a good deal of pleasure without bringing in a great deal of cash. Jane's furniture was what she had been able to salve from the sale.

'*Now*,' she said, turning round from the window. 'Put on the kettle, there's an angel — I'm dying for a cup of tea. And then I'll show you what I got this morning.'

Jeremy put a match to the gas ring and stood up.

'I know what you got — an answer from Box three hundred and whatever it was, because I got one too. I bought it along to show you.'

They sat down side by side upon the sofa and each produced a sheet of rather shiny white paper. The notes were headed Box 3093. One began 'Dear sir,' and the other 'Dear madam'. Jane's ran:

'Your answer to the advertisement inviting the descendants of Jeremiah Taverner who died in 1888 to communicate with the above box number received and contents noted. Kindly inform me of the date of your grandfather Acts Taverner's decease, and state whether you remember him clearly, and to what extent you were brought into contact with him.'

Except for a variation in the name the two letters were identical. Jeremy and Jane gazed at them frowning. Jeremy said, 'I don't see what he's getting at.'

'Perhaps he's writing a family history.'

'Why should he?'

'I don't know — people do. Let's write our answers, then perhaps we'll find out.'

His frown deepened.

'Look here, you'd better let me write.'

Jeremy, how dull!'

'I didn't want you to answer the advertisement.'

'I know – you said so.'

She jumped up and began to get out the tea-things – a dumpy Queen Anne teapot, two Worcester cups and saucers, one of them riveted, a dark blue lustre milk-jug, an engaging tea-caddy painted in pastoral scenes.

Jeremy said slowly, 'What does he want?'

'A family reunion, darling – all our cousins. Perhaps some of them will be rays of sunshine. You are not doing much in that line, you know, my sweet.'

He came over to her and stood there in a very up-in-the-air kind of way.

'I think you had much better drop it. I'll write if you like.'

Jane lifted her eyes. They held a definite sparkle.

'Perhaps you didn't hear me say, "How dull!" '

'Jane – '

'Well, I'm saying it again – dull, dull, dull – ditchwater dull.' Then she stepped back and tapped a warning foot. 'You wouldn't like me to lose my temper, would you?'

'I don't know – '

Dark lashes fell suddenly over the sparkling eyes. A little flush came up under the pale skin.

'I'm too tired.' Then, with a sudden change of manner, 'Oh, Jeremy, don't be a beast!'

Chapter 2

JACOB TAVERNER sat there, as thin as a monkey and with the same alert, malicious look. A good many different climates had tanned and dried his skin. He had kept his hair, and whether by luck or good management, it was not very grey. It wasn't dyed either. No hairdresser would have made himself responsible for its odd dried-grass appearance. His eyes behind the sparkle were hazel. For the rest, there wasn't a great deal of him. He had dropped an inch from his original five-foot-six. Arms and legs had a frail, spidery look. He wore the sort of old clothes which only a tramp or a millionaire would be seen dead in. He wasn't quite a millionaire, but he was getting on that way, and he was seeing his solicitor, Mr. John Taylor, about the disposition of his property. Not that he intended to die – by no means – but having managed to enjoy a great many different things in the course of his seventy years, he now intended to amuse himself with the always fascinating possibilities of will-making with a difference.

Mr. Taylor, who had known him for some forty-five years, knew better than to try and thwart this latest of many preoccupations. Sometimes he said, 'Certainly,' sometimes he said, 'I should advise you to think that over,' and sometimes he didn't say anything at all. When this happened, Jacob Taverner chuckled secretly and the malice in his eyes grew brighter. Silence meant disapproval, and when John Taylor disapproved of him he felt that he had scored, because John Taylor represented middle-class respectability, and when it was possible to give middle-class respectability a brief electric jolt he always enjoyed doing it.

They sat with the office table between them and John Taylor wrote. A pleasantly rounded little man with everything very neat about him, including a head very shiny and bald with a tidy little fringe of iron-grey hair at the back.

Jacob Taverner sat back in his chair with his thumbs in his waistcoat pockets and laughed.

'Do you know, I had fifty answers to my advertisement. Fifty!' He gave a sort of crow. 'A lot of dishonest people in the world, aren't there?'

'There might not be any dishonest intention – '

Jacob Taverner puffed out his cheeks, and then suddenly expelled the air in a sound like 'Pho!' Contempt for his solicitor's opinion was indicated.

'Taverner's not all that common as a name, and when you tack Jeremiah on to it – well, I ask you! "Descendants of Jeremiah Taverner who died in 1888" – that's what I put

13

in my advertisement. I had fifty answers, and half of them were just trying it on.'

'He might have had fifty descendants,' said Mr John Taylor.

'He might have had a hundred, or two hundred, or three, but he didn't have half of those who answered my advertisement. He had eight children – I'm not counting four that died in their cradles. My father Jeremiah was the eldest. The next five sons were Matthew, Mark, Luke, John, and Acts, and the two girls were Mary and Joanna. Mary came fourth between Mark and Luke, and Joanna was a twin with John. Well, there's quite a lot of scope for descendants there. That's what first put it into my head, you know. Old Jeremiah, he kept the Catherine-Wheel inn on the coast road to Ledlington, and his father before him. Up to their necks in the smuggling trade, they were, and made a pretty penny out of it. They used to land the cargoes and get them into Jeremiah's cellars very clever.' He chuckled. 'I remember him, and that's the way he used to talk about it – "We diddled them very clever". Well, he died in eighty-eight and he left everything to my father, his eldest son Jeremiah.' He screwed up his face in a monkey grimace. 'Was there a family row! None of them ever spoke to him again or had any truck or dealings with him. He let the inn on a long lease, put the money in his pocket, and set up as a contractor. He made a pile, and I've made another – and because of the family quarrel I can't make a decent family will without advertising for my kith and kin.'

Mr. John Taylor looked incredulous.

'You don't mean to tell me you don't know anything at all about any of them!'

Jacob laughed his queer dry laugh.

'Would you believe me?'

'No, I should not.'

'Jacob laughed his queer dry laugh.

'You don't have to. I know a thing or two here and there, as you might say. Some of them went up in the world, and some of them went down. Some of them died in their beds, and some of them didn't. Some of them got killed in both wars. Between the little I knew and what was in the fifty

14

letters, I've got them more or less sorted out. Now, to start with – my own generation don't interest me, and they're mostly gone. So far as my money is concerned you can wash them out. They've either made enough for themselves or they've got used to doing without. Anyway I'm not interested. It's the next generation, old Jeremiah's great-grand-children, that I'll be putting my money on, and this is what they boil down to. It's not the whole of them – you're to understand that. I've picked them over and I've sorted them out.'

'Do you mean you've been interviewing them?'

'No, I don't. I didn't want to be mixed up in it personally – not for the moment. As a matter of fact I've taken the liberty of using your name.'

'*Really*, Jacob!' Mr. Taylor looked decidedly annoyed.

His client gave that odd laugh again.

'You'll get over it. I haven't compromised you – only invited the ones I've picked to come and meet you here this afternoon.'

John Taylor tapped his knee.

'To meet me – not you?'

'Certainly not to meet me. I am the great Anon. as far as a personal appearance goes. You can give them my name, but I want to have a look at 'em before they have a look at me. You will interview them, and I shall lurk' – he jerked a scraggy elbow – 'behind that door. I shall hear without being heard. You will place nine chairs with their backs to me, and I shall be able to look through the crack and see without being seen.'

John Taylor leaned forward and said in a perfectly serious voice, 'You know, Jacob, sometimes I really do think that you are mad.'

He got a grimace and a burst of laughter.

'My dear John, I pay you handsomely to prevent anyone else saying so. Besides it isn't true. I have merely retained my youth, while you have become a fogy. It amuses me to gambol, to disport myself, to play tricks. I have a lot of money. What's the good of it if I don't make it amuse me? Well, I'm going to – that's all. And now, perhaps, you will let me get down to brass tacks and tell you about the people who are coming to see you this afternoon.'

Mr. John Taylor pursed his lips, pulled forward a sheet of notepaper, and took up a nicely pointed pencil. His manner showed resignation, with an underlying suggestion of protest.

Jacob let out one of his cackling laughs.

'All set? Well then, off we go! Taverner's the name – Geoffrey and Mildred – grandson and granddaughter of Jeremiah's second son Matthew – brother and sister – some where in their forties.'

John Taylor wrote them down.

'Got 'em? Now we come to the next brother, Mark. Granddaughter of his in the female line – Mrs Duke – Florence – Mrs. Florence Duke.'

John Taylor made no reply. He wrote down, 'Mrs. Florence Duke.'

Jacob rolled his eyes to the ceiling.

'Jeremiah's fourth child was a daughter, Mary. This is where we go up in the world. She ran away to go on the stage and married the Earl of Rathlea – old family, poor wits, twopence halfpenny in his pocket, and a tumbledown castle in Ireland. The family didn't know whether they were coming or going. First she disgraced them by going on the stage, and then they disgraced her by being in trade. One way and another there was no love lost, and what you might call a pretty clean cut. Well, Mary's gone, and the title's gone – last male heir killed in the war. But there's a grandaughter, Lady Marian Thorpe-Ennington.'

John Taylor looked up quickly.

'Lady Marian – '

Jacob nodded.

'Lady Marian O'Hara – Lady Marian Morgenstern – Madame de Farandol – Lady Marian Thorpe-Ennington.'

'My dear Jacob!'

Jacob Taverner grinned.

'Famous beauty – or was. Lively piece by all accounts – varied taste in husbands. Married Morgenstern for his money – no one could possibly have married him for anything else – and he diddled her out of it.'

'I remember. The will made a sensation. He left every-

16

thing to charities – and a secretary.'

'Bit of a sell for my cousin Marian. She married a young de Farandol after that – racing motorist – got himself killed just before the war. Not much money from him. Now she's married to Freddy Thorpe-Ennington whose father's pickle factory has just gone smash. She hasn't had much luck, you see. And now we come down in the world again. The next son, Luke – well, there are quite a lot of his descendants running around. Luke wasn't what you'd call respectable – he took to the roads and died in a workhouse. But one of his daughters married a railway porter at Ledlington, and they had one son. I've picked him. His name is Albert Miller, commonly called Al.'

'What made you pick him?'

John Taylor's tone was mildly interested. He was prepared to maintain, professionally, to all comers that Jacob Taverner was not legally mad. A man who has amassed nearly a million pounds can be allowed his eccentricities. In his private capacity, John was interested to see how these eccentricities worked, and how nearly they might be said to approach the borderline.

Jacob withdrew a pin from the lapel of his shocking old jacket and made small stabbing passes with it in the air.

'Wrote the names on a bit of paper, shut my eyes, and prodded at 'em. Didn't want more than one or two out of any line. The pin went right into Al at the first go, clean through the M in Miller, so I took him. It's a good pin. Do you know how long I've had it – forty-five years. And when in doubt I've always shut my eyes and pricked, and it's never let me down once. Never lost it but once, and I thought I'd have gone off my head. Dropped in my own office, and they said they couldn't find it – slipped out of my hand as I was sticking it back into my coat, and they said they couldn't find it. I had every man jack of 'em up, and I said, "Man, woman, or boy, who finds that pin gets ten pounds, and if it isn't found, everyone gets the sack." A matter of two hours afterwards a smart boy comes along and says he's found it. I took a look at the pin he brought and I said, "I've no room for fools in my office. You can get out and you can stay out".'

'Why was he a fool, and how did you know it was not your pin?'

Jacob cracked his fingers.

'How do you know your children from anyone else's? When you've lived with anything for forty-odd years, nobody's going to take you in. And he was a fool because he brought me a brand-new pin out of a packet. Thought himself smart, and all he got was the sack.'

'But you did get it back?'

Jacob put the pin carefully into his lapel.

'I paid a blackmailing young woman five hundred pounds for it. I'd have paid double. She thought she'd scored me off, but I got back on her. Nobody's ever scored me off and got away with it – nobody. It's too long a story to tell you now. We've done the descendants of Matthew, Mark, Mary, and Luke, and now we come to the twins, Joanna and John. We'll take Joanna first. Her lot is interesting. She married a man called Higgins, and a daughter of hers married a man called Castell – Fogerty Castell – Portuguese father, Irish mother. And I've picked a Higgins grandson, John Higgins – carpenter by trade – bit of a local preacher in his off time. Well, I've picked him, and I've picked the Castells. I said I wasn't going to have anyone in my own generation, but they are the exception that proves the rule. I've picked 'em because they'll be handy. Now for number seven, John. I've got his grandson, Jeremy Taverner – regular soldier – Captain Jeremy Taverner. Then there's number eight, Acts – old Jeremiah took all his children's names out of the Bible – I've picked a granddaughter of his, name of Jane Heron. She's in a shop – tries on the dresses and walks round in 'em so the fat old women and scraggy old maids think they're going to look like she does. There's twice at least this afternoon you've called me mad, John Taylor, but I'm not so mad as the women who go to dress shows and buy the clothes off a girl with a figure they probably never had and certainly don't have now. Well, that's the lot, and I'm off into the next room. Here's the family tree to keep you straight. By the way, the Castells won't be coming. I've my own private arrangement with them, and they're down at the Inn. The others are just about due. Amusing to see

18

who comes first, don't you think? Might be the one that's hardest up – but then sometimes that sort's proud. Poverty, greed, or maybe just plain punctuality – any one of the three might bring 'em here on the dot. Now you get those chairs set out so that I can look and listen, and you ask 'em what I told you to ask 'em, and tell 'em what I told you to tell 'em. And the devil take the hindmost!'

Chapter 3

A YOUNG clerk opened the door and announced, 'Miss Taverner – '

Mildred Taverner took a poking look at the room with its nine empty chairs and came in rather after the manner of an early Christian entering the arena. To be sure, John Taylor would have hardly fluttered the nerves of the most timid martyr, but Miss Taverner became immediately so tied up in explanation and apology that it is doubtful if she noticed his round face, his bald head, or any of the other features which might have had a reassuring effect.

'Oh, dear – I didn't know I was going to be the first. Do you mean to say nobody else has come? I had no idea – I mean I expected my brother – he telephoned and said to be here punctually at the half hour. Nothing annoys him so much as to be kept waiting, and I do try, but it's so difficult. Unless my watch should happen to be running fast – it does sometimes when the weather is warm, but not on a day like this. And I know I am five minutes late, because I broke a shoe-lace just when I was starting, so I didn't expect to be the very first.' She put a limp hand into John Taylor's, and he noticed that she was wearing odd gloves, one being black and the other navy blue. The black one had a hole at the top of the first finger.

As she took one of the nine chairs she dropped her hand-bag, from which there immediately cascaded a bunch of

19

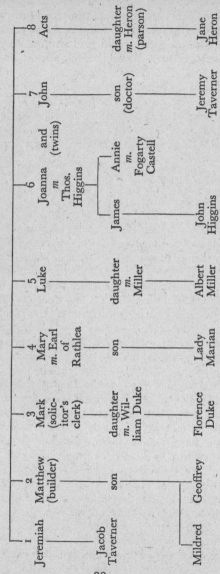

JEREMIAH AND ANN TAVERNER'S EIGHT CHILDREN

1 Jeremiah — Jacob Taverner

2 Matthew (builder) — son — Geoffrey — Mildred

3 Mark (solicitor's clerk) — daughter m. William Duke — Florence Duke

4 Mary m. Earl of Rathlea — son — Lady Marian

5 Luke — daughter m. Miller — Albert Miller

6 Joanna and (twins) m. Thos. Higgins — James — John Higgins / Annie m. Fogarty Castell

7 John — son (doctor) — Jeremy Taverner

8 Acts — daughter m. Heron (parson) — Jane Heron

keys, a pocket comb, a pair of nail-scissors, a bottle of aspirin tablets, three pencils, a couple of crumpled bills, and a rather dingy handerchief. She said, 'Oh dear!' and crammed everything back in an agitated way and without any attempt at arrangement, so that the bag bulged and at first refused to shut.

John Taylor contemplated the performance in an interested manner. He hoped Jacob was getting a good view. He wouldn't have picked Mildred Taverner himself, but then of course he didn't know what Jacob was picking these relatives for. Miss Taverner appeared to be about forty-five years of age. She had a long, stringy figure, she poked with her head, and her fingers were all thumbs. Her fair reddish hair reminded him of Jacob's. It had the same brittle look, and it stuck out at odd angles under a very unbecoming hat. Her rather colourless blue eyes avoided him. They were set under colourless brows in a long, pale face. She wore a navy-blue coat and skirt which had a general air of having belonged to somebody else. The skirt dipped at the back, and the coat rode up in front. Her neck was encircled by a wispy scarf of pink and blue checked wool.

Having taken all this in, he smiled pleasantly and said, 'Well now, Miss Taverner, this is excellent. We can make a good start before the others arrive.' He took up the family-tree, upon which there appeared the names of Jeremiah Taverner's eight children and their descendants, and consulted it. 'Mr. Jacob Taverner wishes me to run over a few points with each of you. You are descended from – '

'Oh, yes, my grandfather was Matthew – the second one. The eldest was Jeremiah, after his father.' She bridled a little, caught his eye, and immediately looked away. Oh *dear*, yes – I know all about the family tree. Old Jeremiah had eight children and he died in eighty-eight – Jeremiah, Matthew, Mark, Mary, Luke, Joanna, John, Acts. And Matthew is our grandfather – my brother Geoffrey's and mine. He was a builder and contractor, and he did very well – quite rich, and very much respected, though a Nonconformist – I, of course, am Church of England. Oh, yes, my grandfather left a very good business, but my father was unfortunate.' She sighed and adjusted the wispy scarf. 'We were in quite reduced circumstances after his death, so I joined a friend in a fancy work shop at Streatham. Geoffrey didn't like it very much, but what was there to do? I wasn't called up in the war, because I have always had a weak heart. Of course Geoffrey is so clever – you have to be in the Civil Service.'

The door opened and Geoffrey Taverner came into the room.

Looking through the chink which he had thoughtfully provided, Jacob Taverner inspected his cousin Geoffrey. Like his sister, and yet not so like after all. They were both fair, thin, and forty, but the sister looked like a bit of chewed string, whereas the brother would pass for a good-looking man. He was a few years the younger. Where she drooped, he was well set-up and well tailored. As he came up to the desk, his expression changed from one of formal but courteous greeting for John Taylor to a definite flicker of annoyance as his eye fell upon his sister.

She broke at once into explanation and apology.

'I quite thought you would be here. I had no idea of coming in by myself – I was really quite upset when I found I was the first. Of course, as Mr. Taylor kindly said, some-one has to be – but I wouldn't have gone in, only I was delayed just as I was starting, so I thought I was late. My watch –'

Geoffrey Taverner said in a repressive tone, 'Your watch is always wrong.'

He took a chair and addressed Mr. Taylor.

'I don't quite know why we have been asked to come here. I answered an advertisement asking the descendants of Jeremiah Taverner who died in eighteen-eighty-eight to communicate with a certain box number, and after a brief interchange of letters my sister and I were invited to come here this afternoon. My first letter went, as I say, to a box number. The reply which I received had no signature, and I must say at once that I should like to know with whom I am dealing.'

'Certainly, Mr. Taverner. You are dealing with me.'

'And you represent?'

'Mr. Jacob Taverner, who is the son of Jeremiah Taverner's eldest son, Jeremiah.'

Geoffrey appeared to consider this. After a moment he said, 'Very well – I'm here. What about it?'

John Taylor balanced a pencil.

'My client informs me that you have satisfied him as to your identity.'

'He has had copies of our birth certificates and of my parents' marriage certificate – yes.'

'I am instructed to ask for a few further particulars. You are, I understand, the grandson of Matthew Taverner, Jeremiah's second son.'

'That is so.'

'Do you remember him?'

'I have already been asked that. I said I did. I was about twelve when he died. My sister was older.'

'I remember him very well,' said Mildred Taverner. 'He had a very bad temper before he had his stroke, but he was much nicer afterwards. He used to tell us stories about the old inn and give us peppermints out of a tin – the striped bullseye kind.'

The young clerk opened the door again, began to murmur inaudibly, and was swept aside. There came in a bright presence and a faint delicious waft of expensive French scent. Something very tall, very elegant, very feminine advanced with a vague but radiant smile. Dark blue eyes with incredible lashes came to rest upon John Taylor. A deep musical voice said, 'I'll have to introduce myself – Lady Marian Thorpe-Ennington. Nobody ever gets it right the first time, and I'm sure I don't wonder. I'm always telling Freddy he ought to drop one of the bits, but he says he can't, in case the relations who might be going to leave him money have their feelings hurt and cut him out of their wills. So I just have to go about explaining, and spelling it. There's an E at the end of the Thorpe, and two Ns in Ennington.' She sank gracefully into a chair. 'And now do tell me – is it you I've been writing to?'

As she moved away from the door, a lank, uncertain figure appeared from behind her. It was a male figure, and it looked very uncomfortable in an awkwardly cut blue suit

23

– too tight, too light, too jaunty. John Taylor, perceiving it, made a shot in the dark, 'Mr Miller?'

Al Miller said, 'That's right.'

He had a cap in his hand and kept turning it and plucking at it in a manner extremely likely to shorten its life. He stood long enough to enable Jacob Taverner to see how nervous he was, and that he had dank hair with too much grease on it, a set of dark irregular features shining with perspiration, and a most distressing tie. All at once he seemed to realise that he was the only person standing, and came down suddenly on the edge of a chair, where he produced a brightly-coloured handkerchief and mopped his brow.

He was still doing so when Jeremy Taverner and Jane Heron arrived together.

Behind his chink Jacob Taverner grimaced. He didn't see they were going to be much use to him, but of course there was no saying. If at first you don't succeed, try, try, try again. They were the youngest of the party by some years. He had seen all their birth certificates and he knew. The Lady Marian woman was thirty-seven. Didn't show it of course, and wouldn't for the next ten years, if then. She was a looker all right – he'd give her that. Complexion out of a box, but quite a good skin underneath. Good hair – you didn't often see that bright chestnut shade. Good teeth, and not spoilt with smoking like threequarters of the women's were nowadays. Fine figure of a woman – good curves. He liked a woman with curves himself, but he thought she'd have to watch her weight when she got into the forties. He hummed to himself inside his mind:

'There will be too much of me
In the coming by and bye.'

Al Miller, he'd be about thirty. Bit of a fish out of water, and a wet fish at that. Young Jeremy Taverner and him cousins – comic when you came to think of it. Good-looking fellow young Jeremy – credit to the family. Twenty-seven he'd be – or was it twenty-eight? No, twenty-seven. And the girl, Jane Heron, would be twenty-two. Graceful girl – very

24

good figure – she'd have to have that to be a mannequin. Not much to look at otherwise – little pale face – scarlet lipstick – rather good turn of the head – dark hair – plain dark clothes.

He cocked an attentive ear, and heard Lady Marian say, 'My grandmother – Mary Taverner? Oh, yes, of course I remember her. I'm supposed to be exactly like her. She ran away, you know, and went on the stage, and married my grandfather. We've got a portrait of her at Rathlea, and everyone says I might have sat for it.' She turned a radiant smile upon the room as if she were collecting applause.

John Higgins received the full impact as he opened the door. It put a slightly bewildered look into his very bright blue eyes. She had looked right at him and smiled, but now she looked away. She was talking to the gentleman behind the desk. He stood where he was and waited for her to be done. Her laugh floated out.

'She was a great beauty, and my grandfather adored her. But an awful warning all the same, because when I remember her she weighed about sixteen stone. *And she didn't care.*' The words were heavy with drama. 'Fatal of course – quite fatal. Because there's nothing like worry to keep you thin – and it's so difficult to worry, isn't it?' There was the least, faintest touch of Irish on the last word. The beautiful eyes went here and there, for sympathy this time. 'She never could worry, and nor can I. She lived to be ninety, and I suppose I shall too. Marvellous stories she used to tell me about her acting days and all.'

John Higgins stood there looking and listening. He couldn't possibly have put it into words, but she gave him the kind of feeling you got when the sun first came to having any strength in the spring. He wouldn't have known what to say about it, but you can know a lot of things you don't know how to say. He didn't say anything, he just stood with those very blue eyes fixed on her, and the thick fair hair which wouldn't lie down no matter what you did to it standing up in a shock all over his head, which was a couple of inches above that of anyone else in the room. Jacob, looking through his chink, put him at six-foot-three, and young Jeremy somewhere between six foot and six-foot-one.

Marian Thorpe-Ennington was still talking when the door handle rattled and the door bounced open. The woman who came in looked big and tall even by John Higgins. She had fine eyes, a lot of dark hair, and the sort of bright, fixed colour which takes a lot of toning down. She was handsome still, but her looks were coarsening. Her dress did nothing to conceal the fact – a royal blue coat and skirt, a white lambskin coat with a plaid lining, a cheerful scarf with a scarlet overcheck, and the sort of hat which you can't get away with unless you are young and slim. She looked all round her, said, 'What – am I the last? Well, good afternoon, all!' and came up to the table.

Mrs. Duke – Florence Duke – that's me – Floss to my friends. I'm Mark Taverner's granddaughter – old Jeremiah's third son. Solicitor's clerk he was. Never made much of a living, but always very kind to us children. I had two brothers killed in the war. My father died when I was a baby. He was a clerk too – William Duke – so we lived with my grandfather.' The words came out one after the other like bubbles rising in oil, not fast but steadily.

Jacob thought, 'She'd be a hard woman to stop if there was anything she wanted to say.'

John Taylor put the same question to her which he had put to the others.

'You remember your grandfather, then.'

'Remember him? I should say I do! I don't know what we'd have done if he hadn't taken us in, because my mother was delicate. I was too as a child, though you wouldn't think so to look at me now, would you?' She gave a deep rich laugh. 'Small for my age too, and so thin I looked as if you could blow me away. Well, it only shows there's hope for all – doesn't it?'

She showed magnificent teeth as she laughed again.

Then her colour deepened. She held her head well up and said, 'If you're thinking about my name – Duke I was born, the same as you'll see if you've got a list of us all, as I suppose you have.'

John Taylor said, 'Yes.' He wondered what was coming.

She went on speaking in her deep, deliberate voice.

'Ellen Taverner was my mother, and William Duke was

my father, so Duke I was born. And Duke is what I've gone back to. I married, and I got a bad bargain, so I went back to my own name that I didn't have any reasons to be ashamed of. My grandfather was dead by then, and I went behind the bar to keep myself. And there's nobody can say a word against me – I've got nothing to hide. I've a little business of my own now, a snack bar, and doing well.' She looked from one to another, not aggressively but with a large tolerance. 'There you are. It's best to say what's to be said and be done with it to my way of thinking, then nobody can cast it up at you afterwards that you weren't straight with them. That's all.'

She gave John Taylor a smile and a nod, and went and sat down between Jeremy and Al Miller. As she did so, John Higgins came slowly up to the table and gave his name.

'I got a letter telling me I was to call here.' He spoke slowly with a pleasant country accent.

John Taylor observed him with interest. There was a puzzled frown between the blue eyes.

'That's quite all right, Mr. Higgins. Just where do you come into this family tree?'

'Well,' – the big work-roughened hands took hold of each other – 'well, sir, my grandmother Joanna, she was one of the twins. Joanna and John they were, boy and girl. And Joanna Taverner, she married my grandfather, Thomas Higgins, head carpenter on Sir John Layburn's estate. Son and daughter they had, James and Annie. James was my father, so that's where I come in. Annie, she took and married a foreigner, name of Castell. Is that what you want, sir? I don't know that there's any more I can tell you, except that I'm a carpenter too, like my father and grandfather before me.'

John Taylor looked him up and down.

'You served in the war, I suppose?'

The blue eyes looked straight back at him.

'Mine-sweeping, sir. They let me do that. It was clean against my conscience to kill.'

He went back to the last vacant chair and sat down beside Jane Heron. Marian Thorpe-Ennington turned her smile upon him, and then allowed it to travel from one end of the line of chairs to the other.

'And we're all cousins,' she said in a voice thrilling with interest. 'We've none of us ever seen each other before, but we're all cousins. All our grandfathers or grandmothers were brothers and sisters, but we don't know anything about each other. Well, I mean to say, it's divine, isn't it? Such a bore to grow up with one's relations, but too wonderful to meet them all ready-made.'

'I think some of you know each other,' said John Taylor, 'Captain Taverner, Miss Heron – I think you do, don't you? Now may I just take down your particulars? Ladies first – '

Jane Heron opened her grey eyes rather widely. A little colour came into her cheeks.

'My grandfather was the youngest. His name was Acts.'

Chapter 4

JACOB TAVERNER was getting bored. He had heard enough – most of it stale stuff which he knew already. 'Your grandfather was John – your grandmother was Joanna – you are in this, that, or the other – ' It was all as dull as a parish meeting. No zip about John Taylor – no go, no sparks flying. He wanted to put his own fingers into the pie and stir it up his own way. He thought he had stood behind the door long enough. He pushed it open, walked in, came round in front of the line of chairs, and said, 'Better introduce me, John.'

John Taylor said, 'This is Mr. Jacob Taverner,' whereupon Jacob walked down the line and shook hands with them all. Some of the hands were hot, and some were cold. Mildred Taverner, Lady Marian, and Jane Heron wore gloves. Florence Duke had taken hers off and stuffed them into a gaping pocket. Geoffrey, Jeremy, and John Higgins rose to their feet. Al Miller sat uncomfortably on the edge of his chair and said, 'Pleased to meet you.' Geoffrey's hand was dry and cold – a thin hand, stronger perhaps than it looked. Al Miller's was so damp that Jacob had no scruple about taking out a cheap brown pocket handkerchief and drying his fingers before offering them to Jeremy Taverner's casual clasp. John Higgins had a warm hand and firm grip.

Jacob noticed everything – that Jane's gloves had seen a good deal of service – that Mildred Taverner had a hole in one of hers, and that the right hand didn't match the left – that Marian Thorpe-Ennington's clothes had cost a packet. A mouthful of a name, an armful of a woman. It would have surprised him very much to hear that she paid her bills.

When he had finished shaking hands he came over to the writing-table and sat informally on the far corner, so that by pivoting slightly he could command his whole audience from John Taylor to Jane Heron. Sitting like that with the cold afternoon light striking in and chilling everything, he really bore an astonishing resemblance to an organ-grinder's monkey. His legs dangled, a shoulder hunched, the bright malicious eyes went from one to another. They made Mildred Taverner fidget with the cotton thread which stuck out an inch from the torn fingertip of her glove, too long not to be noticeable, too short to break off. They made Al Miller mop his brow again. Jane Heron said afterwards that they made her feel as if she was something in a cage being poked at.

It was the affair of a moment. When he had finished looking Jacob said.

'Well, here we all are, and I don't mind betting it's a case of a lot of minds with but a single thought, as the poetry book says. And if you're wondering where I ever read poetry, I'll tell you. Everybody gets top marks for thinking it's not my line. But I once broke a leg on a coral reef. There was a trader took me in, the only white man on the island, and the only mortal book there was in his hut was a thing that called itself Beeton's Great Book of Poetry. Don't ask me where he got it, or why he kept it – he never looked inside it himself. But before I was through I pretty well knew it by heart. I even made some up myself, so you see what I

29

was up against. And to come back to the bit I said just now, what you're all thinking at this moment is, "What has he got us here for?" and, "Why doesn't he come to the point?" '

Marian Thorpe-Ennington fixed her beautiful eyes upon him and said, 'But you're going to now, aren't you? Because of course we're simply dying to know why you advertised. You're not going to let us down, are you? I mean of course you didn't say that we were going to hear of something to our advantage, but naturally one hoped – and when Freddy said it would all turn out to be a do, I told him he was the most utterly unbelieving person, and what was the good of always expecting the worst? I mean, it's too sordid, isn't it? But then of course he's feeling terribly jaundiced, poor lamb. Because of the pickle factory, you know – too completely on the rocks. And what we are to live on, I can't imagine! Freddy says there won't be enough to buy bread, let alone butter – but then, of course, he does worry so, poor sweet. I don't, because what's the use?'

By the time she had finished there was a general feeling that everyone had received a personal confidence. A kind of glow was diffused. Even Al Miller got his share of the warm glance and throbbing voice.

Jacob Taverner waited for her to talk herself out. He was, in fact, enjoying himself. When the last note died upon a fascinated silence he observed drily.

'I'm afraid I can't substitute for the pickle factory. But – ' He made quite an impressive pause, let a swift mocking glance travel over them all, and went on, 'Well, we'll come to that in a minute.'

Mildred Taverner, picking at her glove, had broken the cotton off short, with the disastrous result that another inch of the seam had come undone. She made a small vexed sound and slipped her left hand in the torn black glove under her right in the navy blue which was what she had meant to put on, because the black pair were really not fit to be seen, though she could of course cobble them up and make them do for the household shopping. A glove never looked the same after it had been mended.

Her brother Geoffrey gave her a cold, quelling look.

Jacob Taverner went on.

30

'I have asked you all to come here because I want to make your acquaintance. All your fathers and mothers were my first cousins – the nephews and nieces of my father, Jeremiah Taverner the second. I want to make your acquaintance. When my grandfather, old Jeremiah Taverner, died there was a first-class family row because he left every blessed thing to my father. Any of you know why?'

Quite a bright blotting-paper pink came up into Mildred Taverner's face. She said in an unnaturally high voice, 'It was most unfair! My grandfather always said so!'

Al Miller rubbed his hands together, rolling the handkerchief between them.

'So did mine. He said it was a right-down shame.'

Jacob's mouth twisted.

'I believe there was complete unanimity on that point. It was the only one on which the rest of the family did see eye to eye. The very minute they'd got over telling my father what they thought of him for taking his legal rights, they started a first-class dog-fight over their mother's money.'

Florence Duke said in her deliberate way, 'There wasn't any to speak of.'

He gave his cackling laugh.

'That's just why. Throw one bone in amongst half a dozen dogs and see what happens! As you say, it wasn't a very big bone, and by rights – mark this – by rights it had to be divided among the whole eight children. But my father didn't claim his share. I don't say it was handsome of him – I'm just stating facts. He left his mother's belongings to be divided up among the other seven.'

'Wills are so tiresome,' said Lady Marian in her delicious voice. 'Freddy's father left a simply dreadful one.'

Geoffrey Taverner moved impatiently.

'Just what was there to divide?'

'Nothing to write home about. There was a cottage with a bit of land to it, a few pieces of jewelry, and five hundred pounds in Consols. Matthew, Mark, Luke, John, and Acts, they each got a hundred pounds. Mary and Joanna got a brooch and a bracelet or so apiece, and Joanna got the cottage. She was just going to marry your grandfather' – he addressed John Higgins – 'and when they'd all fought themselves to a standstill and Thomas Higgins had put down another twenty pounds, they took a fiver each out of it and let her have the cottage. Mary didn't come into it, because she was married to Lord Rathlea and safe away on the other side of the Irish Channel. Well, after that there wasn't much love lost. Matthew did well out of his money. He bought a couple of old cottages and doubled his capital on them. House-coping – that was his job.' He glanced maliciously at Geoffrey and Mildred. 'No need to be offended – my father was in the same line. Mark – respectability was his middle name – country solicitor's clerk to the end of his days. Whilst Mary was an ornament to the Peerage, and Luke – well the less said about Luke the better.'

'Why can't you let him alone?' said Al Miller. His dark skin did not seem to be susceptible to a flush. Anger turned him sallow. He rolled the brightly coloured handkerchief between sweating palms.

Jacob laughed.

'All right, all right – least said soonest mended. Joanna lived and died in her cottage in a state of rural felicity. John went up in the world – made a ladder of his brains and climbed. And Acts worked up from rags and bones, figuratively speaking' – he bowed to Jane – 'to quite a nice little antique shop in Ledborough. And there we are.'

Geoffrey Taverner said, 'Very clear and succinct, but I don't know that it gets us anywhere. I think we should all like to know why we have been brought here.'

'Naturally. Now I hope – I really do hope you haven't all been buoyed up with the idea of hearing something to your advantage.'

Marian Thorpe-Ennington sighed in a dramatic manner.

'But of course we have, my dear man. I said to Freddy at once, "Things simply can't go on being as foul as they've been ever since we got married. I mean, if there's a silver-lining, it's simply bound to show up some time, isn't it? And why shouldn't it be now?" I said that at once. But he's so gloomy about the whole thing, the poor sweet, and no wonder, having to go to these dreadful creditors' meetings. That's why he couldn't be here this afternoon. And he simply hated my coming alone, because he always thinks I'll do something stupid. But, as I told him, "There will probably be hordes of us there, and probably some of them will be quite bright people, so it won't depend on me".' She sighed again, even more deeply. 'You don't really mean to say that there isn't going to be anything at all?' Her voice went down into really tragic depths.

Jacob said, 'Well, well –' And then, I'm afraid you may all be rather disappointed. I have asked you here for three reasons. I thought the family quarrel had gone on long enough. I haven't made any ties, and I thought it would be interesting to get to know my kith and kin. For which purpose I want to invite you all to pay me a visit at the old family Inn.'

John Higgins's blue eyes turned on him.

'Twas sold when great-grandfather died, the old Catherine-Wheel.'

Jacob said, 'Ah, but it wasn't. My father never sold it, though I daresay it was put about that he had – I don't say he didn't put it about himself. He gave a lease, and the lease ran out last year, so it's back on my hands, with the Castells running it. Mrs Castell being your father's sister – Joanna's daughter, born Annie Higgins.'

John Higgins said slowly, 'I knew my Aunt Annie was there. It's ten years since I saw her.'

'And you not a mile away in the cottage Joanna got for her share of her mother's property?'

'Yes, I'm in the old cottage.'

'Married, or single?'

A slow smile gave charm to the impassive face.

'There's something you didn't know? Seemed you knew everything. I'm single, and I do for myself. And I haven't seen my Aunt Annie for ten years, though she's living but a mile away.'

Jacob nodded.

'Very interesting. United family, aren't we?'

John Higgins shut his mouth firmly. He sat with a big hand on either knee, quiet and unembarrassed. Jacob said.

'The inn is the Catherine-Wheel on the old Ledlington coast road. Nearest station Cliff Halt – a mile and a half. I'm inviting you all to come and stay with me at this next weekend. Some of you may not find it easy to get away – you may have to engage extra help – you may find it difficult to get leave of absence – you may be put to inconvenience or expense. You will therefore each receive the sum of one hundred pounds as, let us say, some recognition that your grandfathers and grandmothers were shabbily treated under old Jeremiah's will, and that in inviting you for this visit I don't want to put you to any further inconvenience.' He stopped rather abruptly, crossed his right leg over his left, leaned sideways with his hand on the leather-covered table-top, and watched them.

Geoffrey Taverner had a slight frown. Mildred's scarf had slipped, she pulled at it with small ineffectual jerks. Florence Duke's rather heavy features had taken on a look of severity oddly at variance with their previous expression of tolerant good nature. Al Miller had an eager, startled air. John Higgins sat as he had done all through, large, fair, placid, self-contained. Jane had her eyes very wide open, and her lips parted. Her hands held one another tightly in her lap. Jeremy looked angry. The only one to speak was Marian Thorpe-Ennington. She said, 'My dear man – how marvellous!'

'You'll come then?'

'But of course. You do mean Freddy as well, don't you? He won't like it if you don't, and the poor sweet is so upset already.'

Jacob nodded curtly.

'He can come.' He turned to Geoffrey Taverner. 'You can get away? You sister said you were in the Civil Service.'

Geoffrey looked annoyed.

'My sister was inaccurate – she very often is. I resigned some time ago – I am now in private employ. I could manage the weekend you mentioned.'

'And you, Mildred?'

He smiled maliciously at the nervous start which sent her handbag to the floor and once more exposed its contents.

Jacob took in the whole assembly with a dancing gleam of malice and proceeded.

'Since we are all cousins, I propose that we should address one another without handles. Plain Christian names will be

34

sufficient until intimacy warrants some affectionate contraction. But I am afraid I startled Mildred. I apologise. I was merely about to enquire whether she could get away for the weekend.'

Miss Taverner clasped and reclasped the errant bag. A piece of the handkerchief stuck out. It was the one she had intended to put into the wash before she came out. 'Oh dear, oh dear – ' She sought for words in very much the same way as she had fumbled for the overflow from her bag.

'Oh, yes – oh dear – I'm so sorry – the catch should be seen to, but there never seems to be time. My partner, Miss Millington, will take charge, and we always shut on Saturday afternoons. I'm sure it's very kind.' her lips continued to move as they repeated soundlessly, 'Oh dear – a hundred pounds – oh dear, oh dear, oh dear – '

Jacob dismissed her with a nod.

'And you, Florence?'

She gave him the same straight, bold look as she had done before.

'Yes. I'll come. I'd like to see the old place. I've a friend that comes in to give me a hand when I'm pressed, and I don't open Sundays. She'll manage.'

'And you, Al Miller? Let me see you're a railway employee aren't you – Ledlington Station – porter?'

'That's right. I could get off Saturday evening.'

'Jacob nodded.

'The Inn is only three and a half miles out of Ledlington. You've got a bike, I take it. You can come along when you come off duty. That suit you?'

Al Miller thought, 'What's he getting at? A hundred pounds would suit anyone, wouldn't it?' He jerked his head and said it suited him all right.

Jacob said, 'Well, we're getting along. Marian has already told us that she and Freddy can come. Now what about you, John?'

John Higgins said in his pleasant country voice, 'No, thank you, Cousin Jacob.'

The monkey face screwed itself into a vexed grimace.

'My dear chap, why not?'

'I've my reasons, thanking you all the same.'

'Come, come – there's a hundred pounds just waiting to be picked up.'

The blue eyes rested calmly upon him.

'If I'd a good reason for coming, I'd come. Since I've my reasons for staying away, I'll stay.'

'And the hundred pounds?'

'You're welcome to it, Cousin Jacob.'

Jane found her hands clapping themselves together softly in her lap. She looked sideways at Jeremy and saw that he was extremely angry. It was all very nicely controlled, but she didn't trust him a yard. If she didn't take things into her own hands, he was going to put his foot down, or something stupid like that. She reflected that men were quite dreadfully Early Victorian. In point of fact she didn't suppose there had ever been a century in which they didn't throw right back to the cave man and announce that their will was law. Not really civilised, that was the trouble. She gave him a look and said without waiting to be asked.

'I'd love to come, Cousin Jacob. It's frightfully nice of you to ask us. I get Saturday afternoon and Sunday off, but I shall have to be back at half-past nine on Monday.'

Jeremy had a rush of blood to the head. He experienced some primitive reactions. Bounce him, would she? Well, he would show her. And if she thought – if she thought for one minute that he was going to let her go off with this gang and without him to that God-forsaken inn with its shady past and Lord knows what kind of a present, well –

Jacob Taverner was addressing him.

'And you, Jeremy?'

H eanswered with controlled politeness.

'Thank you, sir. I am on leave – I shall be able to come.'

Chapter 5

WHEN they had walked half the length of the street Jane smiled sweetly at an unresponsive profile and said, 'Thank you, darling.'

In a distant voice Captain Jeremy Taverner enquired what she was thanking him for.

'Coming down to the Catherine-Wheel as my chaperon, darling. Having always been accustomed to being wrapped up in cotton wool and sheltered, I do appreciate it. You know that, don't you?'

There was a fair imitation of a flash of lightning accompanied by a smart clap of thunder.

'Just stop talking nonsense, Jane, and listen to me! You can't possibly go!'

'Why can't I possibly go? I am going.'

'You can't – with that gang.'

'No, darling. With you.'

She distinctly heard Jeremy grit his teeth.

'Jane, you can't possibly want to get mixed up with that appalling crowd.'

'They're all the relations we've got.'

'Thank the Lord for that! What a crew!'

Jane's tone warmed a little.

'Jeremy, they're not! You're being a snob. I love John Higgins – he's a lamb.'

'And he isn't going to be there – he's got too much sense. Do you love Al Miller?'

'Not frightfully.'

'Or Geoffrey – or Mildred?'

'Geoffrey might have possibilities. I wouldn't mind exploring them.'

The teeth-gritting was repeated. Jane said hastily, 'On the chilly side though, don't you think? But I rather like Floss-to-my-friends. And Marian – now don't tell me you don't think she's beautiful because I simply shan't believe you.'

37

He made an angry sound.

'I should think she has probably less brain than anything outside a home for the mentally deficient.'

Jane wrinkled her nose.

'Well, I don't know. I think she's got a pretty good idea of which side her bread is buttered.'

'That isn't brains – it's primitive instinct. I grant you she's probably got plenty of that.' His voice changed. 'Jane, stop playing the fool and tell me why you want to go to this damned place.'

She looked up at him with wide, clear eyes.

'Darling, it's too easy. I want that hundred pounds.'

'Jane!'

She mimicked him sweetly.

'Jeremy!' Then she laughed, but when she spoke again her voice was serious enough. 'Don't you realise I've never had a whole hundred pounds in my life before? It's the most marvellous thing that's ever happened.'

'You can't take it!'

'Watch me!'

'Jane – '

'Don't be silly, darling! You don't know what it means. I was ill for six weeks last winter, and I hadn't a penny saved. The insurance money doesn't go on for ever – I began to have nightmares. I didn't know I'd got a relation in the world then. Quite apart from the money, that's why I'm not prepared to go all snob about them like you when they do turn up. I'm going to make friends with them. And I'm going to have my hundred pounds and put it into the Post Office Savings Bank for a nest-egg. So there!'

He put a hand on her arm.

'Jane – why were you ill?'

She said with a touch of defiance, 'Because I hadn't proper shoes, or a warm coat, or enough to eat.'

'Why hadn't you?'

'Because I wasn't in a regular job – just odd dress shows and things. And I had to keep up my insurance, or I'd have been sunk. I just couldn't afford another time like that, and I'm not going to have one. I'm going to have all my kind relations – *and* my Cousin Jacob's hundred pounds.'

Jeremy said nothing at all. She could feel him withdrawing silently behind his frontiers. That she had heard the last of Jacob Taverner, his invitation, and his hundred pounds was so unlikely that she gave it no consideration at all. That he had retired in order to marshal his forces and would presently march upon her with horse and foot, bombs and flame-throwers, was reasonably certain. He might be intending to wait until he had her alone, or he might just pounce with annihilating effect on the top of a bus. She decided on going home by tube, where the facilities for pouncing would be fewer as long as you kept up with the crowd and avoided being marooned with your adversary in an underground passage.

After one or two light-hearted remarks which were received in complete silence she resigned herself and occupied the train journey in sorting out and polishing her own armoury of weapons. Because two things were quite certain. Whatever Jeremy said or Jeremy did, two things were *quite* certain. She was going to go down to the Catherine-Wheel and she was going to have that hundred pounds.

All the way home and all the way upstairs he never said a word. She drew the curtains, she put on the kettle, she laid the table and got buns out of a tin. Jeremy propped the mantelpiece in abstracted gloom until his right trouser leg began to singe at the gas fire, when he came across to her, took a knife out of her hand, laid it down on the table, and said, 'Will you marry me?'

Jane felt as if someone had lifted her up and dropped her again, all very suddenly. Her voice came odd and breathless.

'No – of course not – '

He appeared to be undeflected.

'What's the good of saying "No – of course not," when you haven't given it the least thought? You just blobbed that out without thinking. It's a business proposition, and you've got to think it all out before you say no. And before you can think it out at all you've got to listen to me properly.'

Jane said, 'Oh – ' And then, 'How do I listen to you properly?'

'You sit down on that sofa.'

'And have you somewhere up in the ceiling talking down

on the top of my head? No, thank you!'

'I sit down too. I'm going to turn off the gas under the kettle first, because we don't want to have it boiling over whilst I am proposing to you.'

Jane gave a sort of gasp and sat down. Not so much because Jeremy told her to as because her knees were wobbling and he might think –

She sat down. When he had turned out the gas he came and sat down beside her. He was frowning deeply, and began at once in a businesslike voice.

'I haven't got a great deal to offer you, but they don't kick you out of the Army unless you're pretty bad, and there's a pension. I get a pension when I retire, and you get one if anything happens to me, and if we have any children, they get something till they're eighteen – or twenty-one – I'm not sure which, but I can find out.'

'Jeremy, how frightful! Do stop!'

'It's not frightful at all – it's provision. And you ought to be listening instead of making frivolous objections which put me out. Then I've got three hundred a year private means.'

Jane gazed at him with respect.

'How on earth did you get it?'

'My mother had two hundred, and my grandfather had a life insurance which brings in the rest. It's not a lot, but it's safe, and it makes a lot of difference to have something besides your pay.'

'Jeremy – *please* –'

He frowned her down.

'I do wish you would listen. I think you'd like the life. There's rather a lot of moving about, but you see places, and everyone's very friendly. Anyhow you'd have proper shoes and enough to eat. And you wouldn't have to try on other people's clothes for a lot of desiccated vultures to gloat over.'

Jane looked sideways from between her lashes.

'They're not all desiccated, darling. Some of them bulge.'

He said quite violently, 'It revolts me! It ought to revolt you. I want you to chuck it up and let me look after you.'

Jane gazed down at her hands. There seemed to be something odd about them – they were a long way off. She said in a small obstinate voice, 'I can look after myself.'

'You think you can … girls always do. But they can't. Anyhow you're not going to.'

Jane lifted her eyes.

'Who says so?'

'I do, and you do. How much notice do you have to give your Mrs. Harlowe?'

'I'm not giving her notice.'

'I don't see any sense in a long engagement.'

'We are not engaged.'

He turned a rather daunting look on her.

'You're just being deliberately obstructive.'

She shook her head, and then wished she hadn't, because it made the room go round.

'I'm not. You've been asking me to marry you. I'm saying no.'

'Why?'

'You don't love me – I don't love you – cousins oughtn't to marry.'

He looked away for a minute, and then back again.

'Why do you say that?'

'Because it's true.'

He gave rather a curious laugh.

'That I don't love you? Jane, you're not really a fool – you know perfectly well.'

'I don't. Why should I? You've never said so.'

'I love you like blazes, and you know it.'

Jane said, 'Oh!'

He put his hands on her shoulders. They felt hard and heavy.

'Do you love me? Come along – be honest!'

Jane said, 'No – ' She said it three times in a voice that dwindled until it made no sound at all, because every time she said it Jeremy kissed her. The last kiss went on for quite a long time.

When he lifted his head he said, 'Liar!'

Jane said nothing at all.

41

Chapter 6

CHIEF DETECTIVE INSPECTOR LAMB rose from behind his office table and shook hands with Miss Maud Silver. As always when they met, there was a ritual of polite enquiry.

'I need not ask if you are well, Chief Inspector.'

He had his jovial laugh for that, a sign, if one had been needed, that the proceedings were to be of a not too formal nature.

'My health doesn't trouble me, I'm glad to say.'

'And Mrs. Lamb? I trust she has not felt the inclement weather.'

'She's too busy being a grandmother.'

Miss Silver beamed.

'Ah – Lily's boy – little Ernest. Called after you, is he not?'

'Fancy your remembering that! Well, what do you say to a granddaughter as well? A month old yesterday – little Lily Rose. Pretty, isn't it?'

Miss Silver thought it very pretty indeed.

Detective Inspector Abbott, who had ushered her in and now stood waiting to offer a chair, regarded this interchange with affectionate sarcasm. Lamb's three daughters were the pride of his heart and the surest way to it. But Miss Silver had no ulterior motive, her interest was genuine and perennial. She was now enquiring after Violet, who had a good job at the Admiralty.

Lamb shook his head.

'Just engaged again. My wife says it won't last. She's a pretty girl and a good girl, but she doesn't know when she's well off, and that's a fact. When she's got a young man she thinks she'd like to have a job, and when she's got a job she thinks she'd like to get married. Wants to eat her cake and have it.'

'And Myrtle? Is she still training for a nurse?'

Lamb looked gloomy.

'Yes, she's training, and kept pretty hard at it. My wife says it's too much for her. The fact is, she's our youngest and we miss her in the home. Well, take a chair, Miss Silver. I know you're always ready to help, and there was something I thought perhaps you'd be willing to do for us – privately and without any formality, if you know what I mean. So I thought if we could just have an informal talk – '

Miss Silver seated herself. Her pale, neat features displayed a polite degree of interest. Everything about her was neat, old-fashioned and rather shabby. A breadth of olive-green cashmere showed beneath the black coat. A bunch of brown and yellow pansies, the gift at Christmas of her niece Ethel Burkett, had replaced the purple ones with which her black felt hat had started its career. She wore black knitted gloves, and a tippet of yellowish fur, friend of many years standing, encircled her neck – so warm, so cosy. She settled herself without hurry, arranged an elderly handbag on her lap, and gazed at the Chief Inspector with just the right degree of deference.

'Well,' he said, 'let's get down to it. We've generally met over a murder case, haven't we? This isn't anything so violent, but I think perhaps you might be able to help us. It isn't as if your name had ever got into the papers. Of course you're known to the police, if I may put it that way, but I don't know that outside of two or three people there's been anything that would make you, so to speak, a suspected character so far as the criminal classes are concerned. In other words, speaking generally, I don't think they'd be on to you.'

He was watching her all the time he spoke, wondering if she would take the job or not. Behind a massive façade his mind worked shrewdly. He leaned back in his chair, hands folded at his considerable waistline – heavy, square hands with capable fingers. The overhead light picked out the thinning patch in the strong black hair, and showed up the florid colour in the broad face. The brown eyes bulged a little. Frank Abbott in his irreverence allowed himself to be reminded of peppermint bullseyes.

Miss Silver said, 'Yes?' on an enquiring note.

Lamb brought himself forward with a jerk, leaned across

the table, and said, 'Smuggling.'

Miss Silver looked reproof. During her youth she had been engaged in what she herself called the scholastic profession. It had often stood her in good stead that she looked and talked like an old-fashioned governess. She said, 'Indeed?'

'There's a lot of it going on, you know – bound to be with the customs so high – and in the ordinary way it wouldn't come to us. No, there's more in it than that. First of all there's drugs. Of course we're always up against that, because as long as people will pay a fancy price for their stuff the drug-runner will stick at nothing to get it to them. Now there's a place we've had our eye on for some time – an old inn on the coast road beyond Ledlington. March – let me see, you know March, don't you? He's the Chief Constable down there now. Used to be a pupil of yours, didn't he?'

Miss Silver smiled.

'A long time ago, Chief Inspector.'

'Oh, well, we don't any of us get any younger. He's done pretty well for himself, hasn't he? Does you credit. Well, as I was saying, March has had his eye on this place for some time. It's got an old smuggling history. Then it changed hands. Recently it's changed again – come back to the family that used to own it. But the manager has stayed on. Nothing in that, you may say – nothing against the man, except that he's half Irish, half Portuguese.'

Frank Abbott gazed down into the fire. Lamb's dislike of foreigners never failed to amuse.

The Chief Inspector allowed a bulging gaze to rest for a moment upon his profile, and continued in a louder voice and with a quite portentous frown.

'That's not his fault, of course, and nothing aginst him so long as he behaves himself. He's a British subject, and he's got an English wife. Nothing against either of them. That's the trouble. There's nothing March can get his hands on to anywhere, but there's a kind of feeling about the place – it may be just the old smuggling history, or it may be something new. Well, that's as far as the drug business goes, but now there's something more. All these jewel robberies – you'll have seen about them in the papers – it's not so easy for them to get the stuff out of the country, because everything's being watched. We got just one small shred of a clue after the Cohen affair the other day. You remember old Cohen woke up and fired at the men. He hit one of them, and the others carried him off. We were pretty hot on their trail, and they left him for dead by the side of a country road. We picked him up, and he wasn't dead – not then – but he died before we could get him to hospital. He was muttering to himself. One of the constables had his wits about him and listened. He couldn't make head or tail of most of it, but he did get two words, and he had the sense to report them. They were, "old Catherine". Well, the inn on the Ledlington road is called the old Catherine-Wheel.'

There was a silence. Miss Silver looked thoughtful.

Frank Abbott had not sat down. He stood against the mantelpiece, tall, slim and elegant; his dark suit faultlessly cut, his handkerchief, his tie, his socks, discreet and beautiful; his fair hair mirror-smooth. No one could have looked less like the hardworking efficient police officer that he was. He had a cult for Miss Silver, at whose feet he was content to sit, and a sincere and affectionate respect for his Chief, but neither of these feelings prevented him from considering that their encounters had a high entertainment value.

Miss Silver coughed and said, 'In what way do you think that I can assist you?'

Lamb said bluntly, 'You could go and stay at the inn.'

'On what pretext? It does not sound quite the kind of hotel for a lady travelling alone.'

Lamb gave his jovial laugh.

'Oh, we'll make that all right. Now look here, there's something very odd going on. The man who owns this inn is Mr Jacob Taverner, and he's the grandson of old Jeremiah Taverner who owned it in its smuggling days. About three weeks ago there was an advertisement in all the papers asking the descendants of Jeremiah Taverner to apply to a box number. We followed it up because we were taking an interest in the Catherine-Wheel. The advertisement was put in by Jacob Taverner, and out of the replies he received he has picked out eight people, and he has asked them down to the Catherine-Wheel for this next weekend. What we would like to know is, "Why?"'

Frank Abbott turned his cool, pale eyes upon the Chief Inspector.

'He may be just throwing a party,' he said.

'March says none of the Taverner family have been on speaking terms with each other since anyone can remember. The only exceptions are Luke Taverner's descendants. Luke was old Jeremiah's fourth son and an out-and-out bad lot. He left quite a lot of scallywag disreputable children and grandchildren, most of them with no right to his name. March says they turn up in every shady business in the county. The only legitimate and fairly reputable one is a young fellow called Al Miller who is a porter at Ledlington station, and he's none too steady – likely to lose his job, March says. Well, one of the other lot is barman at the Catherine-Wheel. Nothing against him, but he comes of bad stock. If you could get into the inn whilst this family reunion is going on you might tumble to something. What I'd like is your opinion on the Taverner family circle. If I may say so, that's where you come out strong – you get the feeling of people.'

Miss Silver gazed at him with mild attention.

'Who are they?' she enquired.

Lamb opened a drawer and rummaged.

'Where's that paper, Frank? Oh, you've got it. There you are, Miss Silver. Geoffrey Taverner – travels for a firm called Hobbs and Curtin – all sorts of jims for making housework easy – perfectly respectable people. His sister, Mildred Taverner – old maid running a fancy work shop. Mrs. Florence Duke – a snack bar on the Portsmouth road. Lady Marian Thorpe-Ennington, sister of the last Earl of Rathlea – first husband Morgenstern the financier – he left all his money to somebody else – second husband Farandol, the French racing motorist who smashed himself up about two years ago – now married to young Thorpe-Ennington just going into bankruptcy. That's four of them. Then we have the one I was telling you about, Al Miller, railway porter – they took him back after he was demobbed, but they're not over anxious to keep him. Next, John Higgins, carpenter on Sir John Layburn's estate not more than a mile and a half from the old inn – very high character locally, steady

46

religious kind of chap. And for the last two, Captain Jeremy Taverner, regular soldier, and Miss Jane Heron, mannequin. Nice mixed bag.'

Miss Silver gazed mildly at the sheet of paper with all these names on it and said, 'Dear me –'

The Chief Inspector laughed.

'You're wondering how they'll mix over a weekend. Well, there's one that won't. John Higgins won't go near the place, though he's said to be sweet on a girl who works there and an aunt of his is married to the manager, Castell. The girl is Castell's niece or something. Regular family affair, you see.'

Miss Silver coughed.

'I was wondering why Mr Jacob Taverner should have asked all these people for the weekend.'

Lamb sat back easily.

'Well, you know, there mightn't be anything in it at all. He's a rich man, and he hasn't anyone to leave his money to. So far as the police are concerned, he's got a clean sheet. I don't suppose he's sailed any nearer the wind than a lot of other people who have got away with it and made their pile. He may be wanting nothing more than to have a look at his relations and make up his mind which of them he'll put into his will. That's one possibility. There are others, of course. Maybe he's got a finger in the smuggling pie. Maybe he thinks a family party wouldn't be a bad cover-up for anything that might be going to happen down that way. Maybe he's just got interested in the family history. I don't know, but I'd like to. I want these people sized up, and when it comes to that kind of job – well, we all know you're a wonder at it.'

Miss Silver smiled graciously, but with restraint. A truly excellent man, the Chief Inspector, but sometimes just a little inclined to be patronising. At such moments she was apt to, as it were, recede and become the governess again. Lamb may or may not have felt a slight touch of frost upon the air.

Miss Silver coughed, glanced at the paper in her hand, and addressed him.

'Is Miss Jane Heron young?'

He nodded.

'Yes, bit of a girl – mannequin. Not the sort of job I'd like one of my girls to take on, but there's nothing against her. She and Captain Taverner are said to be sweet-hearting.'

'I believe that I have met her. Some months ago at a friend's house. An attractive girl, and quite young.' She spoke in a meditative tone.

Frank Abbott allowed himself to smile.

'There!' he said. 'What more do you need? We can't offer you a murder, but a love affair with a nice girl in an invidious position should really do almost as well.'

Her glance reproved him.

'Murder is much too serious a thing to make jokes about.'

Lamb said a thought impatiently, 'Well, well, that's true enough. But there's not question of murder. Will you do it? Frank here suggests driving you down. He's got a cousin with a place close by – one of his fancy relations with a handle to his name. He fetches them up like rabbits out of a hat. Beats me where they all come from.'

Frank's fair eyebrows rose.

'Too easy, sir. My great-grandfather had nineteen children. They all married and had large families.'

Lamb grunted.

'Well, this particular cousin's name is Challoner – Sir John Challoner, if you please – and he lives not a mile and a half down the road from the Catherine-Wheel. Frank's idea is – well, he'd better explain it himself.'

Frank Abbott passed a hand over his immaculate hair.

'Well, I drop you at the inn and go on and stay with Jack Challoner. I'm there on the spot quite nice and handy. If you want me you ring up Ledstow 23, and they pass it on, upon which Jack and I drop in for a drink. As far as you're concerned, I lurk until I'm really sure that you've got in. They'll be pretty full up, and they probably won't want strangers. On the other hand, if there's anything illegal going on, they won't want to draw attention to themselves by repelling the bona-fide traveller. Now just how bona-fide can we contrive for you to be?'

Miss Silver coughed.

'My dear Frank, there should be no difficulty about that,
The truth is always best.'

'The truth?'

Miss Silver smiled benignantly.

'I shall ring the bell and say that a gentleman very kindly
gave me a lift and recommended their hotel.'

The Chief Inspector's eyes bulged a little. Frank permitted himself to laugh.

'And what exactly are you doing getting lifts and arriving
after dark at strange hotels? It's going to look funny, isn't
it?'

Miss Silver beamed.

'I tell the simple truth – I have a professional engagement
in the neighbourhood.'

Chapter 7

THE week between being interviewed by Jacob Taverner
and travelling down to Cliff was of a very variable emo-
tional temperature as far as Jeremy and Jane were concerned. It was, in fact, like some of our more versatile
weather forecasts, including gales, bright intervals, frost in
places, and fog locally. There were some sharp clashes, a
major quarrel, a reconciliation which was not without its
softer passages. But in the end there was not very much real
change in their relations, since Jeremy continued to disapprove of the whole Taverner connection and proposed
marriage as an alternative to acquiring what he described as
a lot of riff-raff cousins, and Jane continued to observe with
varying degrees of firmness that it wasn't any good his
putting his foot down, that she meant to have her hundred
pounds, and that everyone said cousins oughtn't to marry.

When the Saturday afternoon arrived there was what
might be described as a fine interval. Since Jeremy possessed a car known to his friends as The Scarecrow, they

were going to drive down to the Catherine-Wheel, and it did seem a pity to waste a fine afternoon quarrelling. As Jane pointed out, Jeremy would probably make himself frightfully disagreeable over the weekend, and there was no point in taking the fine edge off his temper before they got there.

'It would be a pity if you ran out of frowns and things half way through Sunday just by being extravagant with them now.'

Jeremy said briefly that he wasn't in the least likely to run out, after which he suddenly burst out laughing, kissed her before she had time to stop him, and informed her that he would probably be the life and soul of the party.

'Wait till you see me putting down cocktails in the bar with dear Geoffrey and our attractive cousin Al! When I'm well and truly lit I shall make love to Call-me-Floss. When just on the edge of passing out I may even get as far as whispering rude nothings in dear Mildred's maiden ear. I say, what do you think she'd do if I really did?'

'Drop her bag and blush a deep pure puce.'

'Well you watch me!'

Jane giggled.

'You'd better watch yourself. Either Mildred or Floss might feel that they'd like to get about and see places with the Army.'

They were driving down the Great West Road. A pale winter sun shone overhead. The sky was turquoise blue, the air fresh without being cold. Jeremy took his left hand from the wheel and flickered Jane lightly on the cheek.

'I shall be protected by our engagement.'

'We're not engaged.'

'Darling, you can't refuse to protect me. There shall be no misunderstanding. We shall advance hand-in-hand into the bar and announce that we are affianced. The clan will then drink our health in bumpers of synthetic port, after which we shall all expire, the family ghost appearing when we are at the last gasp to mutter, "You had been warned".'

Jane put her chin in the air, but the corners of her mouth quivered.

'We are not affianced. And if it's going to be fatal as quickly as that – '

'Darling, I have a plan. We will pour the lethal draught on to the aspidistra, then everyone else will expire, and we will run the family pub. What shall we do with it? It's had a shady past, so I think we might give it a decorated future.' What shall it be – a gambling hell, or a dope den?'

Jane said primly, 'I was very nicely brought up. I once got a good conduct prize. It was a bowdlerised edition of *The Vicar of Wakefield* with all the bits about lovely woman stooping to folly cut out. I think we'd better make it a tea-garden.'

'Jane, you can't have tea in a garden in England – at least hardly ever.'

'You don't. You have a sort of leaky verandah – only it sounds better if you call it a loggia. The rain drips down your neck and the earwigs get into your tea, but it gives you a nice out-for-the-day sort of feeling, and if the cakes are really good, you just can't keep people away. I make frightfully good cakes. Gramp said I had a natural aptitude. He said I'd inherited it from his mother who was the world's best cook. He made me have really good lessons.'

Jeremy took his hand off the wheel again. It caught hers and held it in an ecstatic clasp.

'When can we be married? I can't wait! I knew that you were lovely and talented, but what's that to the solid worth of a really good cook?'

They went on talking nonsense very comfortably.

The daylight was fading when they passed through Ledlington and took the long flat road out of it which runs through Ledstow to the coast. It is a seven-mile stretch, but the old coast road takes off just short of Ledstow and bears away to the right. It is quite easy to overshoot it, because it isn't much used and the trees have grown in and made it narrow. After a mile the ground rises. There are no more trees, and the hedges are low and bent by the wind off the sea. Cliff is quite a small village, and very few trains stop there. That the railway passes it at all is due to the fact that the land was Challoner property, and at the time the railway was built Sir Humphrey Challoner was someone to be reckoned with. He had married an heiress. And he represented Ledlington in Parliament.

As they ran through Cliff and out at the other side, Jeremy slowed down and looked about him.

'What is it?'

He said, 'Nothing. I just wondered – there's a place my grandfather used to talk about here. As a matter of fact I know the man it belongs to now – Jack Challoner – a very good chap. It's a frightful white elephant of a place. It ought to be somewhere along here. Well, I'd better be lighting up.'

A moment later the headlights picked out two figures walking in the road – a girl with a handkerchief over her head, and a big man, bare-headed with a shock of fair hair. Their arms were linked.

Jane exclaimed, 'It's John Higgins! Jeremy, I'm sure it is! Do stop! Perhaps he's coming after all – they might like a lift.'

Jeremy said, 'I shouldn't think so.'

But he ran slowly past them, drew up, and got out.

'John Higgins, isn't it? I'm Jeremy Taverner. Jane Heron and I are on our way to the Inn. Can we give you a lift?'

Jane arrived in a hurry.

'I do hope you are coming.'

'That's nice of you, Miss Heron, but – why, no.'

'Oh, but you mustn't call me Miss Heron, when we are cousins.'

She could just see that he was smiling and shaking his head. The girl holding his arm spoke up. She had a very pretty voice with something like the ghost of a brogue.

'Miss Jane Heron?'

Jane saw her pull at John Higgins's sleeve. He said, 'Yes,' and turned to Jane.

'This is Eily Fogarty. You'll be seeing her at the Inn. She's related to Mr Castell. My Aunt Annie brought her up.'

'We're terribly short-handed,' said the pretty lilting voice.

Jane could see no more of her than the oval of the face, with the handkerchief hiding what seemed to be dark hair and tied under the chin. There was an effect of charm, but perhaps that was just because she had such a pretty voice.

If John Higgins had not seen his Aunt Annie in ten years, he semed to manage to see his Aunt Annie's *protegée*. The little bare hand never let go of his arm. Jane thought it would be a nice strong arm to hold on to. She said, 'We'd love to give you a lift if you'd like one.'

John Higgins said, 'Would you, Eily?'

The hand plucked at his sleeve. Jane saw him smile.

'Thank you, Miss Heron, but I think we'll have our walk.'

Just as they reached the car Jeremy went back.

'What was that for?' said Jane when he returned.

'I thought I'd ask John about the Challoner place. He says the entrance is about a hundred yards farther on.'

Her little quick frown of surprise came and went unnoticed in the dusk.

'You're very interested in the Challoners, aren't you?'

Jeremy said nothing. He was watching for a pair of tall stone pillars. When they loomed up he slowed the car right down. They hardly broke the encroaching darkness. Iron gates held the space between. Something like an eagle topped the right-hand pillar. The left-hand capital was broken and the bird gone. A few stunted trees and huddled shrubs made a black background. Jeremy whistled and said, 'Poor old Jack!' And then, with a laugh, 'Better him than me.'

Chapter 8

THE old Catherine-Wheel looked up on the edge of the cliff like a bank of cloud. Someone had set a lantern on the wide flagstones in front of the door. There was something dazzling about the circle of light in what was now a dusk so deep as to be more bewildering than actual darkness. There was moss between the flagstones. One of them was cracked in a black jagged line running cornerways. The crack glistened under the light as if a snail had crawled there. The house stood up, an irregular bulk.

53

Now that they were out of the car, the sound of the sea came to them. They stood on the cracked flagstone. Jeremy pulled the bell. Almost at once the door was opened. The man who stood back from it appeared in sihouette against the light of an oil lamp which hung from the ceiling. Jeremy looked, frowned, and said, 'Miller, isn't it – Al Miller?'

And then, as the man turned and the yellow glow struck across the right side of his face, he wasn't so sure. There was a very strong likeness, but this man had a different manner – hardier, bolder, more assured. He was wearing a waiter's grey linen jacket. There was the least trace of a laugh in his voice as he said, 'No, I'm not Al. The name is White – Luke White.'

Jeremy remembered that Luke Taverner had left assorted offspring unrecognised by the law. This was probably some irregular descendant come home to roost. The whole thing took on an added shade of fishiness as he grasped Jane by the arm and followed Luke White along an extremely narrow passage. Jeremy had the idea that it might have been convenient in the smuggling past. It was noticeable that the narrowness had, as it were, been ministered to and increased by such things as a very large stand for coats and hats and a great awkward chest. Where a flight of rather steep stairs ran up, the passage widened into a small hall with doors opening to left and right. The right-hand door was ajar, and from the room beyond there came the sound of voices. Luke pushed the door and stood aside to let them pass.

They came into a fair-sized, fusty room with curtains drawn, oil-lamps adding their flavour to a smell compounded of old drinks, old smoke, old heavy furnishings. There was an immense stuffed fish in a glass case over the mantelshelf flanked by two very large blue china vases. There were framed oleographs of Queen Victoria and the Prince Consort. There was a long table with drinks.

Jacob Taverner sat on the arm of a chair by the fire with a glass of whisky and water in his hand. The entire cousinhood were assembled, and in the midst of them stood Mr. Fogarty Castell, diffusing an aroma of cigars and extreme gratification at this happy reunion of his wife's relations.

Jane and Jeremy were barely allowed to greet Jacob before Fogarty had them each by a hand.

'Captain Taverner – Miss Heron – I cannot at all express how delighted I am! My wife's relations are my relations. Ah – not to intrude, you understand. No, no, no, no, no – a thousand times – but to welcome, to serve, to entertain, to offer the hospitality of the house. What will you drink – Miss Heron – Captain Jeremy – on this auspicious occasion? You are the guests of our friend Mr Taverner – everything is on the house. A whisky-soda – a pink gin – a cocktail? I make the very good cocktail.' He gave a deep-throated chuckle. 'There is one I call the Smugglair's Dream. You will try it – yes – please? Very appropriate, do you not think, since this was a great haunt of smugglairs a hundred years ago. It is a joke – not? I will tell you something, my friends. If you have a shady past, do not cover it up – make a feature of it. Here are your Smugglair's Dreams. As for my wife, your Cousin Annie, accept for the moment my excuses. We are very short-handed – she is in the kitchen. Oh, but what a cook! What a fortune to marry a woman who cooks like Annie Castell! Is it any wonder that I adore her?' He spoke over his shoulder to Luke White. 'Where is that Eily? Send her to me quick! The ladies will wish to go to their rooms. Where is she?'

'Not in, guvnor.'

'Not in? Why is she not in?'

'Mrs. Castell sent her out for somethin' she wanted.'

Jane and Jeremy stood back and watched. The round beaming face with its dark skin and small bright eyes had changed like a landscape overtaken by storm – darkness suffused by anger. The fat, paunchy body balancing jauntily upon small carefully shod feet had become taut. He looked as if he might do some barbaric thing – scream, spring, shout, dash down a glass and stamp his heel upon it. And then all at once the effect was gone. The large face beamed again, the voice was rich with good humour and with its own peculiar blend of accents.

'Ah, my wife Annie – no one can have every virtue. She is an artist, and the artist does not think beforehand – he does not plan, he does not say, "I shall do this or that." He waits for his inspiration and when it comes he must have what he needs for the masterpiece. Annie will without doubt have had an inspiration.' He bounded from the room.

Jane felt a little sorry for Annie. She hadn't cared very much for that moment of threatened storm. She saw Jeremy go and speak to Florence Duke, and was herself caught hold of by Marian Thorpe-Ennington.

'Jane – you are Jane, aren't you? I'm so dreadfully bad at names.'

'Yes – Jane Heron.'

Lady Marian gazed at her soulfully.

'And the man you came in with?'

'Jeremy Taverner.'

'You're not married to him – or divorced, or anything? I mean, it's so much better to know straight away, isn't it, instead of suddenly saying something one shouldn't, and always at the worst possible moment. I'm always doing it, and Freddy hates it, poor sweet. Oh, you haven't met him yet, have you? Freddy, this is my cousin Jane Heron.'

Freddy Thorpe-Ennington had been leaning mournfully against the mantelpiece sipping the last of a series of Smuggler's Dreams. He had a vague impression – he had reached the stage when all his impressions were vague – that the world was full of creditors and relations, and that it might be a good plan to put his head down on somebody's shoulder and burst into tears. He was a small fair man, and when sober, very kindly and confiding. At the moment he was so obviously beyond the reach of conversation that Jane went and sat down beside Jacob Taverner.

'So you've come,' he said.

'Yes.'

'Jeremy didn't want you to.'

'No.'

'What brought you?'

Jane said, 'That.'

'And the hundred pounds?'

'Yes.'

'Do anything for a hundred pounds?'

Jane shook her head.

'Not anything – reasonable things.'

56

'As what?'

'Coming down here.'

He gave a small dry chuckle.

'Thus far and no farther – is that it?'

She looked at him. It was a look that was at once smiling and cool. He was reminded of a child bathing, a bare foot exploring cold water to see just how cold it was. He thought she would go a little farther if she were tempted. He said, 'Well, well, let's talk about something else.'

'What shall we talk about?'

'Your grandfather, Acts Taverner. How much did you really know of him?'

Jane said soberly, 'I lived with him.' Something in her voice said, 'I loved him,' though she didn't use the words.

Jacob was quick in the uptake. He nodded.

'Ever tell you stories about the old place?'

'Yes – lots of them.'

'As what? Suppose you tell me some of them.'

He was aware that she withdrew.

'Why do you want to know, Cousin Jacob?'

He chuckled again.

'Well, I've given up business – I must have something to do. I might have a fancy to write down all I can get hold of about the old family place. It would make quite good reading. What did Acts tell you?'

She answered without any hesitation.

'He said there was a lot of smuggling in the old days, and it went on right down to his father's time. He used to tell me stories of how they outwitted the customs officers.'

Jacob nodded.

'Quite a lot of that sort of thing in the eighteenth century, and well on into Victoria's reign. There was a lot of lace, and silk, and French brandy landed all along this coast.'

'How did they do it?'

All this time she was in the lap of the chair, and he on the arm looking down at her. He cocked his head sideways and said, 'Didn't he tell you?'

Jane looked about her. Everyone was talking hard except Freddy Thorpe-Ennington, who propped the mantelpiece and gazed at his now empty glass after the manner of a

57

medium consulting the crystal. Whatever he saw, it had no reassuring effect. He appeared frowned in gloom, and at intervals shook his head in a despondent manner.

Jane dropped her voice.

'He said something about a passage from the shore – '

'What did he say?'

'He said nobody would find it unless they were shown. He said that it had beaten the Preventive men time out of mind. That's what they called the customs officers in the eighteenth century.'

'And a good bit after. Well, this is getting interesting. Go on.'

Jane's eyes widened.

'There isn't any more.'

'Didn't he tell you where the passage came out?'

'On the shore.'

'But this end – didn't he tell you that?'

'I don't suppose he knew. They wouldn't tell the children.'

Jacob cackled.

'Surprising what children'll know without being told. Sure that's all he told you?'

Jane smiled sweetly.

'I expect he was making most of it up anyhow. He used to tell me a bit of a story every night after I was in bed. Sometimes it was dragons, and sometimes it was pirates, and sometimes it was smugglers. And of course it made it much more exciting to hang the stories on to a real place like the Catherine-Wheel – '

The door opened and Fogarty Castell came into the room with a bounce. He had a girl by the shoulder.

It was the girl who had been walking with John Higgins on the cliff road. Without the frieze coat and the handkerchief over her head she could be seen to have a slim figure and a lot of black hair drawn up into a knot at the back of her head. She wore a dark blue indoor dress, and her eyes were exactly the same colour. She was extremely pretty but at the moment rather pale. Behind the black lashes the eyes had a startled look.

Fogarty Castell took her up to Lady Marian, to Florence

Duke, to Mildred Taverner. He kept his hand on her shoulder.

Jacob finished his drink and said drily, 'Fills the room, doesn't he? A bit of a mountebank, our Cousin Annie's husband. But why not? It pleases him so much more than it hurts us. Half Irish, half Portuguese – and under all than nonsense quite an efficient manager. And here he comes.'

He came up with a flourish.

'This is Eily Fogarty – me grandmother Fogarty's second cousin twice removed but she calls me uncle, and she calls your cousin Annie aunt, seeing it's all the uncles and aunts she's got, and all the fathers and mothers too. And if there's anything you or the other ladies are wanting, you'll ring your bells and Eily will see to it. Or if you'd like to go to your rooms – '

Jane felt quite suddenly that she had had enough of Jacob Taverner. She said, 'Yes, I would,' and saw the look in Eily's eyes change to relief. She thought, 'She was afraid I was going to say I had seen her before.' And then she was out of the chair and crossing the room.

The door closed behind them, and they went up the stair. Eily said in a quick whisper, 'You didn't say you'd seen me?'

Jane shook her head.

'Aren't you supposed to go out with John Higgins?'

'No – no – I'm not.'

'Why?'

They had come out on a square landing. There was a side passage with four irregular steps going up to it – doors on either side of it, and a passage going off to the left – two steps up, and two steps down again farther along. All very bewildering.

Eily turned into the right-hand passage. At the top of the steps she opened a door, disclosing a large gloomy bathroom with worn brown linoleum on the floor and a painted Victorian bath profusely stained with rust and furnished with a broad mahogany surround.

'It's the little room next door I've given you. Lady Marian and her husband are beyond, and Captain Jeremy and Mrs. Duke and Miss Taverner opposite.'

She stood aside to let Jane enter a small room almost entirely taken up with a very large double bed. It was lighted, like the bathroom, by a wall lamp which diffused a warm oily smell. It was a forbidding little room. A battered chest of drawers painted mustard yellow, a tarnished looking-glass standing on it, two chairs, and a shabby wash-stand, were all the furniture. There was a huge flowered ewer in a small plain basin. Half a dozen rickety hooks behind a yard or two of limp chintz supplied the only hanging accommodation. The window curtains of the same material swayed in an unseen draught. The pattern of the carpet had long ago been obliterated by dirt and age.

Eily shut the door and said, 'It's no place for you at all. John said to tell you that.

Jane had so much of the same feeling herself that she found this rather undermining. She put out a quick thought in the direction of the hundred pounds, and said with spirit, 'Well, you're here, aren't you ? What's the difference?'

Eily said in her pretty mournful voice, 'He doesn't like my being here.'

'Then why do you stay?'

'I can't be leaving Aunt Annie.' A pause, and then after a dreadful sigh, 'I'd not dare. He'd have me back.'

Then, before Jane could say anything at all, she was gone, opening the door and slipping out without any sound.

Chapter 9

JANE was drying her hands, when there was a knock on the door. As soon as she said, 'Come in!' Jeremy was in the room. He shut the door, came up close, and said, 'We're just staying as we are. I suppose you're getting into a dress.'

'I thought I'd better.'

'All right – hurry! There's a little room half-way down the stairs – I'll meet you there. Don't take too long over the face – it's quite good as it is.' And then he was gone again.

Jane hung up her suit on two of the hooks behind the limp curtain, improved the face, slipped on a grey dress with an amusing rose-coloured curlicue coming down off the left shoulder, and went down to the little room on the half-way landing.

She found Jeremy walking up and down like a hyena in a cage.

'Why do women take hours to do the simplest things?'

'Darling, they don't. What is it?'

'What is what?'

'Why the assignation?'

'I had to see you.'

'You *are* seeing me.'

'Jane – what were you talking about to Jacob Taverner?'

'Gramp's bedside stories.'

'What did you tell him?'

'I said there was one about a passage from the shore.'

'Was there?'

She nodded.

'What did Jacob say?'

'Wanted to know where it came out this end. So I said I didn't suppose Gramp knew and sheered off. And then Eily came in with Castell.'

Jeremy said, 'Look here, he asked me the same sort of thing – did my grandfather tell me stories about the old place – if he did, what stories?'

'What did you say?'

'I spread a fairly thick fog.'

She dropped her voice to a whisper.

'What did your grandfather say?'

'Lots of things. What did yours?'

'That's telling.'

'Aren't you going to tell?'

'Not unless you do – and not here – not now.'

'Why not?'

They had been standing quite close together, his arm half round her. Now he drew away frowning.

'Because I don't like this place. You've no business to be here.'

61

'Jeremy – really!'

'Jane, we've got to clear out tomorrow. We ought never to have come.'

'Yes, darling – you've said all that before. Do you know, I've got a sort of feeling that I might get bored if you don't stop soon.'

He gloomed.

'There are worse things than being bored. If ever I saw a bad lot in my life, it's that fellow Luke White. The man Castell is an offensive bounder, and that girl Eily looks scared to death. I don't know what's going on here, but it's something shady, and we're leaving tomorrow.'

Jane opened the door and walked out. Jeremy had all the makings of a trampling bully, and she had no intention of being his door-mat.

She said, 'Goodbye, darling,' and waited for Florence Duke who was coming down the stairs. She had caught only a glimpse of her when they arrived, and she had thought there was something odd about her colour. She couldn't very well turn pale, but the heavy red in her cheeks had a curious undershade of purple. She now wore a remarkable garment of very bright red silk profusely patterned with pink and green. It was rather tight and rather short, and it had seen fresher days.

As they went down the stairs together, a cloud of strong pungent scent accompanied them. Jane was just thinking that she really preferred paraffin, when Florence said under her breath,

'Do I look all right?'

Jane took in the heavy untidy hair, the overdone make-up, the dress, the shoes with their tawdry buckles, and said the only thing that it was possible to say, 'Oh, yes.'

She wouldn't have found it convincing herself, but it seemed to go down all right with Florence. She put a large coarse hand with bright fingernails on Jane's arm and said, her deep voice lower still, 'I've had a most awful turn.'

'What sort of a turn? What can I do for you?'

Florence shook her head.

'Nobody can't do anything. That's the way when you're in a fix. You get yourself in, and you've damn well got to

62

get yourself out – nobody can do it for you.' She stood on the bottom step but one and swayed a little. 'Oh, gosh – why did I have to come!'

Jane thought, 'She's tight. We *are* going to have a jolly purty.'

Forence gazed at her with tragic eyes and swayed. Jane said briskly, 'Those cocktails were much too strong. We'll feel a lot better when we've got some food inside us. There's the gong now. Come along and see how Cousin Annie cooks.'

The dining-room was opposite the lounge. Dark panelling rose to within a foot of the ceiling, which was crossed by massive beams. Above the cavernous hearth a wide brick chimney-breast ran up. It supported an irregular trophy composed of old flintlocks, bayonets, and heavy horn-handled knives. There was a long table covered with a coarse linen cloth. Someone had set a tankard full of evergreens half-way down the narrow board. For the rest, the service might have been described as rag-tag-and-bobtail – here and there a heavy silver fork or spoon amongst cheap electro-plate, old knives worn down to a point and three inches of blade, the flimsiest modern glass mixed up with half a dozen old cut beakers. The chairs were as mixed – rush-bottomed, Windsor, common kitchen. There were places laid for nine, with Jacob Taverner at the top of the table in a massive old chair carved with lions' heads. A lamp hung down from the central beam and made of the table and the people round it an island of light.

They took their seats – Marian Thorpe-Ennington on Jacob's right, and Florence Duke on his left; Geoffrey Taverner beyond Lady Marian, then Jane; Jeremy opposite Jacob at the end of the table, with Freddy Thorpe-Ennington on his right; and beyond him Mildred Taverner, leaving an empty place between her and Florence Duke which was obviously destined for Al Miller whenever he happened to arrive.

Luke White served them with soup in a variety of odd plates, and after the first spoonful Jane was aware that Fogarty Castell had made no vain boast of their Cousin Annie's cooking – the soup was a dream. She looked across the table anxiously to see whether Florence was getting it down, and was a good deal relieved to find that she was. If the rest of the dinner was anything like up to this sample, there would be no need to worry any more about the Smuggler's Dreams.

As her eye travelled back, she became aware with concern that Freddy Thorpe-Ennington had not so much as taken up his spoon. She kicked Jeremy, but before she could do any more about it Lady Marian was calling down the table.

'Freddy – Freddy, my sweet – the most marvellous soup! Jeremy – that's your name, isn't it? – do make him have some!'

Freddy stared at her with glazed eyes. That recourse had been had to the sobering properties of cold water was obvious – his fair hair shone wet under the lamp. That the remedy had been ineffectual was also obvious. He swayed where he sat, and on a repetition of his wife's appeal pronounced very slowly and distinctly the only two words which anyone had heard him utter:

'Bilge – water – '

It was at this moment that the door opened to admit Al Miller. He had taken time to change out of his porter's uniform and was wearing the suit in which he had attended at John Taylor's office. It was also unfortunately apparent that he had taken time to have a few drinks. He was not drunk, but he was definitely exhilarated and all set to be the life of the party. After hailing Jacob from across the room with a wave of the hand and a 'Cheerio, Jake!' he advanced to slap Jeremy on the back, and casting an 'Evening, all!' at the rest of the company, steered himself to the vacant place with a hand on the rail of Mildred Taverner's chair and saluted Florence Duke as 'Ducks'. After which he took his soup noisily and with gusto.

Jane said to herself, 'It's going to be the most frightful evening – it really is.' And then all at once she wanted to laugh, because Midred Taverner was obviously quite petrified at finding herself between Al and Freddy. She sat with her elbows well drawn in and picked at her food with an expression of concentrated gentility.

The soup-plates were removed and Fogarty Castell produced a napkined bottle of champagne with a flourish and filled Lady Marian's beaker. As he passed round the table, Jane saw Florence Duke lift her glass and drain it, an example quickly followed by Al Miller. Miss Taverner took a birdlike sip and returned to picking at a pea.

'*Freddy* – ?' said Marian Thorpe-Ennington in rich poignant tones.

Freddy uttered again. Dividing the words with care, he enquired, 'What's – marrer?'

'My sweet, you know champagne doesn't agree with you.' He shook his head solemnly.

'Absolutely – not.'

'Freddy, you'll be ill!'

'Absolutely.' He took up the glass with an air of serious purpose and emptied it.

Lady Marian said, 'Oh, well, he'll pass out now,' and apparently ceased to take any further interest.

Jane found herself engaged in a conversation with Geoffrey Taverner. It was a very dull conversation all about the things he travelled in, his dry, precise manner doing nothing to enliven the subject.

'We have a washing-machine which I do not hesitate to say is twenty-five per cent better than any other on the market – gas-controlled eleven pounds seven and six, electrically controlled thirteen pound ten, which, you will realise, is a considerable reduction upon the standard price.'

Here there was a hiatus, because Jane's attention was diverted to Jacob Taverner owing to the fact that she had just heard him say to Florence Duke, 'Didn't he tell you where it came out?' The words were spoken in an undertone, and why they should have reached her through the buzz of conversation, she had no idea. But reach her they did. She felt them slipping into her mind like small round lumps of ice, she didn't know how and she didn't know why. They gave her a cold, lost feeling.

She came back to Geoffrey Taverner talking about something that did your washing-up for you, by which time Fogarty Castell was going round with more champagne. Her own glass was untasted, and as he came by, she asked if she could have some water.

Geoffrey was saying, ' "Halves the labour and doubles the pleasure." Would you think that a good slogan? Or perhaps, "You give the party, we do the washing up." Which of those would catch your attention and make you look a second time at an advertisement?'

'Well, I think, perhaps the one about the party.'

He nodded complacently.

'That was my own opinion. I am glad to find that you agree with me. I have given a good deal of thought to the advertising side of the business, and some of my suggestions have been adopted.'

He embarked upon a full and particular description of the bright ideas which he had put up to Messrs. Hobbs and Curtin and the rather disappointing manner in which most of them had been received. Mr Hobbs, it appeared, was old-fashioned. 'What was good enough for my father is good enough for me – you know the style.' And Mr. Curtin was noncommittal and timid. 'The pain of the new idea, if you take me. But as I ventured to submit, a business without new ideas is a business without new customers. I am sure you will agree with me on that.'

Jane was wondering whether it was she or the firm which was to agree, and had just made up her mind that it couldn't possibly do any harm to say, 'Oh, yes,' when the voice of Al Miller came into the conversation with loud irrelevance.

'Where's Eily?'

Fogarty Castell leaned between him and Florence Duke, champagne bottle poised.

'And where would she be if she wasn't helping her aunt in the kitchen?'

Al picked up his glass, gulped, and set it down with a bang.

'Prettiest girl anywhere round about,' he said thickly – 'prettiest girl anywhere. Oughtn't to be in a kitchen – ought to be here.' He pushed back his chair. 'Going to look for her – going to bring her here – good as anyone – better than half your society ladies.'

By this time everyone was looking and listening. Jacob Taverner said, 'Sit down, Al Miller! If you wish to see Eily you can do so presently.'

There was nothing in the words. The tone had an edge on it.

Whilst Al hesitated, Florence Duke put up a strong hand to pull him down. As he dropped back, she said not at all inaudibly, 'You won't get your hundred pounds if you don't behave.'

Fogarty patted him on the shoulder.

'You'll be seeing her,' he said, and passed on.

The dinner proceeded – turkey stuffed with chestnuts – bread-sauce and vegetables so beautiful that they might have served as a pattern to any chef. One at least of the family could do something supremely well.

Jeremy relaxed so far as to lean across the corner of the table and murmur the word, 'Genius! What do you suppose she's like?'

Jane laughed.

'Let's go and see, shall we – after dinner? She's almost an aunt, and we ought to thank her.'

On the other side of her Geoffrey was saying, 'Every hotel in the country ought to have our patent plucker.'

Jane discovered that she was too hungry to care who talked about what.

When the plates had been taken away Jacob Taverner waited a moment, and then got to his feet.

'It is, perhaps, just a little early in the evening for speeches, but I propose to make a short one and to give you a toast. I am sure that you must all have been feeling curious as to why you have been asked here. Well, I am going to explain. It is really all very simple. Here we are, a lot of cousins most of whom have never met before. I thought it would be a good thing if we did meet. In the course of two world wars family ties all over the world have been strained, wrenched, and generally bombed to blazes. Annie Castell and I are the only two left in our generation – the only surviving grandchildren of old Jeremiah Taverner. He had eight sons and daughters, and we two are all that are left of his children. We are the grandchildren, and all the rest of you are great-grandchildren. I have no other kith and kin, and as I can't take my money with me when I die, I thought

I had better get to know you all before I set down what I want to happen to it. I naturally intend to live as long as I can, and as I don't feel any older than I did twenty years ago, I should say I was good for at least another twenty. That is the first instalment of my speech, and at this point I will ask you to drink to the Family. Fogarty has just filled your glasses. Here is the toast –

The Family.'

Jane touched her glass with her lips and set it down again. Everyone drank except Freddy Thorpe-Ennington, sitting slumped in his chair and quite obviously dead to the world. Jacob's bright malicious glance travelled down the table. He repeated the words of the toast, 'The Family,' and added, 'May it never be less.' Then he went on briskly, 'Well, now I know you all, and you know each other.'

Jane thought, 'How much does he know – how much do any of us know? I know Jeremy, and Jeremy knows me. He's raging under that polite look. What he'd really like to do is to drag me out of the room and beat me, but he can't, poor lamb. Too bad. I shall have to make it up to him somehow. I always know just what he's thinking. But the others. . . . Something's the matter with Florence, but I don't know what. She looks as if someone had hit her over the head and she hadn't quite come to. Al's drunk, and he wants Eily. Mildred' – a little inward laughter shook her – 'in a way she's hating every moment – Al on one side of her and Freddy on the other – two drunk men, and she's miles and miles away from her little fancy work shop. But in a way she's thrilled. I don't suppose anything has ever happened to her before, and I don't suppose anything will ever happen to her again, so she's simply got to make the most of it. . . . I wonder what Geoffrey's thinking about. Perhaps a slogan introducing the word Family – "Our Potato-peeler – every Family needs one" . . .'

Marian. . . . No need to guess about Marian. There she was, magnificent in Parisian black with three rows of pearls dripping down into her lap and her beautiful eyes gazing soulfully at Jacob. She had in fact taken the stage and was discoursing richly.

'My dear man, I couldn't agree more – I really couldn't.

68

We all need to get closer together, don't we? After all, if we can help each other – that's what we're here for, isn't it? I've always said so. And as to wills, we don't need to talk about them, because everybody lives to a simply incredible age nowadays if they don't get killed by a bomb or something. My first husband, Morgenstern, would have been alive now if he hadn't *insisted* on flying over to the States in the middle of all those air attacks. That's why I really *do* feel a little prejudiced about wills, because, you know, he left simply everything to charities and to his secretary, a horse-faced woman with streaky hair. It only shows you never can tell – doesn't it? *Nobody* could have imagined she wasn't perfectly safe.'

'My dear Marian, I am supposed to be making a speech.'

She gave him a warm, indulgent smile.

'You were doing it so well too. Men are so good at that sort of thing. René used to make wonderful speeches – my second husband – after he had won a trophy or something. But I always knew he would kill himself racing, and of course he did. So there I was – a widow for the second time and not a penny.'

Florence Duke on Jacob's other side said deep and slow, 'Some people have all the luck.'

Marian Thorpe-Ennington took no notice. It is doubtful if she even heard. She flowed on.

'So you see why I don't like wills – so dreadfully undependable. Of course René hadn't any money at all, and now Freddy isn't going to have any either. And what I always think is, how much better to see what a lot of pleasure you are giving whilst you are here to enjoy it, instead of waiting until you are dead. I mean – '

Jacob's smile became suddenly malignant. He said softly and coldly, 'Thank you – I know exactly what you mean. And I am now going to go on with my speech.'

He leaned forward and rapped upon the table.

'Now that you have all had a breathing-space I will go on. I am sorry if you thought it was all over, but I'm going to be brief, and I'm not going to be dull – at least I hope not, but of course you never can tell. I expect you have all noticed that I have asked a good many questions as to how

69

much you know about the old Inn. All your grandfathers and grandmothers seem to have known something about its smuggling past.' He paused for a moment to address Castell. 'All right, Fogarty, go on – serve the ice-pudding. Annie will never forgive us if we let it melt.' Then, turning back, he resumed. 'They could hardly have helped knowing something, since they were born and brought up here, and had the advantage for a good many years of old Jeremiah's company and example. What I have wanted to find out was how much of what they knew they had handed on. Anybody got any contribution to make?'

The ice-pudding was quite terribly good – all the food was terribly good. Jane felt really sorry for Freddy, who was missing it. She looked sideways at Jeremy, and found him giving a polite attention to his host. She wasn't sure if there wasn't a momentary flicker in her direction, or whether it was merely that she knew with what energy he was saying, 'No!' to the question which had just been put to them all. She transferred an innocent gaze to Jacob's face.

Nobody answered, nobody stirred. Mildred Taverner divided a small piece of her ice-pudding into three. Delicious – really delicious. She savoured the mouthfuls slowly, laid down a thin old silver spoon, and said in her high voice, 'There used to be a passage from the shore.'

Her brother Geoffrey looked across the table and said, 'Those old stories!' His tone was bored and contemptuous.

Jane had the oddest conviction that behind the coolness and the boredom there was a sharp edge of anger. Yet Mildred had really said nothing that had not been said before by one or another of them.

Jacob grinned his monkey grin.

'I wondered whether the old stories hadn't been handed down, and it seems they have. Now just how much did my Uncle Matthew tell you, Mildred?'

Mildred Taverner said in a confused voice, 'Oh, I don't know – there was a passage – the smugglers used it – '

'Is that all?'

'I think – ' she broke off – 'yes, I think so.'

The grin became more pronounced.

'Well, that's pretty vague, isn't it? I can do better than

that, because I can show you the passage.'

Everyone moved or made some involuntary sound – a shifting of the balance, a leaning forward or back, the faint rattle of fork or spoon as a hand released its hold, a quick involuntary intake of the breath. Jane saw Geoffrey Taverner's hand close hard and then very deliberately relax.

Jacob nodded, delighted with his effect.

'Surprised – aren't you? I thought you would be!' He chuckled. 'I could see you all thinking you'd got hold of a shocking family secret, and all the time it wasn't a secret at all. As soon as everyone has finished, come along and I'll show you. We'll go and look at the passage while Annie is sending the coffee up, but before we go – We've drunk to the Family, and now we'll drink to the Family Secret, it's smuggling past, and its harmless present –

The Secret!'

Chapter 10

THEY went trooping through a green baize door at the back of the hall, to find themselves in a confusing rabbit-warren of stone-floored passages. There was a smell of cooking, and of mould from old walls which held the damp. One passage ran straight ahead, not narrow like the one which had led from the front door, but wide enough for two men to walk abreast and carry a load between them. All the passages here had this convenience of width – and no difficulty in guessing why. The smell of food came from a half open door on the left, carried out and away by the heat of a noble fire.

But Jacob Taverner turned into a cross passage which went away to the right. Doors opened on either side of it, a stair came down on the right. The middle door on the left disclosed a cellar stair going down easily into the dark with wide shallow steps.

Fogarty Castell had a bright electric lamp. He stood at the bottom and lighted them down. Eighteen steps, and they were in a wide hall with doors opening on three sides of it. The floor was dry and dusty under foot, and the air warm. Fogarty went ahead with his lamp and stopped at a door which was locked on the outside. He turned the key – a heavy old thing like a church key – and took himself and his light into a long, narrow cellar with brick walls and a stone-paved floor. It was quite empty except for one or two small wooden boxes lying in the corner.

Jeremy had Jane by the arm. He thought, 'What is he getting at?' and he kept her near the door.

Jacob took the lamp and went to the far end of the cellar. He said, 'All right,' and Fogarty Castell did something in the corner where the boxes were. They couldn't see what he did. Nobody could, because they were all looking at Jacob and the light. Castell might have bent down and straightened up again. Jeremy had the impression that that was what he had done, but he couldn't be sure, and in the next moment he had something else to think about, because Jacob Taverner laughed and pushed hard against the brick wall at the end of the cellar. He pushed hard with both hands on the right side, and it gave and swung in. A long black gap showed all down that side. The whole end wall of the cellar moved – eight foot of it – the right-hand side going back, and the left swinging out until it stood endways on, with a four-foot passage on either side.

Jacob held up the lamp for everyone to see.

'Well, here's the old back door of the Catherine-Wheel. Ingenious, isn't it? The wall looks solid enough, but it's only a door built into a wooden frame and pivoted on an iron bar. There's a simple locking arrangement, and when it's locked no one can get in from the shore. There were some rough characters in the smuggling game, and our fore-fathers took precautions against waking up some fine night with their throats cut. Well, there's the road to the shore. The cliff's about forty foot, and we're ten foot underground here, so there's another thirty foot to go before you get down to shore level. But they didn't bring the cargoes in off the shore. There's a cave right under here, no size but very convenient. They used to run a boat in at high tide and land the stuff where the passage comes out. So you can cut off another eight or nine feet. That leaves a twenty-foot drop, and with the help of a few steps they've managed a passage with quite an easy gradient. Anyone want to come along and see? I don't advise it for the ladies, because it's all pretty foul from not being used, and they'll be apt to spoil their dresses. I don't suppose anyone's been into it a dozen times since Jeremiah died.'

Mildred Taverner, standing very near the middle of the cellar, said in that high voice of hers, 'But I thought – '

Nobody had spoken whilst Jacob spoke. Everyone listened, and when he stopped speaking there was a hush. Mildred's 'But I thought – ' came right into the middle of it. When she caught herself up, everyone was looking at her. She said, 'Oh!' with a sort of gasp, and stood there.

Geoffrey Taverner said, 'No, I don't think the ladies ought to go.'

Jacob moved, passing between Geoffrey and Florence Duke. He said, 'Mildred was saying – What was it you were saying, my dear Mildred?' His tone sharpened on the question.

There was confusion in her manner and colour in her face – ugly, flat colour. She said in a hurry, 'Oh, nothing – nothing at all.'

'You said, "But I thought – " What did you think?'

'I don't know – I'm sure I don't know why I said it – it must have been the excitement. It's very exciting, isn't it? And my dress won't hurt. I should like to see where the passage comes out. These patterned silks are so useful – they don't show marks.'

In the end they all went down except Marian Thorpe-Ennington.

'Not that I'm not interested, my dear man, because of course it's too utterly thrilling, but as this is probably the last garment I shall ever be able to buy from Dior, I really should hate to get it spoilt with slime and seaweed and things. They never really come out – too devastating. And of course the very minute Freddy goes into bankruptcy nobody will give us any more credit – so unfair, I always think.

73

Only I can't stay here in the dark.'

'Fogarty's got a torch – he'll take you back. I'm afraid we must stick to the lamp.'

One underground passage is very much like another. Jane wouldn't have stayed behind for the world, but she had never hated anything quite so much in all her life – the dark descent, the shadows cast by the electric lamp, the smell of the cave coming up on a salt breath, the smell of decaying seaweed that might easily have been something worse. There might have been murders in a place like this – a knife stuck suddenly between someone's ribs, and dead men's bones left lying in the dark. It was like all the worst nightmares she had ever had, the kind where something chased you in deep places where there isn't any light. She held Jeremy's arm in a painful grip. He felt her heart beat as she pressed against him. His whisper at her ear had a laughing sound.

'If you'll stop mangling my arm, I can put it round you.'

It came round her, and she held on to his jacket instead. They were behind the others. He said, 'Silly!' still in that laughing whisper, and kissed the back of her neck.

The smell which she kept telling herself was only seaweed got stronger. There was an oozy feeling under foot. The lamp stopped a little way ahead, and they were called forward one by one to look out over a lip of rock and see black water moving under the light a couple of feet below. The walls of the cave went away up out of sight. They glistened with moisture. The light glittered on the water. Jane felt as if at any moment the whole cliff might tilt and drown them. The glittering and the glistening and the oozy feeling under foot began to run together in her mind. Just for a minute she didn't know where she was, or that it was only Jeremy's arm that kept her on her feet.

When the giddy feeling passed they were going back up the slope. She said, 'I'm all right now. Oh, Jeremy, I do hate secret passages.'

'I rather gathered that. Sure you're all right?'

'Yes, quite.'

He let her take her weight again. They came out into the cellar and up the cellar stairs to the warmth from the kitchen door and the wholesome smell of food. The door was still half open, as it had been when they went down. There was a fragrance of coffee. Jane said close to Jeremy's ear, 'Let's go and see Annie Castell.'

It was quite easy to fall back and let the others go on. They pushed the kitchen door and went in, to find themselves in a big room with a stone floor and a low ceiling crossed by heavy beams. The beams had big hooks in them here and there, and in the old days there would have been hams hanging up to cure. Now there were only strings of onions and bunches of dried herbs.

Annie Castell turned round from the range. She was a heavily built woman of middle height with a flat pale face which reminded Jane of a scone, and flat pale hair dragged back into a scanty knot behind. At first it was difficult to say whether it was fair, or grey, or somewhere betwixt and between. She looked at them out of small nondescript-coloured eyes which had no expression at all. The few sandy lashes did nothing to shade them, and the wide colourless eyebrows showed like smudges on the pale skin. If Jane had stopped to think she would have felt discouraged. But she was too full of a sense of escape. The warm room and the smell of coffee were too heartening. She said in her prettiest voice, 'We're some of the cousins. This is Jeremy Taverner, and I am Jane Heron. We want to say thank you for the lovely dinner, Cousin Annie.'

She put out her hand as she spoke. Annie Castell looked at it, looked at her own, wiped it slowly upon the washed-out overall which enveloped her, and then just touched Jane's fingers in a limp, hesitating way. She did not speak at all.

Jane persevered.

'It was a most beautiful dinner — wasn't it, Jeremy?'

'I don't know when I tasted anything better.'

Annie Castell made some kind of a movement, but whether it was intended to be a modest disclaimer, or a mere acknowledgment of compliments received, it would have been difficult to say. For a moment nobody said anything. Then a raw-boned elderly woman emerged from what was evidently the scullery. She had a battered-looking hat on her head, and she was buttoning up a man's overcoat some sizes too large for her.

'I got through,' she said in a hoarse confidential tone. 'And if you're really not wanting me to do the silver – '

Annie Castell spoke for the first time. She had a country accent and a very flat, discouraged voice.

'No, Eily can do the silver. You've done the glasses?'

'I didn't know I had to.'

'Yes, please.'

The woman bridled.

'I'm sure I don't know that I can. Mr. Bridling, he won't half carry on if I'm late. But there, if I must, I must, and no good having a set-to about it. I'll tell him you kept me.'

'Thank you.'

Annie Castell turned back to Jeremy and Jane.

'The coffee has gone through,' she said in her flat mono-tone.

They were dismissed, and, as far as it was possible to tell, without acquiring any merit. As they shut the kitchen door behind them, Jeremy said, 'Effusive person our Cousin Annie.'

'Jeremy, do you suppose he beats her?'

'Who – Fogarty? I shouldn't think so. Why?'

'She's got that crushed look. People don't look like that if they're all right.'

Jeremy put his arm round her.

'Sometimes I like you quite a lot. But talking about looks, you've got a green smudge – you'd better slip upstairs and do something to the face.'

They separated at the foot of the stairs. As Jane turned into the passage which led to her room she heard a man's voice. She didn't get any words, only the voice. There was something about it that made her angry. She came up the four steps where the level of the passage rose, and heard Eily say, 'I won't!'

Just at this point she realised that the voices came from her own bedroom, and that one of them belonged to Luke White who certainly had no business there. Eily, she sup-posed, would be turning down the beds, and if either of them thought of Jane Heron at all, they would expect her to

76

be taking coffee in the lounge or whatever they called that big room downstairs. In the circumstances, she didn't feel the least bit ashamed of standing still and listening.

Luke White said with an odious drawling sound in his voice, 'And what good to you think you're doing by saying you won't?'

Eily sounded breathless.

'I'm saying it because I'm meaning it.'

'And what good do you think you're doing by meaning it? I'll have you in the end. If you'd a grain of sense you'd know that and come willing.'

He must have reached out and caught hold of her, because there was a half-stifled 'Let me go!'

'You'll listen to me first! And you'll give me a nice kiss, and then you can go – for this time.'

She said, 'I'll scream. You've no business here. I'll tell Aunt Annie.'

'Annie Castell – that makes me laugh! And what do you think you'll get out of telling Annie Castell?'

Her voice wavered.

'I'll tell Uncle.'

'You won't! If you want to start anything like that, there's two can play at telling. Where had you got to this evening when I spoke up for you and told Castell Annie had sent you out on an errand? I lied for you and got you out of the mess you'd have been in if he'd known where you was. Along of John Higgins, wasn't it? Keeping company like – sweethearting like – holding hands and kissing, or perhaps a bit more. For all he's so pious, I bet you don't sing hymns all the time you're with him!'

'Luke – let me go!'

'In a minute, when I've said what I want to. Here it is. You go snivelling to Castell or you go running away to John Higgins, and I'll cut his heart out. If you want to wake up some night and find your bed a-swimming in his blood, you run off and marry him and that's what you'll wake up to some fine night. I'll not swing for him neither – you needn't think it – I'd not give you that satisfaction. I'll have an alibi that the two Houses of Parliament couldn't break, not if they tried ever so. And I'll have you too, whichever way it

77

goes and whatever you do. You can choose whether you'll come willing and now, or whether you'll let it come to what I said and have John Higgins's blood on you first. And now you'll kiss me proper!'

Jane went back down the four steps, and made a noisy stumble on the bottom one. Just as she did so she heard Eily cry out. Hard on that Luke White cursed. Jane ran, and almost bumped into him as he came out of the bedroom looking dangerous and nursing a hand. When he saw her he stopped for a moment and said, 'Eily called me in to see to the catch of your window. It slipped and caught my finger.'

Jane watched him nearly to the end of the passage before she shut the door.

Eily stood by the chest of drawers which served as a dressing-table. She had a fixed sick look, her eyes staring, her face dead white. She was holding Jane's nail-scissors. There was blood on the blades. She was wiping it off with her finger and staring at it.

Jane went close up to her and put an arm round her shoulders.

'I heard what he said. Why do you stand it?'

Eily went on wiping the blades with her finger.

'There's nothing else I can do.'

'Of course there is! You ought to tell Mr Castell and your aunt.'

A faint shudder went over Eily like a ripple going over water.

'You don't understand.'

'You could walk out of here and marry John Higgins. He wants you to, doesn't he?'

'I can't be doing that.'

'Because of what Luke said? He was just trying it on. You could go to the police. There, that's three things you could do. And you can put those scissors down – they give me the creeps. You stuck them into his hand, didn't you?'

The dark blue eyes widened. There was another of those slow shudders. Jane said half impatiently, 'I shouldn't worry – he was asking for it.'

She turned round to the glass, exclaimed at what it

showed her, and began to get busy with cleansing tissue.

Eily put the scissors down and moved a step or two away. All the time Jane was doing her face she was aware of her, standing there with that fixed staring look.

When she was ready, Eily was still there. Jane began to feel that she needed shaking. A girl who was chambermaid at an inn which certainly contained some odd people ought to be a bit tougher than that. The Catherine-Wheel was no place for a sensitive plant – very few places were. If you had your living to earn you had to learn how to look after yourself, but it oughtn't to have to come to stabbing, not even with nail-scissors. She said rather briskly, 'Come along, Eily – there's no harm done.'

Eily looked down at the blood on her forefinger.

'It was only the little pair of scissors,' she said, 'and no harm done at all.'

'Then what are you worrying about?'

She said, 'Suppose I'd had a knife –'

This time the shudder was in her voice.

Chapter 11

As Jane passed the turn of the stairs on her way down, a cold wind came blowing up to meet her. She stopped half-way, and saw the front door open and Luke White standing there with his back to her. She could see that it was Luke because of his grey waiter's jacket. His left hand hung down and there was a handkerchief around it. His voice came back to her with the blowing wind – quite a polite, civilised voice for someone who had just been talking about cutting people's hearts out.

'I am sorry, madam, but I am afraid we have no room.'

Beyond him, still upon the doorstep, Jane could see a woman's figure. A voice said, 'Dear me!'

Jane came down the rest of the way into the hall and took

a step or two along the narrow passage to the front door. There was something familiar about the voice with its very clear enunciation. She came right up to the door and saw a little woman in dowdy old-fashioned clothes, a well worn fur tippet about her neck, a shabby handbag in one hand and a small fibre suit-case in the other.

She said, 'Oh!' And then, 'But I've met you, haven't I – at Mrs Moray's? Your name – '

There was a faint prim cough.

'Miss Silver – Miss Maud Silver. And you are Miss Jane Heron?'

'Yes. Do come in, won't you?'

'We haven't any room, Miss Heron,' said Luke White. He spoke smoothly, but with an underlying impertinence which brought Jane's head up.

Miss Silver stepped past him and set down her case.

'Pray shut the door.' Her tone was one of quiet authority. She addressed herself to Jane.

'The wind is extremely chilly. I was on my way to keep an appointment, and after some difficulties with which I need not trouble you a gentleman very kindly gave me a lift in his car and recommended this hotel. He himself was going to stay with a Sir John Challoner who resides in this neighbourhood, so it has all turned out most conveniently. I really do not feel able to proceed any farther tonight – so inclement, and I have no conveyance. But I shall be quite content with an armchair if there is no bedroom available.'

She had been walking down the passage as she spoke. They now emerged upon the small square hall. From the lounge door half open on the right there came the smell of coffee and the sound of voices. As Miss Silver turned with a pleased smile in this direction, Luke White pushed past her.

'That's a private party in there. And we've no room – I told you we haven't.'

Miss Silver coughed.

'I have no wish to intrude – ' she began with dignity.

But before she could say anything more the half open door was thrown wide. Between Jeremy, who obviously intended to come out, and Jane, who obviously intended to come in, there really was no room for Luke White. He had a look of black anger as he slid past Jeremy into the lounge and made his way to where Fogarty Castell was standing beside the coffee-tray.

Jane had slipped her hand inside Miss Silver's arm.

'Jeremy, this is Miss Silver whom I met at Mrs Moray's. She got held up on the road, and that horrible Luke White says there isn't any room here. But we can manage something, can't we?'

'I expect so. Come in, Miss Silver, and have some coffee with us.'

Miss Silver gave him the smile reserved for the polite and attentive young.

'Most delightful – most refreshing,' she said.

As they advanced into the room they encountered Fogarty Castell, all smiles and apologies.

'My excuses, madam, but we really do not have any room that we can offer you. Mr Taverner's party has taken up all our accommodation. Captain Taverner will tell you that this is so.'

Captain Taverner frowned. He could see just what Jane had landed him into, and he didn't see any way of getting out of it. He would have to give up his room. The thought was sweetened by the fact that this was, for some reason, going to annoy Luke White to whom he had taken a considerable dislike. It was also, apparently, going to annoy Fogarty Castell. He made his offer pleasantly enough, received the gracious thanks of Miss Silver and the approbation of Jane, and then had to meet some suave opposition.

In the end it was Miss Silver herself who decided the matter. Speaking with the quiet precision with which she had so often in the past quelled an unruly schoolroom, she observed that if there were any question of the intrusion of a stranger into some private family affair, she would of course withdraw.

Forgarty threw up his hands.

'But there is no private affair! There is a family reunion – you can see it. I will speak to Mr Taverner. He is the owner, you understand. The inn is his, the party is his – I am only the manager.' He made another of those foreign gestures and was gone. They could see him waving his hands as he talked to Jacob Taverner.

Jane spoke on a sudden impulse. 'He didn't like your saying that about its being a private affair, did he? Look here, come and sit down, and Jeremy will get us some coffee. How odd that the man who gave you a lift should be going to stay with Jack Challoner. He's a friend of Jeremy's.'

The room was a good size. There were chairs scattered about over the floor-space in groups of twos and threes. Heavy plush curtains masked the windows, giving out a smell of must and tobacco. Even under the softening influence of lamplight both they and all the other furnishings had a drab and dingy look.

Mildred Taverner was sitting by herself at a small table upon which she had placed her coffee-cup. She was thinking how shockingly in need of spring-cleaning and whole place was. Her head felt queer and light, but not quite so queer and light as it had done before she drank her coffee. It was very good coffee – very good indeed. All the food and drink was very good. Without meaning to, she gave a little giggling laugh. The champagne was very good. She had never had champagne before. It made you feel funny afterwards, but it was very good at the time. Might have been a bit sweeter. She would have liked a spoonful of sugar in it herself, but there wasn't any on the table, and if there had been, she wouldn't have liked to make herself peculiar. she would have liked another cup of coffee, but she didn't feel too sure about getting up and going over to ask for it. She thought perhaps she would, and then she thought she wouldn't.

She looked about her. Geoffrey was standing with his back to her talking to Lady Marian. Funny to think they had a cousin who was an earl's daughter. But she didn't think much of that Mr. Thorpe-Ennington. Awful to be married to a man who got drunk like that. Drunk? He might have been dead the way he was lying in that chair. She wondered how they had got him in from the dining-room. Al Miller wasn't much better. Noisy, that's what he was – noisy and vulgar – laughing too much, and talking too loud to the waiter and Mr. Castell. The waiter – Luke White – one of the Luke Taverner lot. Not at all a nice family connection. She didn't really care about any of them, and they didn't care about her. Nobody came and talked to her. She didn't want them to – she had much rather they didn't – she liked looking on.

Jeremy Taverner and Jane Heron were having their coffee with the governessy-looking person who had come into the room with Jane. Such an unfashionable hat, such a shabby fur tie. She remembered her own fur, bought just before the war in a January sale, kept very carefully in a drawer with moth-ball and only worn on special occasions. She kept all her clothes in moth-balls, and had become so used to the smell that she no longer noticed it. It was diffusing itself now like the quality of mercy and contending not unsuccessfully with the odours indigenous to the room.

She was mentally pricing the rest of Miss Silver's attire, a process which gave her a pleasantly superior feeling, when Jacob Taverner came and sat down beside her. The superior feeling petered away and left her fluttered and wishing herself anywhere else. His eyes were so bright they made her quite giddy, and there was something about his voice – as if he was laughing at you, only of course there wasn't anything to laugh at.

'Well, my dear Mildred, Annie Castell makes good coffee, doesn't she? You're none the worse, I hope, for your visit to the Smuggler's Cave?'

She bridled a little, lifting her long neck out of its habitual poke and drawing in her chin. He was a cousin of course, but to call her 'My dear Mildred' like that – well, it was only the second time they had met. It wasn't really quite nice. Too familiar, that's what it was, and it wasn't a thing she had ever cared about or encouraged. And then it all went out of her head, because he was saying, 'What did you mean when you said, "But I thought – "?'

At once she became quite dreadfully confused. Men made her feel nervous. Though he was two years younger, Geoffrey had always bullied her. She could still feel the place on her arm where he had pinched her down in the cellar. As if she had said something dreadful. He oughtn't to have done it – she was sure she was going to have a very bad bruise. What she had said was nothing really – anyone might have said it. She hadn't meant to.

83

'Well? Why did you say it?'

'I don't know –'

'You were surprised – was that it?'

'Oh, yes.'

'You didn't think there was a passage?'

She looked as confused and nervous as she felt. Because of course she had always known there was a passage, and Geoffrey had always told her not to talk about it.

Jacob Taverner didn't give her any time.

'No, it wasn't that. You knew there was a passage, didn't you? But you didn't know that it opened out of the cellars. Was that it? You said, "But I thought – " Did you think it opened somewhere else?'

The questions came as quick as peas out of a pea-shooter. That's what they reminded her of – Geoffrey shooting peas at her out of his pea-shooter when he was eight years old and calling her a cry-baby because she burst into tears. As if anyone wouldn't cry if they thought they were going to have their eyes shot out! She had a moment's terrified recollection of just how frightened she had been.

Jacob fired that last question at her again.

'Did you think it opened somewhere else? Where did you think it opened?'

The champagne was still in her head. She didn't mean to speak, but before she knew that she was going to she had said, 'Upstairs –'

His bright, twinkling eyes were much too near. He had his elbows on the table, leaning across it. She didn't like anyone to be so near her.

He said, 'Why?'

'I don't know –'

'Come along – you must know why you thought it was upstairs. What made you think so?'

It was like being pushed into a corner. His eyes twinkled at her and made her feel giddy. It was like being pushed. She hadn't any resistance left.

'My grandfather said so.'

'Matthew? What did he say?'

'It was when he was very old – he liked talking. He said he woke up in the night and heard something. It was all in the dark and he was frightened – he was only a little boy. Then he saw a light coming from a hole in the wall. He was dreadfully frightened, and he ran away back to his bed and pulled the clothes over his head.'

'And where did he see this hole in the wall?'

She shook her head.

'He didn't say.'

'Didn't you ask him?'

She shook her head again.

'That's what Geoffrey said, but I didn't think about it. It was when I was helping to nurse him before he died. Geoffrey was angry, but I didn't think about it at all – not like that. I thought he'd been dreaming. I didn't think there was a passage. But when you said there was – then I thought perhaps it really happened. Only I didn't think he could have gone all the way down to the cellars – not a little boy like that, in the dark. And that's why I said, "But I thought – "'

The twinkling eyes fixed hers.

'That was all?'

She nodded.

'It wasn't anything really.'

He took his elbows off the table and sat up. Such a relief to have him farther away.

'No, it wasn't anything,' he said. 'You were right about what you thought the first time. He'd been dreaming. And whether he dreamed what he told you when he was a kid or when he was in his second childhood doesn't make a ha-porth of difference. The passage has always opened out of the cellar just the same as you saw it tonight. Seeing's believing. And first to last what Matthew told you would be just something he'd dreamt.'

He began to get up out of his chair. 'Not that it matters anyway,' he said, and went over to the group beside the coffee-tray with her empty cup in his hand.

Chapter 12

FLORENCE DUKE was standing there. She had been standing there ever since they came back from the cellars – not talking to anyone, just standing there drinking coffee, sip after sip, quite slowly until the cup was empty, and then sip after sip again after it had been filled up. She had the look of a woman among her thoughts, listening intently. It was plain that she was taking no part in what was going on around her – Geoffrey Taverner's conversation with Marian Thorpe-Ennington, Al Miller's noisy talk and laughter, or the sometimes angry, sometimes tactfully intended remarks of Fogarty Castell. Not even when he turned to her with one of his foreign gestures and said in a passionate undertone, 'This Al Miller, we are going to have a scene with him, I tell you. Why can't he take his drink quiet and go to sleep on it like the other one?' – not even then did she really come back. Her eyes looked past him as she said in that slow way she had, 'He's all right. Let him alone.'

She reached for the coffee-pot and filled her cup again. Fogarty wondered if she was drunk. She wasn't flushed. As much of her colour as she could lose was gone. Now and again the drink would take someone that way. Her hand was steady and she stood like the figurehead of a ship, a big, bold woman, solid and firm. But there was something. . . . He shrugged, and went back to Al Miller, who hadn't stopped talking.

'Where's Eily? I want Eily. Got something I want to tell her.'

Fogarty threw up his hands.

'Didn't I tell you she's busy? You wait a bit and you'll see her fast enough. Do you think my wife has three pairs of hands? You leave Eily be till she's finished her work!'

Al hitched a leg over the corner of the table and sat there swaying. He began to sing in a weak falsetto.

' "Eileen alannah, Eileen asthore – " ' That's the song for

her! Irish song for Irish girl. We've got an Irishman up at the station, he sings it – name of Paddy O'Halloran. He says I can't sing.' He caught Castell by the lapel and swayed. 'Who says I can't sing?' He lifted his voice again, ' "Eileen alannah – " ' then as suddenly broke off. 'I say I want Eily – something to tell her – '

'She's busy like I said. You have another drink. What is it you're wanting to tell her?'

Al let go of the lapel, fumbled for a handkerchief, and mopped his face. He said, 'I don't mind if I do,' and tilted the proffered glass. He took a deep draught and blinked. He said, 'I'm not drunk.'

Fogarty said nothing. He hoped this drink would do the trick, but of course you never could tell.

Al finished the tumbler and set it down just over the edge of the table. When it fell and smashed he laughed unsteadily and repeated his former remark.

'I'm not – drunk.'

'No one said you were.'

'Better not – thass what I told them. Nobody's going to say I'm drunk. Give me the sack, will they – say I'm drunk and gimme the sack?' He put a hand on Fogarty's arm. 'I'll – tell – you who's get'n the sack. They are. I'm – get'n – out. No one's goin' to say – I'm drunk.' His voice rang loud.

'No one's saying it.'

Al stared.

'If I was drunk – I'd talk. Not drunk – not talking – only to Eily. If there's anything there – we'll get it. If there ishn't – no harm done – we'll get married allersame – married on prosheeds.'

Fogarty said, 'You come along with me, and I'll get Eily. Another little drink, and then I'll get her.'

Al shook his head.

'All right here.' Then he suddenly advanced his lips to Fogarty's ear and said in a penetrating whisper, 'Like to know – what I know – wouldn't you? Well, I'm – not tell'n.' He let go suddenly, lost his balance, and slumped down, half on, half off a chair.

All this time Luke White had stood behind the table, his face expressionless, his manner unconcerned. He might have

87

been listening to Marian Thorpe-Ennington telling Geoffrey Taverner the story of her three marriages. He might have been watching Jacob talking to Mildred Taverner. Or he might have been watching Jane and Miss Silver and Jeremy, or Florence Duke. He might have been listening to Al Miller. When Jacob came across and put down Mildred Taverner's cup he lifted the tray and went out by the service door at the end of the room.

Castell had got Al Miller on to the chair. He wouldn't talk any more for a bit. Luke looked back, holding the door with his shoulder, and then let it fall to again.

Florence Duke straightened up, felt at her sleeve in a vague, abstracted manner, and said slowly, 'I haven't got a handkerchief.'

It was not said to anyone, and nobody took any notice. She walked round the table and out at the service door.

Back in the room Jane was saying, 'I expect you think it's a very odd kind of party. We're all cousins, descended from old Jeremiah Taverner who used to keep this inn. It belongs to Jacob Taverner now. That's him over there by the table. He's giving the party. He's a grandson, and the rest of us are great-granchildren. Most of us haven't ever seen each other before. Jeremy and I have of course, but that's all. Because of family rows. Cousin Jacob advertised for his grandfather's descendants, and here we are.'

Jeremy said, 'A job lot!' and Jane gave her pretty laugh. 'Would it amuse you to be told who's who?'

Miss Silver coughed and said with perfect truth, 'It would interest me extremely.'

Down in the kitchen Eily was putting away the glass and silver. She wasn't being as quick as usual, because every now and then a very bitter salt tear escaped from between her fine dark lashes and ran slowly down over a white cheek. Sometimes the drop splashed upon spoon or glass, and she had to polish it again. Annie Castell was busy over the range. All her movements were slow and dragging. It was a wonder how she ever got done. There was no word spoken between them until at the end of it she turned round and said in her toneless voice, 'What's the good of your standing there crying? It never helped anyone that I heard tell.'

Eily said, 'There's no help at all – '

Annie Castell took the lid off a saucepan with porridge in it, gave it a good stir round, and covered it again. Then she said, 'It's that Luke?'

Eily said, quick and choked, 'If he touched me, I'll die.' She snatched a breath, 'Or I'll kill him.'

Annie Castell made a clicking sound with her tongue against the roof of her mouth, but she didn't say anything for a piece after that. She heard Eily fetching her breath quick, but she didn't say anything. In the end she put a question, 'Has he touched you?'

Eily began to cry like a lost thing.

'He came up into the room where I was. I was turning down Miss Heron's bed. And I said to go away, but he wouldn't. And I said I'd tell, and he dared me. He said' – she fought for her breath and got it hard – 'he said if I went to anyone else, he'd come in the night and cut his heart out.'

Annie Castell was clearing the kitchen table. When she had everything off it she took an old clean cloth out of the drawer and spread it. She took knives and forks and laid them neat and orderly, and set glasses. Then she said, 'Men talk a deal of nonsense.' And after a pause, 'I'd lock my door nights.'

'Do you think I don't?'

Annie nodded. She said, 'Mrs. Bridling left her scarf. Fetch it through from the scullery and put it handy on the dresser and come and have your supper. No knowing when Luke and Fogarty'll be down. You have your supper and get off to bed.'

Eily said nothing. She went to the scullery, and she came back again empty-handed.

'It isn't there.'

A slow frown came between Annie Castell's eyes.

'It's there, at the end of the drip-board. I let it out of my hand when I was bringing it through.'

'It's not there.'

Annie Castell said, 'She must have come back for it. Sit down and have your supper.'

89

Chapter 13

Miss Silver looked about her at the room which Captain Taverner was so kindly relinquishing.

'Very comfortable,' she said, – 'and most good of you. Mrs. Duke next door, and then Miss Mildred Taverner, you say? And Lady Marian and her husband opposite?'

Jeremy said, 'Not quite. It's Jane who is just over the way from you, and the Thorpe-Enningtons beyond her. The bathroom's on Jane's other side.'

'So very convenient. You really are too kind. These old houses are sometimes so confusing. There are some more bedrooms, are there not, across the landing?'

Jeremy wondered why elderly ladies took so much interest in other people's affairs. He said, 'Yes. Mr Taverner's over there, and Geoffrey – and I suppose the Castells, and that girl Eily.'

Miss Silver coughed.

'And Mr Miller?'

Jeremy was packing his bag. Jane was sitting on the end of the bed. She wrinkled her nose and said, 'Thank goodness no! He's gone.'

Jeremy turned round with a shaving-bush in his hand. 'How do you know?'

'Eily told me. He was – well, you saw what he was – and just to keep him quiet, that wretched Castell wanted Eily to come and see him, and she wouldn't. She had already had a scene with Luke White, and Al was the last straw. She ran out of the room in the end, and a little while after Fogarty told her he'd gone home.'

Miss Silver put her head on one side like a bird and repeated the last word in an interrogative manner.

'Home?'

'Ledlington. He's a porter at the station – I told you. He's got a room in some back street.'

Jeremy reached for his pyjamas and pushed them down on the top of his shaving tackle.

'Long odds against his making it. Drunk and incapable in a ditch would be the form, I should think. As a matter of fact I saw him go, and if he doesn't sober up, I shouldn't think he'd get half a mile. He was still singing "Eileen alannah".'

Jane said, 'It's nonsense Eily staying here. She ought to marry John Higgins and get out of it.' She turned to Miss Silver. 'He's another of the cousins, but he won't come here. Perhaps he's afraid of not being able to turn the other cheek to Luke White. He's a sort of local preacher when he isn't being Sir John Layburn's head carpenter. Eily and he are in love, and he'd make her an awfully good husband. Quite a nice change after Luke and Al.'

Jeremy picked up his case.

'I've plumped for the room half way down the stairs.' He took Jane by the wrist and pulled her up. 'If you're good, you can come and help me unpack. Good night, Miss Silver.'

They went down the short flight to the room where they had talked before dinner. A bed had been made up on the deep old-fashioned couch. It really looked very comfortable.

Jeremy shut the door, and said with frowning intensity, 'Why on earth were you spreading yourself like that?'

'Why on earth was I spreading myself like what?'

'Like you were to Miss Silver.'

'I wasn't!'

He said contemptuously, 'Of course you were! I want to know why.'

Jane softened. She had been looking rather haughtily at a point just above his head. She now allowed her eyes to meet his for a moment, then looked down and said in a tentative manner, 'Jeremy – '

'Well?'

'There's something – and I don't know whether to tell you – ' She paused, and added thoughtfully, 'or *not*.'

Jeremy threw his bag on to the couch. He turned back to say, 'Look here, what's all this?'

'Well, perhaps it's nothing – '

'All right, if it's nothing, you'd better go to bed.'

'No – I'll tell you. It's only – you know – I met Miss Silver at Mrs. Moray's, and I thought just what anyone would think, that she was a sort of Edwardian specimen governess and really ought to be under a glass case in the British Museum or somewhere, but rather a lamb, and we'd been getting on like a house on fire.'

'Darling, is all this going to get us anywhere? Or shall I just go quietly off to sleep until you arrive at the point?'

'I have arrived at it. That's what she seemed like, and that's what I thought she was. But she isn't. At least she is really. That's why it's so convincing. I mean, she used to be a governess and all that sort of thing, so it's the most marvellous protective colouring – like insects pretending to be sticks – '

'Jane, you're raving!'

'No, darling, I'm only leading up to it gently.'

'Leading up to what?'

She gave a little gurgle of laughter, put her lips quite close to his ear, and said, 'She's a detective.'

'You're pulling my leg.'

'No – really. Mrs. Moray said she was marvellous. Charles said so too – they both did. They said the Criminal Investigation Department at Scotland Yard thought no end of her.'

'You're not spoofing?'

She said indignantly, 'As if I would!'

'You might. Then – '

They looked at each other. Jane nodded.

'I know – that's what I've been thinking – about her being here. It might be accidental like she said, or it mightn't. She might be detecting.'

Jeremy said in an exasperated tone, 'I told you there was something fishy about this place. You oughtn't to have come.'

'The theme song!' She blew him a kiss. 'So I thought if there is any dirty work going on, she might just as well know which of us is which and have some sort of an idea of the lay-out. Because – well, I didn't tell you about Luke White, did I?'

She proceeded to do so, finishing up with, 'It really was – *horrid*. And don't keep saying I oughtn't to have come, because that's nonsense. It's Eily I'm thinking about. You could see what a shock she'd had. You know, really it isn't civilised to go round throwing your weight about saying you'll cut people's hearts out and drench them with blood if they marry somebody else.'

Jeremy said, 'Not very,' in rather an odd tone of voice. Then he tipped Jane's chin up and kissed her in a good hard kind of way. It was agreeable, but undermining. It was still more undermining when he said in a different voice, 'Let's get married soon.'

Jane didn't want to be undermined, but she felt it coming on. She hadn't ever realised before how dreadfully easy it would be to say yes. She kissed him back once, and pulled away. And ran out of the room.

Chapter 14

EVERYONE began to go to bed. The downstairs rooms were left to darkness and silence except for the glimmer of a wall-lamp in the small square hall. Old houses settle slowly to their rest. Floors upon which many generations have walked, furniture which has been a very long time in use, walls which have borne the stress and weight of old beams for centuries, have a way of lapsing into silence by degrees. There are small rustling sounds, creakings, movements – a whispering at the keyhole of a door, a stirring amongst spent ashes of a fire, a sighing in the chimney – and all in the darkness which has been there night after night for perhaps three hundred years. Thoughts, feelings, actions which have left their impress come to the surface. The life of today no longer dominates these empty rooms. The past comes stealing back.

Upstairs Miss Silver braided her hair and pinned it up neatly for the night. She had spent a very instructive evening. She folded her crimson dressing-gown, made in the last year of the war from utility cloth but most warm and comfortable and ornamented with the handmade crochet lace which was practically indestructible and had already served two previous gowns. Her slippers were new, a present from her nephew's wife Dorothy, who had brought them home from the East. So very kind, and just the right shade of red. They had black pompoms on the toes, and of course these would not wear so well as the slippers, but could be replaced. She arranged them neatly side by side before getting into bed, after which she put on a warm blue shawl with an openwork border over her long-sleeved woollen nightdress, and read a chapter from the Bible before blowing out the candle and composing herself to sleep.

Mildred Taverner also wore a long-sleeved nightgown of a woolly nature. She had embroidered a spidery bunch of flowers on either side of the front opening, which she had trimmed with little ruches of lace. She lay in the dark and wished that she had drunk less champagne. The bed really was not steady at all, and she felt far from well. She tried to remember what she had said to Jacob Taverner.

In the big double bed over the way Freddy Thorpe-Ennington could just hear his wife's voice going on and on. He wasn't asleep, because he could hear Marian talking, and he wasn't awake, because he wouldn't have been able to answer her even if he had wanted to. He didn't want to. He wanted her to stop talking and put out the light, which hurt his eyes. He wasn't drunk – he had walked upstairs, hadn't he? All he wanted was to go to sleep. Why couldn't Marian let him alone and put out the light? He wished she would stop talking, because every now and then he couldn't help hearing what she said. She said things like, 'Freddy, my sweet, you know you really shouldn't drink so much,' and, 'You'll feel rotten tomorrow – you know you will.' He didn't want to hear what anyone said. He wanted to go to sleep.

Marian Thorpe-Ennington finished creaming her face and put on the chin-strap which she wore at night though it was really dreadfully uncomfortable, tied a cap over her hair to preserve the waves, and slipped her hands into soft wash-leather gloves. When she had done all this she took off the cape which she had been wearing to protect her nightgown.

It was worth protecting – white triple ninon smocked at the shoulders and at the waist in a delicate apple-green. She put on the matching apple-green coatee and took a casual look at herself in the glass. The chin-strap rather spoilt the effect, but anyhow you had to cream your face, and it wasn't as if there was anyone to see you. Freddy, poor sweet, never knew how you looked or what you had on.

This happened to be true, because having once made up his mind that she was the most beautiful woman in the world, he remained in that simple belief, and nothing she did or omitted to do had the slightest effect upon it.

Marian Thorpe-Ennington gave a fleeting sigh of regret to the days when her complexion owed its astounding brilliance to her own youth and to the soft water and softer airs of Rathlea and when she didn't have to bother about a double chin. Then she got into bed, kissed the back of Freddy's head, and blew out the candle.

On the other side of the landing Geoffrey Taverner was reading in bed. He wore neat grey pyjamas, and a grey dressing-gown edged with a black and white cord. He had only two pillows and he had been at some pains to arrange them comfortably. He wore pale horn-rimmed glasses. He was reading a thriller with the intriguing title of *Three Corpses and a Coffin.*

In the room next to Miss Silver Florence Duke hadn't undressed. She sat on the edge of the bed with her hands folded in her lap. There was a lighted candle on the chest of drawers which served for a dressing-table. The flame moved in the draught from the window. It made the candle gutter. The flame, the guttering wax, and the candle itself were reflected in the tilted glass. There were two wavering tongues of fire, two little caves running with melted wax, two candles thickened with what old wives' tales call winding-sheets. Florence Duke stared past them at the wall.

Jane felt the air come in cold and salt from the sea. It hadn't taken her five minutes to undress. Now she was here in the dark with the wind blowing in, a wind from a long way off. She lay in the dark and watched the oblong of the window form upon the darkness until it hung there like a picture in a frame. The frame was there, but the picture was

95

all a soft blur of grey, without form and void. That was in the Bible, in Genesis. Her thoughts began to drift. Under the drifting thoughts she was warm and happy. Jeremy had kissed her as if he loved her – very much. Cousins oughtn't to marry – perhaps it wouldn't matter if they did – perhaps –

She came awake with a start. There was a soft knocking on her door, and then the door opening, the wind rushing through and Eily's voice saying, 'Miss Heron – please – '

Jane sat up. The door shut, the wind stopped rushing. She said, 'What is it? Look here, shut the window, and I'll light a candle.'

The window closed, and at once the room fell still. The curtains came together, and by the candle-light Jane saw Eily in her blue dress. She had some things gathered up in her arm, a nightgown, a dressing-gown. She stood halfway between the window and the bed, catching her breath, her eyes fixed on Jane's face, her own as white as milk.

Jane said, 'What is it?' again.

Eily came up close.

'Miss Heron – if you'd let me stop here – I'd sit in the chair and not make a sound.'

'What is it?'

Eily said in a shaken voice, 'There's no key in my door.'

'Do you mean there isn't one ever, or there isn't one now?'

The shaken voice sank low.

'It's gone. Aunt Annie told me to lock my door. She didn't need to say so – I've always locked it – since that Luke's been here. But tonight there's no key – it's gone.'

'You must tell your aunt.'

'I can't – they're in the one room together, she and Uncle. If you'll let me stay – '

'Of course you can stay. Get your things off and get into bed! It's big enough for half a dozen.'

Eily caught her breath.

'I didn't mean that – or to trouble you – only to stay in the room. He said to ask you.'

Jane took her up quickly.

'He? Who?'

'It was John, Miss Heron – John Higgins.'

'When?'

'Miss Heron, you'll not tell? There's no harm, but you'll not tell? There's once in a while he'll come out here and go by whistling to let me know he's there. It's a hymn tune he whistles – Greenland's Icy Mountains – and I'll look out of my window, and he'll say, "Are you all right, Eily?" and I'll say, "Yes". But tonight – oh, dear, he was in a way!'

'Why?'

Eily shrank.

'You know what happened up here tonight with that Luke. I went down and I told my Aunt Annie. Mrs. Bridling that comes in to help when we're busy, she'd finished up and gone home, and I was putting away the silver. I didn't know there was anyone there. But Mrs. Bridling came back. She'd left her scarf, and she came back for it, and she heard what I said when I thought it was just Aunt Annie and me, the two of us alone.'

'How do you know?'

Eily sat down on the edge of the bed. It was just as if she couldn't hold herself up any more. There seemed to be the weight of the world on her. She went on telling Jane about Mrs. Bridling.

'She went right back to Cliff and saw to Mr. Bridling – he's in his bed and can't get out of it. Then she began to think about what she'd heard me tell Aunt Annie, and when she'd thought about it for a bit she went along next door and told John Higgins, and John came out here right away. I've never seen him in such a taking.'

'I don't wonder. Elly, why don't you marry him like he wants you to? He does, doesn't he?'

Eily looked at her, a long mournful look.

'And have his blood on me the way Luke said?' She shook her head. 'I'd rather jump off the cliff – I told him so tonight.'

'And what did he say to that?'

Eily's voice went lower still.

'He said I'd lose my soul and go to hell, and he said he'd come after me – there or anywhere. And he said, "God forgive me, but it's true." I've never seen him like it before. What's the matter with men, Miss Heron, to get worked up about a girl the way they do? There's Al, and Luke, and even John – what gets into them at all?'

Jane bit her lip. She wanted to laugh, and she wanted to cry. She remembered Jeremy kissing her that hard way.

Eily went on in her pretty grieving voice.

'He wanted me to come out by the side door. He said he'd take me out to Mrs. Bridling and we could be married in three days. And I said I couldn't leave Aunt Annie. You'd never think he'd carry on the way he did. I just said no, and no, and no, and at the last of it he said would I give my solemn promise I'd go along to your room and ask you to let me stay, and he'd come out in the morning and talk to uncle, so I said I would – ' Her voice trailed away.

Chapter 15

EILY slipped in on the far side of the big bed and felt warmth and safety close round her. She said, 'Thank you, Miss Heron,' on a soft breath, and heard a laugh from the neighbouring pillow.

'Oh, drop the Miss Heron! We'll be cousins when you marry John Higgins.'

Jane lay there thinking how odd it all was. She knew the moment when Eily fell asleep, but she herself was broad awake. If you scare your first sleep away, it doesn't readily come back. Her mind went over all the things that had happened since they came to the Catherine-Wheel – the old house, the dark passage to the shore, Al Miller's drunken laugh, Eily, Luke White nursing a bleeding hand, Jeremy kissing her in the little room half way down the stairs. They came back as thoughts, but the thoughts changed to pictures, and the pictures went with her over the edge of sleep. In the last of them she was out of bed standing at the door of the room. The door was open. She looked into the passage, and it was empty – empty and dark. But there was a light at the end where the stair went down. She went along as far as the landing and looked over the stair. The door of the little room half way down was open and someone was coming out. It was Jeremy. That is what she thought when she saw him. And then she wasn't sure. His hair was much longer, and he looked so ill. He had on a big loose coat and a high dark stock. His hands were pressed hard against his side, the blood ran between his fingers. It wasn't Jeremy – it couldn't be Jeremy. He came out of the room and looked up at her standing there. She knew that he was going to die. She screamed, and the scream waked her.

She was sitting up in the big bed in the dark with her hand at her throat and the scream ringing in her ears. For a moment the dream hung there – Jeremy looking up at her, and the blood running down – and the scream. It was her own scream. Or was it? The dream went back into the place from which it had come, and she wasn't sure. She remembered Eily. If she had screamed like that, why hadn't Eily waked?

She stretched out a hand across the bed to feel for Eily, and she wasn't there. From the time of her waking to that time was a matter of seconds. It takes too long to tell. To live through, it had taken no longer than to lift a hand and let it fall again. In the moment she knew Eily wasn't there she heard the scream again. It came from somewhere in the house.

Jane was at the door before she knew how she had got there. The passage stretched away dark to the landing – dark and empty. It was just like her dream, except that in her dream she hadn't known whether it was hot or cold, and now she was so cold that she could hardly get her breath. Her heart thumped and her breath caught in her throat. She must have picked up her dressing-gown, because she had it clutched up against her. She must have caught it up from the foot of the bed without thinking what she did. She huddled it about her shoulders, and heard the house wake round her. A bed-spring creaked, doors opened. Miss Silver came out of her room fastening the cord of her crimson dressing-gown.

Jane ran past her to the head of the stairs and halted. It

was just as if she had gone back again into her dream, because the door of the little room halfway down was open and Jeremy was coming out. Terror went over her like a cold breath. And then it was gone, and the dream with it. This was Jeremy, very much alive and on the spot, in blue and white pyjamas, with his hair standing on end.

Jane ran down the half-flight and caught his arm. She said, 'Jeremy!' – or she began saying it and then stuck. With her lips parted and half his name froze on them, she looked down into the hall. There were three people there. One of them lay sprawling in the middle of the floor. He lay on his face as if he had tripped on the bottom step and pitched forward with his arms spread wide. There was a handkerchief twisted round his left hand. He was in his stocking feet, but he wore dark trousers had a grey linen coat. The rough horn handle of a knife stuck up under his left shoulder. The yellow light of the hanging lamp showed all the grey linen on that side horribly stained. The lamp hung on three brass chains and it had been turned low, but it showed Luke White lying there dead with a knife in his back.

It might have been Florence Duke who had screamed. She stood just past the newel of the stair where the passage went on to the baize door. She was dressed as she had been at dinner. The scarlet dress with its flaring pink and green pattern gave her a most ghastly look. The old make-up put on hours ago stood out from the pallor of her face with shocking effect. She held her hands a little away from her and stared at them. The fingers were red.

Eily was on the bottom step of the stair, crouched down with her face in her hands.

In the moment that it took Jane and Jeremy to see all this Miss Silver passed them. She went straight down into the hall and touched one of those outflung wrists. As she straightened up again, Fogarty Castell came running down, dishevelled past belief, red pyjama jacket open at the neck, plaid dressing-gown flapping. At once the whole frozen scene broke up. His noisy agitation swamped it. Ejaculations, protests, asseverations set the air throbbing.

'My poor Luke! What has he done that this should happen to him? Who is the assassin? And why should it happen to me, in my house – my respectable house? And Mr Taverner here – and the party – the reunion! What a reunion! We must have a doctor – why does nobody send for a doctor? Perhaps he may be restored perhaps he may speak – if it is only one word – if it is only the name of the murderer who ruins me by arranging an assassination in my house! My poor Luke – such a waiter – such a hand with a cocktail!' He ran his finger through his already distracted hair and produced an epitaph in a single word – 'Unreplaceable!'

It was at this moment that Geoffrey Taverner made his appearance, an unruffled figure, his grey dressing-gown neatly fastened, his hair immaculate. The horn-rimmed glasses had been removed and left behind in his room. They marked the place at which he had been interrupted in his reading of *Three Corpses and a Coffin*.

Jacob Taverner followed a step or two behind, overcoated and muffled as if about to take the road, his face puckered up with cold. Or perhaps it wasn't cold but something else which gave him that yellow tinge under the tan. He came round the bend of the stair on Geoffrey Taverner's heels, and heard Miss Silver say, 'He is quite dead, Mr Castell. The police must be rung up immediately.'

Chapter 16

EILY didn't move. Jacob Taverner stepped past her into the hall. He stood there looking down at the prostrate figure.

'Luke White – eh?' He turned sharply on Miss Silver. 'You say he's dead. How do you know? Not a doctor, are you?'

Miss Silver's air of authority had left her. She coughed in a deprecating manner and said. 'There is no pulse. And the position of the wound. I may have spoken too decidedly.' She produced a slightly flustered impression. 'I was in

London during the war. One could scarcely avoid some painful experiences.'

Jacob said, 'H'm!' And then, 'We ought to get him out of here.'

Miss Silver became very flustered indeed. With all the wish in the world to remain unobtrusively in the background, she really could not acquiesce in the removal of the body. she gave an excellent imitation of something very feminine and clinging.

'Oh, do you think so? Of course you will know best, but I have always understood that nothing should be disturbed until the arrival of the police. So extremely inconvenient, but I have always been under that impression.'

From the half open dining-room door came the raised exasperated voice of Fogarty Castell.

'Yes, I have said it twice – Ledlington police station! . . . Is that Ledlington police station? . . . I have an assassination to report. . . . I say an assassination! A man has been stabbed with a knife! He is dead!'

Jacob Taverner crossed over to the dining-room and went in, shutting the door behind him. They could no longer hear what was said.

All this while Florence Duke had not moved at all. Eily still sat with her face in her hands. She was wearing a faded pink dressing-gown over her nightdress, and a pair of old bedroom slippers on her bare feet. Her dark hair was loose upon her shoulders. Jane sat down on the step beside her and put her arm round her. She could feel then that Eily was shuddering. Long tremors went over her like waves coming in on a low tide.

As Jeremy stepped down into the hall he felt a touch on his arm. It might have been accidental, but he thought not. Miss Silver stood just within the open doorway of the lounge. He thought that it was she who had touched him. As she stepped back, he moved forward. The darkness and warmth of the empty room were behind them. The fire still glowed upon the hearth. Whilst in full view of the hall, they were to all intents and purposes alone.

Miss Silver said in a very composed manner, 'Captain Taverner, I am not anxious to put myself forward. You are

102

accustomed to some authority. Will you assert yourself if it is necessary? Nothing should be moved or touched before the arrival of the police, and if it is possible, everyone should come in here and await their arrival.'

He nodded.

'The girls aren't dressed – none of us are, except Florence Duke. She ' He broke off suddenly.

Miss Silver coughed.

'She has blood on her hands. That does not prove anything, you know. If she found him, she may have attempted to stanch the wound. She has certainly received a severe shock. I think I had better go to her. The police should be here within half an hour. Pray do your best to get everyone into the lounge.'

She crossed the foot of the stairs and came to where Florence Duke stood motionless, her eyes on her reddened hands. She did not move when Miss Silver touched her.

'Mrs. Duke, will you come into the lounge and sit down. The police will be here before long. They will want to see everyone. You have had a shock.'

The arm she was touching jerked under her hand. Florence Duke made a choking sound in her throat. There were no words. Then on a deep, hard-won breath they came, not pouring out, but in her old slow way, like bubbles rising.

'He's dead – I found him – '

'Yes. The police will want to know anything you can tell them. Come and sit down in the lounge.'

Florence did not move. She went on looking at her hands. She said, 'She was there – that girl Eily – she came from the lounge – she screamed. She said, "It's Luke! He's dead!" And I said, "You never know your luck." '

Miss Silver coughed.

'Why did you say that?'

Florence moved for the first time – moved and shifted her gaze. The fine dark eyes rested for a moment upon Miss Silver. They had a blank look. She said in that slow way.

'Well, you don't, do you? Perhaps she doesn't know hers. Perhaps it will catch up on her. It does sometimes when you're not expecting it.'

Miss Silver said, 'Dear me! Now what did you mean by that?'

Something flickered in the dark eyes. The heavy, monotonous voice said, 'Wouldn't you like to know?'

She turned with a jerk and walked into the lounge.

Geoffrey Taverner was lighting the wall-lamps. As the light came on it showed Florence Duke standing over the fire. She had a handkerchief, and she was rubbing her hands and wiping them dry. When she had finished she dropped the handkerchief into the fire, where it presently blazed up and fell away to a light ash.

Jeremy was getting everyone into the lounge and doing it very well.

Jacob Taverner came over from the dining-room with Castell and said that the police were on their way. He looked like a mummified monkey, but his manner was brisk and businesslike. He was very much in command, and was pleased to approve what had been done.

'Quite right, quite right! The police will want to see everyone — they said so. And of course nothing must be touched. But we're not all here. Who's missing? I don't see Mildred — or the Thorpe-Enningtons. . . . Yes, that's it — Mildred, and the Thorpe-Enningtons, and Annie Castell.'

Fogarty bounded into the conversation. He didn't exactly run his hands through his hair and tear it out, but he gave the impression that he might do so at any moment.

'Annie?' he said on a piercingly interrogative note. 'And what has Annie got to do with it? Does anyone imagine that she rises from her bed in the middle of the night to assassinate the best waiter we have ever had? I am her husband, and I can tell you that when she is in her bed she stays there, and that when she puts on her clothes it takes her three-quarters of an hour.'

'Then she had better start now,' said Jacob drily. 'The police will probably want to see her.' He frowned and looked about him. 'Someone had better see about the Thorpe-Enningtons and Mildred Taverner. I should have thought they'd have been down. There's been enough noise to wake the dead.'

104

There was a gasp from Eily. Jane had got her into one of the big chairs by the fire. She sat on the arm of it herself with her hand on Eily's shoulder. Eily leaned towards her, her head against Jane's knee, her face hidden.

Jacob touched Miss Silver on the arm.

'You, madam I don't know your name, but you seem to have a head on your shoulders – will you go upstairs with Mr. Castell and see if Miss Taverner and Lady Marian Thorpe-Ennington and her husband are all right. They'd better come down.'

Miss Silver said nothing at all. Even if she had wanted to, Fogarty Castell would have given her very little opportunity. He talked with passion about his house, his reputation, his loss, the purity of his motives, his devotion to the interests of the public and his patron, the excellency of his wife Annie as a cook and her virtue as a woman.

This got them to the Thorpe-Enningtons' door, where Fogarty tapped and met with no response. When repeated knockings, each louder than the last, had failed to elicit a reply, Miss Silver turned the handle of the door and opened it halfway.

If there had been any anxiety, it was immediately dispelled. The deep blended sound of two persons snoring filled the room. There was quite unmistakably a male snore and a female snore. Fogarty Castell threw up his hands.

'What do we do? You can hear? They are asleep – the two of them. As to him, I could have told you it would be ten o'clock in the morning before he was awake. And the Lady Marian – am I to assault her, to wake her up, to shake her by the shoulder? If she is like my wife Annie who is her cousin she will not wake for anything less than that.'

He held a lighted candle. Miss Silver took it from his hand and entered the room.

In the big four-poster bed Freddy Thorpe-Ennington lay with his face to the wall. His fair hair stuck up all over his head. He looked young and defenceless. His mouth was wide open, and he snored in irregular jerks. Lady Marian lay on her back. She looked exactly like a lady on a tomb, with her hands folded on her breast and a long dark plait lying outside the bedclothes and reaching almost to her knee. In

105

the wavering candlelight even the chin-strap added to the medieval effect. She looked beautiful and imposing, and she snored in a deep, harmonious way.

Miss Silver allowed the candlelight to shine upon the closed lids. Except for the fact that it displayed the magnificence of Marion Thorp-Ennington's eyelashes, nothing happened.

Miss Silver coughed and retreated.

'I think they may be left until the arrival of the police,' she said in her natural tone. 'It can then be decided whether it is necessary to rouse them.'

Fogarty threw up his hands.

'What a gift! If I could sleep like that! What a magnificent woman! What a heart – what lungs – what a digestion! It is worth all the fortunes in the world to be able to put your head on your pillow and not to think again until the morning! My wife Annie is like that too, but for me, I will be thinking, and tossing round, and tossing back, and turning everything upside down in my mind a hundred times in the night. And that is how I can tell the police who is the assassin. If I am asleep I do not hear him. But I am awake. I am thinking that the house must be painted outside without fail in the spring, and that the spring is a bad time for the outside painting, because if by some miracle we have a hot summer, the paint will blister. And that if I cannot have the best paint it will not be worth while to have it done, because for bad paint it is not worth the labour expenses. Over and over, and round and round, it goes in my head. And then I hear him go whistling past the end of the house.'

They were in the passage. Miss Silver still held the candle. It illuminated her small prim features, her neat hair, the crochet edging of the warm red dressing-gown. She said, 'Dear me!' And then, 'Who was it?'

Castell made an expansive gesture.

'It will be for the police to say. But when they hear that he comes round the house at night whistling under my niece Eily's window, and always the same tune – ' He pursed up his mouth and rendered very melodiously the first two lines of Bishop Heber's celebrated hymn. 'Does he come in the day? He does not! It is in the night that he comes and whistles under Eily's window – like that. And when I ask my wife Annie she says it is a hymn tune called "Greenland's Rocky Mountains".'

Scholastic tradition was too strong for Miss Silver. She coughed and said, '*Icy.*'

Fogarty looked outraged.

'Icy – rocky – it is all one what you call it! I do not sing hymns. It is John Higgins who sings them, and whistles them under Eily's window. And my poor Luke who is in love with her, wouldn't he be angry now? Wouldn't it come to words between them, and maybe fighting? And maybe a knife in the back? And Eily out of her bed and downstairs there in the hall where she had no business to be in the middle of the night!'

Miss Silver coughed again.

'You will have to say all that to the police, Mr. Castell. Do you not think we should knock on Miss Taverner's door?'

They knocked and received no reply. This time Miss Silver did not wait to knock again. She opened the door and stepped across the threshold.

The room was of a fair size and sparsely furnished. The bed, a small modern one, stood back against the right-hand wall. It was empty, and so was the room. Mildred Taverner wasn't there. Her clothes were neatly folded on a chair at the foot of the bed. The room offered no place of concealment. She wasn't there.

Miss Silver came back into the passage, leaving the door ajar. From where she stood she could see that the bathroom door was open, and that the room itself was dark. She went along past Jane's door and her own and looked in. There was certainly no one there.

As she stepped back, her eye caught a movement in the corresponding passage on the other side of the landing. Like the one in which they were standing, it was dark. But someone was coming along it towards the light. In a moment Mildred Taverner emerged. Her hair was wild and her manner distracted. She wore a heliotrope dressing-gown.

'Oh, Mr. Castell, what has happened? I woke up, and there was such a noise. I went along to find Geoffrey, but he wasn't in his room. Is it a fire? Have I time to pack my things?'

Chapter 17

A COLD winter daylight came in through the single window of Fogarty Castell's office. Beyond the fact that it possessed a large, plain table which supported a blotting-pad, an inkstand, and a pen-tray, there was nothing to differentiate it from any other small shabby room tucked away in the irregular plan of an old house. It was dull, it was bare. It had a square of dirty carpet on the floor and a peeling paper on the walls. A fly-spotted engraving of the Duke of Wellington directing the battle of Waterloo hung on the chimney-breast which cut off a corner of the room and gave it an uneven shape.

There were two doors, one leading through from the lounge, and the other giving upon a cross passage to the kitchen. The hotel register lay on a chair by the window, the table having been cleared for the accommodation of the police.

Inspector Crisp from Ledlington, small, wiry, and dark, sat before the blotting-pad with a pencil between his fingers and the alert expression of a terrier watching a rat-hole. Round the corner from him at the side of the table, with his chair at an angle which permitted him to stretch his long legs, Inspector Abbott of Scotland Yard leaned back in as easy an attitude as the chair permitted. He had his hands in his pockets. His dark blue suit was unwrinkled, the trousers had a perfect crease. The tie was just what it should have been, adding a discreet touch of colour to an otherwise sombre scheme. His fair hair, mirror-smooth, was slicked back from a high, pale brow. He was beautifully shaved. There was, in fact, nothing about his appearance to suggest a police officer who has been up most of the night dealing with a murder case.

The third occupant of the room was Miss Maud Silver, who had also been up all night, and showed it as little. Her hair with its Alexandra fringe in front, its coils behind, and its controlling net, was the last word in neatness. Her olive-green dress was fastened by a cherished ornament in the shape of a rose carved in bog-oak with an Irish pearl at the centre, a legacy from her aunt Editha Blake, who had departed from a sedate family tradition by marrying a wild Irishman and breaking her neck in the hunting field. Editha's rose had come a long way and changed a pretty harum-scarum mistress for a prim and practical one. It remained one of Miss Silver's most valued possessions.

She sat on a low upright chair of the kind produced in the early years of Queen Victoria's reign. A capacious knitting-bag lay open on her lap, and she was knitting rapidly without once glancing at the busy needles. About four inches of bright china-blue wool depended from them like a frill. When completed, the garment would be a warm woolly dress for her niece Ethel Burkett's youngest, little Josephine, now just two years old. Since she was a fair child with rosy cheeks and round blue eyes, Miss Silver considered this bright blue wool a very happy choice.

Inspector Crisp was speaking.

'Inspector Abbott suggests that we should run over the statements with you and see whether there is any point which strikes you. The position, as I understand it, is that you are here unofficially at Chief Inspector Lamb's suggestion.'

Miss Silver inclined her head.

'That is the position.'

'He also tells me that you have worked confidentially with the police on previous occasions.'

Miss Silver made a slight verbal correction.

'I have worked confidentially upon cases with which the police were connected.'

A faint sardonic smile appeared for a moment on Frank Abbott's face. Inspector Crisp put his head on one side and looked alert. He didn't get the point, but he thought there was one, and that it had got away. He didn't like things to get away. He pounced on one of the papers in front of him and turned to get the light on it.

'Now here's Castell's statement – a lot about it and about. What it boils down to is this. He's been manager here for

109

five years, first under a Mr. Smith, and then under Mr. Jacob Taverner whose father had granted the lease of the Catherine-Wheel to Mr. Smith's father. The original lease ran out a good many years ago, after which Mr. Smith had a yearly tenancy. On his death Jacob Taverner took over the control. Castell's wife is his cousin. Castell identifies the dead man as Luke White – barman, waiter, general handy-man at the hotel. Says he's been here three years and he has found him satisfactory. But he belongs to a family with quite a bad name in the neighbourhood – and they are illegitimate connections of the Taverner family. Everyone in this case is a connection of the Taverner family.'

Miss Silver intervened.

'They are all grandchildren or great-grandchildren of Jeremiah Taverner who kept this inn until his death in eighteen-eighty-eight.'

The Inspector's eyebrows twitched.

'I've got a list of them – a kind of a family tree. But I suppose you don't need to see it.' His tone was sharp.

Miss Silver smiled disarmingly.

'I have had some time to get it by heart. And then I have met the people, which makes it so much easier.'

The paper in Crisp's hand rustled as he turned it.

'Well, all this party came down yesterday. You arrived at about nine o'clock, and the party broke up some time after ten. One of the guests, Albert Miller, was not staying in the house. He left in an intoxicated condition at half past ten. Did you notice his condition?'

Miss Silver coughed.

'It would have been difficult not to do so. He behaved in a very noisy and illbred manner. Mr. Castell was doing his best to keep him quiet.'

'Were there any words betweeen him and Luke White – any quarrel?'

'I did not see any quarrel. He was calling out for Mr. Castell's niece, Eily.'

'And Luke White was sweet on her, wasn't he? There might have been a quarrel over that.'

Miss Silver shook her head.

'Luke White did not seem to be taking any notice. He was

110

standing by the coffee-tray attending to the guests.'

Crisp tapped with his pencil.

'Well, Castell says Miller left the hotel just before half past ten. Captain Taverner confirms this – says Castell drew his attention to the state Miller was in. They were in the lounge at the time, and Captain Taverner says they looked out of the window and watched Miller go off down the road. He says he was walking unsteadily and singing some song about a girl called Eileen.'

Miss Silver's needles clicked.

' "Eileen alannah". He was singing it in the lounge.'

Crisp said shortly, 'I don't know one song from another. But it seems Albert Miller's out of it. He left here before half past ten, and his landlady, Mrs. Wilton, 6, Thread Street, Ledlington, she says, and her husband corroborates, that Al Miller came in drunk just before half past eleven. They say he made a lot of noise and kept singing this song. The Wiltons are respectable people. Mr. Wilton called up to him to say they'd had enough and he could find himself another lodging in the morning. And Miller said he was clearing out anyhow – used language and said he was fed up with the place and his job and everything – said he was getting out and wouldn't be back in a hurry. This was on the stairs, him at the top and Mr. Wilton at the bottom. Then he went into his room and banged the door, and Mr. Wilton went down and locked the front door and took away the key because he didn't want any moonlight flittings. Seven o'clock in the morning Miller came down, paid a week's money, and said he wouldn't be coming back. Said he'd send for his things when he got a job. Mrs. Wilton wasn't dressed. Mr. Wilton opened the bedroom door a bit and took the money. When he saw it was all right he gave Miller the key to let himself out. Miller went up to the station, where he was supposed to be on duty for the seven-thirty. He walks in as bold as brass in his plain clothes and says he's had enough – says what he thinks about the station-master and the whole bag of tricks and walks out. Nobody's seen him since. We'll pick him up of course, but there doesn't seem to be any chance of his being mixed up in the stabbing, because – to get back to Castell – he says he and

111

Luke White were together for some time after Miller left. He says he went up to his room at about ten to eleven, and left White alive and well. White had a downstair bedroom opposite the kitchen. There doesn't seem to be any reason why Castell should give Miller an alibi if it isn't true.'

Miss Silver said, 'At such an early stage motives may be very obscure.'

Crisp came back sharply.

'Does that mean you have any reason for suspecting Castell?'

She appeared mildly surprised.

'Oh dear no, Inspector.'

He looked at her suspiciously for a moment, and turned again to the paper in his hand.

'Castell says he didn't get to sleep at once. He was lying awake, when he heard footsteps coming from the direction of Cliff – that's the next village along the road. He has a window that looks out at the front. He says the footsteps turned off and went down the other side of the house and round to the back. He says he got up and went along to the lavatory window, which looks out that way. He heard someone come along whistling a hymn tune – "Greenland's Icy Mountains", he says. So then he went back to his bed, because he know who it was. It seems John Higgins, who is another of these Taverner relations, is courting this girl Eily Fogarty, and once in a way he'll come along like that and whistle under her window and they'll have a word or two. Seems he always whistles the same tune. Castell says he doesn't approve – says the girl has been in two minds between Higgins and Luke White. But he says she's of age and can please herself, and he isn't prepared to have a row about it. He goes back to bed, and he can't fix the time any nearer than that it must have been well after eleven.'

He paused, put the paper down, and took up another.

'Now we'll take the girl Eily's statement. She says she went up to her room between half past ten and a quarter to eleven. she undressed, and was going to lock her door, when she found the key was gone. She says she was frightened – says she always locked her door at night.' He ran his eye down the page. 'Here we are – "I dressed and put on my

112

shoes and stockings. I was frightened to go to bed. I didn't know what to do. I put out my candle and sat by the window and looked at the sea. I don't know how long it was before I heard John Higgins whistling. If he wanted to speak to me any time he would come along and whistle Greenland's Icy Mountains under my window. We can talk like that without anyone hearing, because my room is at the corner, and there's the lavatory, and the linen-room, and the back stairs before you come to another room that side. I told John I was frightened about my key, and he said to go along to Miss Heron and ask her to let me stay with her, and he would come in the morning and take me away and Mrs. Bridling would take me in until we could be married. He said he'd got it all fixed up." Asked what she was frightened of, she said Luke White had threatened her.'

He laid the paper down.

Miss Silver had been knitting rapidly, her hands low in her lap, the needles held after the Continental fashion. She said now, 'I believe that is correct.'

Crisp nodded.

'Yes – Miss Heron confirms it. She says the girl came into her room, and seemed frightened, so she told her to stay. She says Eily undressed and got into bed, and they both went to sleep. She woke up, thinking she'd heard a scream, and Eily Fogarty wasn't there. When she'd heard a second scream and ran down to the half landing Luke White was lying face-downwards in the hall with a knife in his back, and the girl Eily was sitting on the bottom step with her head in her hands. Mrs. Duke was standing by the newel with her hands covered with blood.'

Miss Silver inclined her head.

'That is correct. I was just behind Miss Heron. She remained on the half landing with Captain Taverner who had just come out of his room there, whilst I went down into the hall. There was no one else present. Mr. Geoffrey Taverner and Mr. Castell came down later, and then Mr. Jacob Taverner. Afterwards Mr. Castell and I found Mr. and Mrs. Thorpe-Ennington very deeply asleep.'

'They really were asleep?'

Miss Silver looked across the clicking needles.

'Undoubtedly.'

'And you met Miss Taverner returning from her brother's room?'

'Yes. She was much disturbed, and enquired if the hotel was on fire.'

Frank Abbott said with a suspicion of a drawl in his voice, 'And what do you suppose made her think of that?'

Miss Silver gave her slight cough.

'I cannot say. She is an extremely nervous person.'

Inspector Crisp rustled among his papers.

'When I asked this girl Eily in what way Luke White had threatened her she burst into tears and I could get no coherent statement. Now it looks to me as if she may very well have done more than talk to John Higgins out of a window. Suppose she came downstairs and let him in. She says she was up and dressed. Suppose she meant to go off with him – she'd had some sort of a fright, you know. Or she may have just meant to let him in and have a good cry on his shoulder.'

Frank Abbott shook his head.

'That won't do, because she went along to Jane Heron's room and undressed and went to bed there. Miss Heron confirms that, you know.'

Crisp said in a dogged tone, 'She may have gone to bed, but she got up again. She was down in the hall in her night-gown when the man was murdered – or as near as makes no difference.'

Abbott nodded.

'Just let Miss Silver hear what she says about that. I'd like to hear it again myself.'

Crisp read from the paper before him, his sharp voice making an odd contrast with Eily's faltered words.

' "I went to sleep almost at once, I was so tired. Then I woke up. I thought I heard something. I went to see what it was. I saw Luke White lying there in the hall. I didn't know what had happened. I screamed, but he didn't move. Then I saw the knife. I ran into the lounge. I thought – they'd had drinks there earlier – I thought of getting something to help him, but everything had been cleared away. I

114

came back. Mrs. Duke was there bending over him. Her hands were all red. I screamed again. Everyone came down." '

Frank said in a considering tone, 'Well – it might have happened like that – '

'Doesn't sound natural to me,' said Inspector Crisp. 'What did she go into the lounge for? They'd been having drinks there!' He made a sound of contempt. 'There were windows there, and she could have been letting John Higgins out that way.'

Frank nodded again.

'It could be. Let's hear what the other woman says — Florence Duke.'

'Well, here we are. "I hadn't undressed. I got thinking about old times – I suppose because of the old inn. My grandfather used to tell me about it. I'm accustomed to sitting up late. I didn't think I could sleep if I went to bed. I had taken off my watch and wound it up, so I didn't take any notice of the time. I got restless after a bit. I thought I'd go down and see if I could raise a drink, or if I couldn't get a drink I might lay my hands on a paper or a magazine. It was getting me down, being the only one awake and all the old stories about the inn. I went downstairs, and there was a light in the hall. There wasn't anyone there. I went into the lounge. It was all dark, but I had my bedroom candle. The drinks had been put away. I hadn't much hope of getting one, but you never know your luck. I went over to the dining-room. Same thing there. Then I went through the baize door and along to the kitchen. I found a bottle of sherry, and I had some. Then I had a look round. I was curious to see the old place after hearing so much about it. I don't know how long I was out there. I'm not any good at noticing the time, and I didn't look at the clock. I could hear it ticking, but I'd have had to go right up to it with my candle to see the hands. After a bit I thought I'd go back to my room. Just as I came to the baize door I heard someone scream. The candle dropped out of my hand and went out. I lost time finding it. When I got it again I remembered I had no matches to light it with. I dropped it down and went through into the hall. Luke White was lying on the floor
115

with a knife in his back. I went up to him to see if he was dead. I got his blood on my hands. Then I saw Eily Fogarty coming out of the lounge, and she screamed.'

Chapter 18

Doesn't get us much forrader, does it?' said Frank Abbott. 'If the Duke woman stabbed him, why didn't she get away while the going was good? She wasn't there when Eily came down. If she killed the man, why should she come back and allow herself to be caught, quite literally, red-handed?'

Crisp frowned.

'Say the girl Eily's statement is correct. What she hears is the sound of the man falling. Mrs. Duke hears her coming and dodges back through the baize door, keeping it open a chink. She sees Eily go into the lounge, and thinks she'll have time to get away up the stairs.'

Frank's fair eyebrows rose.

'And she is found bending over the body. No – you can't make it fit.'

Miss Silver coughed in a gentle deprecating manner.

'You suggested that I should comment upon any point which I considered significant, Inspector.'

He said, 'Yes,' with some appearance of reluctance.

Miss Silver, perfectly well aware that he would have preferred to continue his argument with Frank Abbott, remarked that a point had occurred to her.

'In Eily Fogarty's statement she says that Luke White had threatened her. I gather from Miss Heron that she overheard a scene between them just before my own arrival at the hotel.'

'What kind of a scene?'

Miss Silver said very composedly, 'You had better ask Miss Heron. The point that occurred to me is this. The

116

threats which frightened Eily were not made until nine o'clock in the evening, yet John Higgins seems to have known about them when he came here at some time after eleven.'

'The girl told him of course.'

Miss Silver's needles clicked.

'Quite so, Inspector. But Eily says that he had already arranged with Mrs. Bridling to take her in until they could be married. Mrs. Bridling is, I believe his next door neighbour. She is in the habit of coming in to assist Mrs. Castell when the hotel is full. She was here last night.'

'She left before nine o'clock.'

'Yes, but she came back.'

'What!'

Miss Silver gave him a glance of mild reproof. Quite an intelligent officer, but inclined to be abrupt. She said, 'I find that she left a scarf in the pantry. She must have come back for it, because when Mrs. Castell told Eily to bring it through – it had been left on the drip-board – the scarf was gone. It will, of course, at once occur to you that if Mrs. Bridling had returned to fetch her scarf at the time that Eily was alone with her aunt in the kitchen, she may have overheard some particulars of this scene with Luke White. If she did so, and if she repeated what she had heard to John Higgins, it would account both for his coming out here to speak to Eily, and for his decision to remove her at all costs from the danger of any repetition of such a scene. It also accounts very satisfactorily for his having arranged with Mrs. Bridling to take Eily in. It seems quite plain to me that he had seen Mrs. Bridling after her return from the Catherine-Wheel, and that something which she then told him made him resolve to get Eily away with no further loss of time.'

Crisp said abruptly, 'We'll have to see the two of them – Higgins and Mrs. Bridling. And we don't want them cooking up a story either. Cooling had better take the car and fetch them along. We can be seeing Miss Heron.'

He got up and went out to give his orders.

Frank Abbott raised those fair eyebrows and looked across at Miss Silver with half a smile.

'All zeal, isn't he?' Then, 'Well, here you are, right in

117

the middle of it. And the Chief said he was giving you a nice change from murder! Are you going to tell me who did it?'

Miss Silver looked shocked.

'My dear Frank!'

He said in a bantering voice, 'Don't tell me you don't know!'

She said reprovingly, 'It would be quite improper to advance an opinion at present. There are a good many possibilities. It is difficult to avoid the suspicion that the motive for the murder is to be found somewhere in the background which we were sent down here to investigate. Taking the family history into consideration, this man Luke White's connection with it, and the fact that he has been employed here for the last three years, there is the possibility that he had acquired some dangerous knowledge, and was murdered either to prevent his informing or, more probably, because he was attempting to use his knowledge for the purpose of blackmail. There is also the possibility that he was murdered for purely personal reasons either by John Higgins or by Eily Fogarty. I should give more weight to this theory if the wound were such as might have been received during a struggle. But a girl like Eily would be very unlikely to stab a man in the back. From what I hear of John Higgins, it would be equally out of character in his case.'

'And what do you hear of John Higgins?'

'He comes of good local yeoman stock. He is head carpenter on Sir John Layburn's estate, as were his father and his grandfather before him. His father was Mrs Castell's brother and a grandson of old Jeremiah Taverner. He seems to bear a very high character, and has struck Captain Taverner and Jane Heron as being rather an exceptional person.'

Frank gave a short laugh.

'Some kind of a local preacher, isn't he? There's no saying what the most exalted character may do if somebody threatens his girl.'

Inspector Crisp opened the door.

'This way, Miss Heron. If you will take a chair – there are just a few questions we should like to ask you.'

Jane sat down. She faced the Inspector and the window.

The pale, chilly daylight had not brightened. It showed her pallor and the dark marks under her eyes. It occurred to Frank Abbott that she would have done better not to paint her lips. He did not, however, attach any importance to the fact that she had done so, an ample quota of female cousins having taught him that a girl feels quite immodestly undressed without her lipstick, the natural lip being as sedulously concealed as was the Victorian ankle.

Inspector Crisp picked up his pencil and balanced it.

'Now, Miss Heron – Eily Fogarty says in her statement that this man Luke White had threatened her. She gives this as her reason for being afraid to stay in her own room last night, and for coming along to yours.'

Jane said nothing. Her bright lips were a little parted. Her eyes went in a quick glance from Frank Abbott to Miss Silver, from whom she received an encouraging smile, and came back again to Inspector Crisp and his pencil. 'Nervous', was his mental comment. He made it with satisfaction, since a nervous witness handled with just the right amount of severity could usually be relied upon to spill the beans. In his official capacity he would not, of course, have employed such a vulgarism, but thought is apt to be less formal than speech.

'Well now, can you corroborate that?'

'I don't quite know what you mean by corroborate.'

Frank Abbott had a fastidious ear. He found Jane's voice extremely pleasing.

Crisp said, 'Do you know that Luke White threatened her?'

She hesitated, and then said, 'Yes.'

'Will you tell us what you know about his threat.'

'I don't know ... ' The words came out slowly and reluctantly.

Miss Silver said with mild firmness, 'Truth is always best. It harms no innocent person.'

Jane didn't feel so sure about that. She was remembering how Eily had looked at her nail-scissors, and how she had said, 'Suppose they had been a knife.' But she wouldn't ever tell that. She was distressed and uncertain.

Crisp said, 'Come now, Miss Heron!'

She said, 'Luke White did threaten her. I heard him.'

'Where did this take place?'

'In my room. Eily was turning down the bed, and he followed her in. Mr. Taverner had been showing us the old smugglers' passage. When we came back Jeremy – Captain Taverner – told me I'd got a smudge on my face, so I went up to my room. The door was half open and I could hear Luke White talking to Eily. I didn't exactly like to go in – I thought it would be embarrassing for Eily. I stood where the steps come up – '

'He was threatening her?'

Jane's voice had steadied.

'He said he would have her whatever she did, and she'd better come willingly. He said if she married anyone else, he'd come in the night and cut the man's heart out. He talked about her being drenched with his blood. It was horrible. Then, I think, he caught hold of her. She called out, and he swore, and I made a noise on the steps as if I had stumbled. He came out then, and I went into Eily. She was very much upset.'

Inspector Crisp made a little stabbing pass in the air with his pencil.

'The dead man had his left hand tied up in a handkerchief. There was a small wound just short of the knuckles. Do you know how he got it?'

'I saw him with his hand tied up.'

'When did you see that?'

'When he was letting Miss Silver in.'

'And that was when?'

Miss Silver said, 'Nine o'clock, Inspector.'

'And how long after this scene in your room?'

'Just after. He was letting Miss Silver in as I came down.'

He made that stabbing pass again.

'Come, come, Miss Heron, I don't think you are being frank. Did you know where Luke White got that wound?'

'I didn't see him get it.'

'No – for you were outside your bedroom, and he and Eily Fogarty were inside. You heard her cry out, and you heard him swear. And then you saw him come out of the room. Could you see his left hand?'

120

'Yes.'

'What was he doing with it?'

'He was holding it with the other.'

'Did he say anything?'

'Yes, he said the window had stuck and Eily had called him in to help her. He said he had hurt his hand on the catch.'

'Did you believe him?'

After a long pause Jane said, 'No.'

She pushed back her chair and got up.

'I'm afraid that's all I can tell you,' she said, and walked out of the room.

Chapter 19

MRS. BRIDLING, in the chair pushed back by Jane, sat bolt upright and met Inspector Crisp's questioning gaze with the agreeable consciousness that no one had ever been able to say a word they shouldn't about her nor any of her family. Go where they would and ask what they liked, they'd only be told the one thing. Bridlings or Bents – she herself had been a Bent – there was only the one thing to be said about them – they were good-living, hardworking people, Chapel members for the most part, and nobody could say different. She was buoyed up by these thoughts, and by the fact that she had kept Constable Cooling waiting whilst she put on her Sunday dress, a bright royal blue, her good black coat, and the hat which she had had for her mother-in-law's funeral three years ago with a nice bunch of berries at the side to take off the mourning look. Her gloves had been bought for the same occasion and were still very good indeed, being too uncomfortable to wear except upon high days and holidays. They pinched her fingers, and it was a dreadful struggle to get them on, but they gave her a good deal of moral support. She was a tall, thin woman with a screwed-up knob of hair under the funeral hat. She had pale eyes, a long pale nose, and very pale lips.

Inspector Crisp looked hard at her and said in his rather jerky way, 'You were helping Mrs. Castell last night, Mrs. Bridling?'

'That's right. I've got my husband bed-ridden and my hands full, but he's willing for me to oblige Mrs. Castell. We went to school together when she was Annie Higgins and I was Emily Bent.'

'Old friends – eh? Well, you were here helping. What time did you leave?'

Mrs. Bridling smoothed down her black kid gloves.

'It was every bit of a quarter to nine. I'd reckoned to get off by the half hour, but she asked me to stay and do the glasses.'

'You're sure it wasn't later than that – it wasn't after nine?'

'I wouldn't have stayed as late as that. I'd Mr. Bridling to see to at home. I'm sure I don't know when I've been so put out.'

'What put you out, Mrs. Bridling?'

'The same as would have put anyone out – getting all behind.'

Miss Silver gave a gentle cough and looked at Inspector Abbott, who immediately responded by enquiring in a languid voice, 'If you left at a quarter to nine you were not so very late. But you had to come back for your scarf, had you not?'

Mrs. Bridling nodded.

'Left it on the drip-board. I don't know when I did such a thing, I'm sure. And why I didn't notice it sooner was on account of my coming over so hot with my hands in the boiling water. "Come out hot, go home cold", as my father used to say. So I ran back for it sharp. I didn't like keeping Mr. Bridling waiting, but I knew how he'd carry on if I came in without my scarf. Very particular he is about my keeping my throat well wrapped up, because he says, "If you go and get yourself into hospital through acting silly, well, it's all very well for you", he says. "You'll be comfortable enough and waited on hand and foot," he says, "but who's going to look after me?" so I thought, "If he's going to be put about, it had better be because of me being late, and not bring all that up again about the hospital not being able to keep him on account of his being a chronic case," so I just came back for my scarf.'

Crisp said, 'What time did you get back to the inn?'

The pale eyes dwelt upon him.

'It'd be after nine. I'd gone a good bit of the way.'

'Did you see Mrs. Castell?'

'No. Her and Eily were talking – Mr. Castell's niece, Eily Fogarty.'

Crisp said, 'Ah!' And then, 'Did you hear what they were saying?'

Mrs. Bridling looked down her long, pale nose.

'I'm not one to listen at doors,' she said in a virtuous voice.

Frank Abbott's lip twitched. He had never encountered an eavesdropper who did not preface his statement by explaining just how abhorrent it was to him to overhear what was not meant for his ears.

Inspector Crisp made the accustomed response.

'I'm sure you're not. But if the door was open –'

She nodded.

'Well, it was and it wasn't. I was looking round for my scarf, and I couldn't help but hear what Eily Fogarty was saying.'

'And what was she saying?'

'You may well ask! I'm sure I never heard such goings-on. The poor girl was all of a shake. Seems that Luke White followed her into one of the bedrooms, caught hold of her, and used dreadful language, and if it hadn't been for Miss Heron coming along there's no saying what might have happened. Eily said she had to pick up Miss Heron's nail-scissors and run them into his hand to make him let her go. And all Annie Castell had to say was, "Lock your door nights." Well, I thought the sooner the girl's out of that house the better, and I didn't wait to hear any more, I just picked up my scarf and ran.'

Frank Abbott said, 'You live next door to John Higgins, don't you? Did you tell him what you had heard?'

123

She turned her pale gaze on him.

'Indeed I did, and before I slept last night. I told Mr. Bridling about it whilst I was getting him his cup of cocoa and getting him comfortable for the night. "Emily," he says, "if anything happens to that girl, you'll have it on your conscience for ever. Nothing but an abode of iniquity, that's what that place is, same as it always was, and you can't get from it. And I don't care if you went to school with Annie Castell ten times over. I've been willing for you to keep up with her and oblige when short-handed, but I'll not have you going over there again," he says, "not if there's that kind of shameless goings-on, and Annie Castell with no more to say about it than 'Lock your door nights'. She was brought up in a God-fearing home, and she did ought to know better," he says.' She looked round enjoyably. 'I don't know when I've seen Mr. Bridling so worked up. Quite cheered him up having something he could disapprove of so thorough – kept on talking about it and hindering me. "There'll be a judgment," he said. And when the news come this morning you couldn't hold him. "The triumphing of the wicked is short," he says.'

Crisp stemmed the flow.

'Did you in fact tell Higgins what you had overheard?' She gave a vigorous nod.

'Mr. Bridling wouldn't have given me a minute's peace if I hadn't. I'd him to see to, and a bit of washing to do, and then I went in and told John Higgins.'

'How did he take it?'

Mrs. Bridling tossed her head.

'The way you'd expect any man to take it that was a man – clinched his hands up and turned as red as fire and then as white as a bit of curd. I don't know how he kept himself, but he didn't say anything, not till he'd got a hold of himself. I said, "You'll have to get her away, John. It's no place for a good-living girl." And he says, "No." And then he says, "Mrs. Bridling, you'll take her in if I can get her to come away tomorrow? We'll be married as soon as I can fix it up, but you'll take her in till then?" So I said I would, and glad to do it, for he's a good neighbour and a good-living man if there ever was one, and she's a lucky girl to get him for a husband. Many's the time he's been up half the night with Mr. Bridling when he's had one of his turns, so as I could get a bit of rest. So I said to him, "If there's anything I can do, you know I'll do it and be glad of the chance".'

'Thank you, Mrs. Bridling,' said Inspector Crisp.

Chapter 20

Mrs. Bridling left with regret. She didn't know when she'd enjoyed anything more, but like all the great moments of life it was over too soon. There was a hymn they used to sing in Sunday school:

> 'Fleeting ever, fleeting onward,
> Earthly joys will never stay.'

The lines came to her mind regretfully. Over it was, but it would be something to tell Mr. Bridling when she got home.

She came through the door between Castell's office and the lounge and sat down to wait until they should be finished with John Higgins. After due consideration she had rejected the idea of going through into the kitchen to see Annie Castell. For one thing, here she was in her best, and with Annie working it wouldn't seem hardly friendly not to give her a hand. She wasn't ever one to stand by and watch other people work, but risk spotting her best dress was more than could be expected. The lounge was empty. She picked a comfortable chair and sat down to wait.

John Higgins was in the office, sitting with a hand on either knee, his fair hair standing up in a shock and his blue eyes steady on the Inspector. Frank Abbott thought, 'Solid, dependable chap. Hope he didn't do it. Not the type to stab a man in the back. Unless — ' Suppose the fellow had caught hold of Eily Fogarty and John Higgins had come upon them struggling. No, that wouldn't do. There was no doubt where the knife had come from – that trophy on the chimney-breast in the dining-room. Whoever used it had got to get it from there. It wouldn't be lying about in the hall to be snatched up on the spur of the moment.

John Higgins said, 'Yes, I walked over last night to see Miss Fogarty.'

Crisp balanced his pencil.

'Mrs. Bridling told you that there had been a scene with Luke White?'

'Yes. I went over to tell Miss Fogarty that she must leave in the morning. It wasn't fit for her to be there. We are going to be married, and I told her she could stay with Mrs. Bridling while I got it all fixed up.'

'Did she tell you that the key of her room was missing?'

Angry colour swept up to the roots of the fair hair.

'Yes. I told her to go along to Miss Heron's room and ask if she could stay there.'

Crip's bristling dark eyebrows rose.

'Do you know Miss Heron? Is she a friend of yours?'

John Higgins said, 'I was sure that she would let Eily stay with her.'

Crisp stabbed at the blotting-paper.

'You had quite a talk with Miss Fogarty, didn't you?'

'We talked.'

'For how long?'

'I couldn't say.'

'An hour?'

John Higgins shook his head.

'Not near so long.'

'Half an hour?'

Another slow head-shake.

'More like a quarter, but I won't swear to it.'

'And where did this conversation take place?'

'Eily was up at her window.'

'And you?'

'Down underneath.'

'Sure she didn't let you in?'

The blue eyes looked at him very directly.

'She wouldn't do that, and I wouldn't ask her to.'

'That's no answer. Did she let you in last night?'

'No, she did not.'

'Sure about that?'

John Higgins said in a hard, steady voice, 'It's five years since I've been over the threshold of this house till I came here today.'

'Why?'

He gave the same answer that he had given in John Taylor's office.

'That's my business.'

Crisp stabbed at him with his pencil.

'Nobody's got any private business in a murder case. Mrs. Castell is your aunt, isn't she? What's your quarrel with her?'

'I've no quarrel with my Aunt Annie.'

'Then with Castell — what's your quarrel with him?'

'I've no quarrel with him. I don't like his company. He would tell you that he doesn't like mine. We go our own ways.'

Crisp shifted impatiently in his chair.

'We've got away from the point. You know that a man was murdered here last night — the barman, Luke White?'

John Higgins nodded.

'That kind of news travels fast.'

'You had a quarrel with the man, hadn't you?'

'I had no quarrel with him.'

'Not after you'd heard what Mrs. Bridling had to say?'

The muscles of the big hands lying on either knee tensed, the knuckles stood up white. John Higgins said in his steady, deep voice, 'He was an evil-liver. It wasn't fit for Eily to be under the same roof. I'd have fetched her away as soon as it was day.'

Crisp repeated the last words.

'As soon as it was day. But what about last night? You came out here hotfoot after you'd seen Mrs. Bridling. Are you going to say Eily Fogarty didn't let you in?'

'I've said so.'

'And you sent her along to Miss Heron's room and didn't see her again?'

'I didn't see her again.'

'Do you think she stayed with Miss Heron?'

'Of course she did.'

Crisp gave another of those darting stabs.

Then how do you account for the fact that she was found down in the hall in her nightgown, and Luke White not a yard away from her with the knife in his back?'

The blood rushed powerfully to John Higgins' face. He sprang to his feet and stood there, his hands on the table edge, gripping it hard.

'Eily — ' he said. His voice caught on the name. He tried for it again, and as he did so, the hot blood drained away and left him ashy pale.

Miss Silver laid her knitting down on the floor beside her chair and got up. At the touch of her hand on his arm he turned and looked at her, an agonised question in his eyes. She said in a kind, cheerful voice, 'You have no need to be anxious, Mr. Higgins. Eily is quite safe.'

His look went blank for a moment.

'Safe — '

'She is perfectly safe, Mr. Higgins. Nothing has happened to her — nothing at all.'

He said in a stumbling voice, 'She was down there — with that man — '

'She heard a noise and came down and found him. It was a shock of course, but she is quite safe.'

Frank Abbott had a moment of unreasoned admiration for his Miss Silver. At what she considered the dictates of humanity she would without hesitation sacrifice a point in the game. She had in fact just done so, and it was annoying Inspector Crisp very much. He said with an angry edge to his voice, 'I think you had better leave this to me, Miss Silver. We have no evidence to support Eily Fogarty's statement. If I may say so, you had no business to repeat it.'

Miss Silver turned a look of calm rebuke upon him.

'I beg your pardon, Inspector!'

Nothing could have been more proper than the words, yet in some singular manner Inspector Crisp had the feeling that his collar was too tight, and that he did not quite know what to do with his hands and feet. These were sensations which had afflicted him in his teens, now many years behind him. He had hoped never to experience them again, but during the moments that he had to support Miss Silver's gaze they were uncomfortably prominent. It was with a good deal of relief that he saw her turn back to John Higgins. She gave a little cough and said in a confidential voice, 'You really need not be troubled about Eily. Miss Heron is with her all the time. They are doing the bedrooms together.' After which she resumed her seat and her knitting.

Inspector Crisp's collar returned to its normal size. He felt an urgent need to assert himself. His tone was brusque as he said, 'Sit down, Higgins! Eily Fogarty says she heard a noise and came downstairs. If that's true, the noise may have been made by the murderer. Suppose there was a window open in the lounge. I'm not saying who opened it, or for what purpose. I'm not saying it was Eily Fogarty, but it could have been. I'm not saying anyone came in that way, but you can see for yourself that someone might have done, and you can see for yourself that it might have been you. Eily Fogarty was seen to come out of the lounge with Luke White lying dead in the hall. She could have been shutting that window after you.'

John Higgins shook his head.

'I neither came in nor went out,' he said.

Crisp made a sharp thrust with his pencil.

'There was a window unlatched in the lounge.'

Chapter 21

THERE were a good many more questions and answers, but the result was the same. In a perfectly deliberate manner John Higgins stuck to it that somewhere about eleven o'clock he had stood under Eily Fogarty's window and talked to her for something like a quarter of an hour, and that he had then gone home. He had not then or at any time during the past five years set foot inside the Catherine-Wheel. He had not at any time during the past twenty-four hours either seen Luke White or had any communication with him.

When they had let him go Crisp said in his most didactic manner.

'You may depend upon it that's the way it was. There was that window unlatched – the one just through there.' He pointed at the door going through to the lounge. 'All the others were hasped – that one wasn't. Castell says he checked them all over when he shut up for the night.'

Frank Abbott gazed abstractedly at his beautifully polished shoes.

'I don't know that I should want to hang a dog on Castell's evidence,' he observed.

Crisp nodded quite good-humouredly.

'Oh, yes. But that's what you're down here for, isn't it – to find something against Castell? He's a slippery customer, and British subject or no British subject, he's got foreigner written all over him.'

Frank said, 'Cosmopolitan, if you want to be polite – mongrel, if you don't. Portuguese father, Irish mother. Born more or less by accident in some London purlieu, and brought up for the most part in Marseilles, where his parents kept what may pass for a boarding-house.'

Miss Silver coughed.

'That would account for the fact that his turn of speech is often decidedly French.'

Crisp gave a short laugh.

'Give a dog a bad name!' he said. 'You can't hang Castell because his mother was no better than she should be. He may have a finger in this dope-smuggling pie that you people are so set on, but for that very reason he'd keep clear of a thing like murder. And where's the motive? The two men were as thick as thieves.'

Frank Abbott smiled.

'You've said it – they were as thick as thieves. Haven't you ever heard of rogues falling out?'

When John Higgins left the office he walked through the lounge into the hall. It was five years since he had been in the house, but he knew his way. He took a look round the screen at the dining-room door, found the room empty, and then walked up the stairs. On the halfway landing he checked, and stood for a moment listening. There was the sound of voices. He knocked on the door of the room in which Jeremy had slept the night before and went in.

Eily and Jane Heron was making up a bed on the old-fashioned couch. Jeremy was at the table writing. Eily gave a cry of surprise. She stood where she was, very pale, and made no move to come to him, not even when he said, 'Eily!' – only caught her breath and moved a step closer to Jane. There was a short uncomfortable silence. Then Jeremy said, 'Hullo! I suppose you've heard?'

John nodded.

'The police sent for me, and for Mrs. Bridling. Seems we were both here last night. Along with a good few other people.' He turned to Jane. 'Miss Heron, I've to thank you for helping Eily. That Miss Silver that was down with the police, she told me you were looking after her.' He put a hand on Eily's arm. 'Will you come down into the dining-room,' he said. 'There's things I want to say to you, and you to me.'

She went out with him and down into the dining-room. Seen by daylight it was like a gloomy cave, the light all at one end where two straight windows faced the door. Dark panelling drank the light. Nothing had been done about the fire. The ash of last night's logs stirred in the chimney draught.

There is a nature drift even to a dead hearth. John and Eily came up to it and stood there, a little apart. Behind them, masking the door to the hall, was one of those screens covered with pictures cut from old papers and magazines, some coloured and some plain, but all glazed this hundred years in a varnish which time had deepened to amber. It served to keep the worst draughts from the room when the front door stood open. It did very little to mitigate them. A cold current of air moved in the room, appearing to come now from the hearth, now from the windows, and now from the masked door.

John Higgins didn't notice it at all, but Eily shivered as if the air could move her bodily. She looked frail enough, standing there and holding out shaking hands to the cold hearth. His arms came round her.

'Eily – darling – what is it? He didn't hurt you? Say he didn't hurt you!'

She stood quite passive in his embrace, not yielding to it at all, but stiff, as if she was holding herself against the shaking and against him. She said in a faraway voice, 'He didn't hurt me. He was dead when I came down. They think I hurt him.'

'Eily, what made you come down?'

He felt the beginning of a shudder, and the way she wouldn't let it come. He was reminded of a creature shamming dead because it was so frightened. Wild things would do that if you got your hands on them, but Eily had nothing to be frightened of with him.

He laid his cheek against her hair.

'What is it? What's frightening you? I must know, or how can I help you? Tell me, my little dear. You went along to Miss Heron like I told you?'

'Yes – ' It was more like a sigh than a word.

'Then why didn't you stay there? Eily, I told you to stay.'

Her head had been bent so that he couldn't see her face. she lifted it now and stared up at him.

'You know – '

'I?'

'You – called me – '

'Eily!'

'You came under the window whistling. I heard you, and I went along to my room. When I looked out of the window you were going round the corner of the house – '

He stopped her.

'Eily, what are you saying?'

She said it again, like a child that repeats a lesson.

'You went by whistling. When I saw you go round the corner of the house I came downstairs. I was going to open one of the windows in the lounge and tell you to go away – but he was there in the hall – he was dead. John, why did you do it?'

He lifted his big hands and put them on her shoulders.

'Why, my little dear, what made you think that of me?

Do you think I'd touch you like this if I'd blood on my hands? No, no — don't you think it! I won't deny when I heard what Mrs. Bridling had to say that the old Adam got up in me pretty strong, and I thank the Lord I didn't meet him then. Not but what he deserved a good hammering, for he did, and if I'd met with him, that's what he'd have got. But not a knife in the back my dear — don't you think it! Don't you let it trouble you, for that's a thing I couldn't do, not however much my blood was up. I'm not denying I might have struck him and found it hard to be sorry afterwards. The servant of the Lord mustn't strive, but there's times when it comes hard — I'm not denying that. But not knives and suchlike, and stabbing a man in the back. You've no call to be frightened I'd do anything like that.'

Insensibly his warmth, his voice were reassuring her. When she spoke her tone was more natural.

'Why did you come back?'

'I didn't, my dear, I didn't.'

'I heard you.'

He said grimly, 'You heard someone whistling my tune. It might be someone who wanted you to come down, but it wasn't me. After I'd said good night to you I went right back to Cliff and stayed there. I knew you'd be safe with Miss Heron for the night, and I was coming to fetch you in the morning. Why should I come back?'

'It — wasn't you?'

'No, my dear.'

He put his arms round her again, and this time she came close to him and put up her face to be kissed. After a little he said, 'Tell me, my dear. You said you saw someone go round the corner of the house, and you thought it was me, and you were going to open one of the windows in the lounge and tell me to go home. Did you open that window?'

'Oh, no, John.' The shudder took her. 'He was there in the hall — he was dead.'

He held her warm and close.

'You didn't go into the lounge?'

She said, 'Oh!' and then, 'Yes, I did.'

'Why?'

'I don't know. I told the Inspector it was because there

had been drinks there, and I thought about getting something for Luke. I don't know if it was true – I don't really. I just said it, but I don't know whether I thought about it or not. I couldn't tell him about seeing you go round the corner of the house and wanting to tell you to go home – I couldn't tell him that.'

'You should have told him the truth, my dear.'

She had begun to cry, tears flooding up into the dark blue eyes and brimming over.

'You can't tell what you don't know. I was too frightened to know why I did it. I did think about the drinks, but I did think about you being there and wanting to get to you. And then it came over me that you'd done it, and I was too frightened to go on. So I went back, and seeing him – like that, dead – ' She clung to him, sobbing.

'There, there, my dear, don't you take on. You're coming back with me now like I said, and Mrs. Bridling will look after you till we're married, and then I'll look after you myself.'

She pulled away from him at that, rubbing at her eyes with the sleeve of her overall.'

'Oh, John, I can't!'

'Eily – '

She shook her head.

'But we're ever so short-handed. I can't – not with all these people in the house. Miss Heron's helping me.' She smiled suddenly and dabbed her eyes again. 'She says to call her Jane, because we're going to be cousins – if I marry you.'

He said indulgently, 'Aren't you going to marry me, Eily?'

Her smile came, and went, and came again.

'Not with all this going on in the house. There's no need for me to go away now that I can see. I'll be all right. It was Luke I was afraid of, but he's dead.'

Her movement as she pulled away from him had left him facing the door and the screen which partly covered it. As he stood he could see the panelling above the door. He should have been able to see an inch or two of the door itself. But there was nothing there – only two fingers of emptiness. The door was open, and a draught blowing in from the hall.

Just when it had opened, or who had opened it, there was nothing to show. Eily and he had been too far away to know or care.

He left her and ran out into the hall. Mildred Taverner was on the stairs.

Chapter 22

SHE was on the fifth or sixth step. She had both hands on the balustrade and stood there pressed up against it looking down into the hall. It was impossible to say whether she had been going up or coming down. When she saw John Higgins she poked with her long neck and said in a discontented voice, 'It's quite terribly cold, isn't it? I've been in my room, but it is so very chilly there. Do you suppose there is a fire in the lounge?'

He wondered whether it was she who had opened the door to see if there was a fire in the dining-room. He said gravely, 'Yes, there is a fire in the lounge. Did you think there would be one in the dining-room? Was it you who opened the door just now?'

She was immediately very much flustered. The three separate chains which she wore, one of rather large gold links, one of sky-blue Venetian beads, and one of some kind of brown berry strung upon scarlet thread, all jiggled and clanked. The berries became entangled with each other and mixed up with a very large silver brooch which was rather like a starfish. She came down the stairs, plucking nervously to disentangle them.

'Oh, no. I've been up in my room. I didn't really feel – I mean it's so very awkward, isn't it? Such a dreadful thing to have happened – and no knowing who did it. So if you are with anyone, you can't help thinking, suppose it was him, or her, or them, as the case might be. So I went up to my room, but when you are alone you can't help having the feeling

that there might be someone under the bed or in the ward-
robe, even if you've looked there before – or perhaps creep-
ing along the passage with their shoes off.' She shivered, and
the chains all clanked again. 'So I thought perhaps the
lounge. Do you know if there is anyone there?'

He opened the door for her. There was certainly a fire,
and a comfortable chair drawn up to it. But Mrs. Bridling,
who had been sitting there, had got tired of waiting and gone
home. There was Mr. Bridling to see to.

There was only one person in the room, and that was
Freddy Thorpe-Ennington. He was standing by a window
immediately opposite the door with his hands in his pockets
looking out. He turned round as Mildred Taverner came
in, stared at her as if he had never seen her before, and went
back to looking out of the window.

John Higgins shut the door upon this ill assorted couple.
Eily had come out of the dining-room. She stood there,
troubled and uncertain. He took her by the arm, and along
through the baize door by the other way into Castell's study.

Inspector Crisp was on his feet, and Miss Silver was putting away her knitting. Frank Abbott, who had been making
a note, looked up, pencil in hand. They all looked up.

John Higgins said in a firm, cheerful voice, 'Now, Eily,
you'll tell the Inspector what you've just been telling me.'

He felt her whole body jerk with the start she gave. He got
a glance of passionate reproach. She began to tremble and
to trip over her words.

'It wasn't anything – it wasn't anything at all. I told the
Inspector – '

Miss Silver gave her little cough.

'It seems, perhaps, that there is something you did not
tell. There very often is. Sometimes it is quite important.
There is nothing to be afraid of. Just tell us what it is that
you have remembered.'

As Eily stood there catching her breath, John Higgins said,
'She's upset – she's had enough to make her. It's just this,
Inspector, and it may be important. Eily came down last
night because she thought I was whistling for her.'

Crisp said, 'What!' very abruptly. Frank Abbott stopped
in the act of putting the notebook into his breast pocket.

John nodded.

'She went along to Miss Heron's room like I told her. They went to sleep. Then Eily woke up. Reason she woke was someone was going past under the window whistling Greenland's Icy Mountains. That's the tune I always whistle when I come over to have a word with her. So she went along to her room and opened the window, thinking it was me, and all she saw was someone going round the corner of the house. The lounge is that side, so she ran down to call to me out of the window there. But when she got into the hall, there was Luke White dead. Tell them Eily, what you did.'

She was pinching his arm – angry enough to pinch as hard as she could, and frightened enough to want to hold on to him. She found some odds and ends of a voice.

'That's true, Inspector. I thought it was John – or I'd never have come down.'

'You came into the lounge and opened the window?'

'No – no – I didn't. I was going to, but I didn't. He was dead, and it came over me. I thought about the window, but I didn't get there. And I thought about the drinks like I told you, but they'd been put away. And I came back into the hall and I saw the knife. And I couldn't go on – I came over giddy, and I sat down on the stair.'

Miss Silver slipped the handle of her knitting-bag over her arm. It was of flowered chintz, a very pretty pattern, the gift of her niece Ethel, not new but very well preserved. They had all remained standing.

When Eily's voice had faded out on a sob she took a step towards John Higgins, and he put his arm about her.

'That's how it happened, Inspector,' he said.

Crisp snapped out, 'Then why didn't she say so at once?'

If they had been alone, or with only Miss Silver present, Frank might have made an enemy for life by permitting himself a classical quotation. The words 'Elementary, my dear Watson,' were upon his lips, but he restrained them. He did not quite restrain a faint sarcastic smile.

John Higgins neither smiled nor trifled. His answer was simple and direct.

'It would be because of me, Inspector – on account of not wanting to get me into trouble, as she thought. When she heard that tune it never came to her for a moment that it would be anyone but me.'

'You say it wasn't you?' Crisp was very short and sharp.

'I say the same as I've said all along. I went straight back to Cliff after Eily had talked to me out of her window, and there I stayed till Wat Cooling fetched me along this morning.'

'That's your story?'

'It's the truth.'

'And the first you knew about Luke White being murdered? Well now, what was the first you knew?'

'When Wat Cooling came along and fetched me.'

Crisp fairly glared.

'Cooling told you?'

'I've known him all his life. I don't want to get him into any trouble.'

'He'd no business to talk! So you came here knowing all about it – time, place, weapon, everything, I suppose!'

'He said it would be one of those knives out of the dining-room.'

Crisp pounced.

'Oh, you knew about the knives in the dining-room? I thought you said you hadn't been inside the place for donkey's years.'

This time John did smile, showing strong white teeth.

'Five years, Inspector. And those knives have been there a sight longer than that – nearer the hundred, I'd say.'

'But you knew they were there. You knew where you could lay hands on a knife.'

'That's not to say I'd use it.' He stood up straight. 'That's all I've got to say. I didn't come back, I didn't set foot inside the inn, I didn't set eyes on Luke White. And I'd like to take Eily away. She's upset.'

When they were gone, Crisp turned his angry stare upon his fellow Inspector.

'Well, what do you make of that? What put him up to bringing the girl in here and making her tell how she'd heard him come along whistling the second time?'

Miss Silver made a verbal amendment.

'She thought that it was he whom she heard.'

He pursed up his lips.

'Who else would it be?'

Frank Abbott smiled.

'Almost anyone. Greenland's Icy Mountains is one of the easier tunes to whistle.'

Crisp made a sound half derisive, half vexed.

'Easy to turn it off with a joke! What I want to know is, what's behind it? What's he about, bringing the girl in here to say she heard him under the window and came down to let him in round about the time the murder was done? What's he getting at?'

Miss Silver said gravely, 'It might be the truth, Inspector.'

He made the same derisory sound again.

'When you've seen as many criminals as I have you won't be in such a hurry to believe what they say!'

Frank Abbott slid his hand across his mouth. He had seen Miss Silver deal with disrespect before, and had found it an enjoyable spectacle. Impossible to say just how it was done, but done it was. There was no raised voice, for she did not speak. There was no flashing glance, for her eyes were not made to flash – she would, in fact, have considered it a very unladylike proceeding. There was a certain distance, a certain dignity, which relegated provincial Inspectors to their very minor place in the service of the law. A sense of authority diffused itself. Even Chief Inspector Lamb had on occasion felt himself carried back to the village school in which he had first learned that two and two make four.

The picture which confronted Inspector Crisp was of a slightly different but no less chastening kind. He had received his education at Lenton Grammar School. There came vividly to his mind a winter's day and a group of boys throwing snowballs. A massive back presenting a too tempting target, he had let fly. There had been a direct hit, a snowy explosion, and, sudden, majestic and awful, the face of the headmaster looming up from the ensuing flurry. The memory was as momentary as it was vivid, but an oppressive sense of delinquency remained. He said abruptly, 'There isn't much more to be done till we get the result of the post-mortem. Not that there's likely to be a lot in it. He couldn't have been dead very long when we got here at one-thirty.

Not much doubt it had just happened when the house was roused. You would agree with that?'

He was addressing Miss Silver. She answered him with the air of a teacher who, having reproved, is now willing to overlook the fault.

'I am not an expert. When I touched his wrist it was cold. But the night was a cold one.'

Crisp nodded.

'We were half an hour getting here, and the blood wasn't dry.'

Miss Silver said a surprising thing.

'Do you think he was killed where he was found?'

Frank Abbott's cool blue eyes took on an interested look.

'What makes you think of that?'

She said in a deprecating manner – the little dowdy spinster who looked as if she could be snubbed with impunity, 'It seems such a curious place to kill him,' she said.

Chapter 23

IT was one of the longest Sundays that any of the twelve people shut up together in the Catherine-Wheel could remember. Perhaps Jane and Jeremy felt it least, since each was still exploring the other's territory and finding it full of new and exciting things. They were also helpfully bent upon making themselves useful, laying and clearing meals and washing up with efficiency and despatch. In the evening Mrs. Bridling returned to oblige, having conducted an all-day battle against Mr. Bridling's scruples as to her doing so on the Sabbath. She had emerged victorious, not only on account of her own prowess, but because of some fifth-column assistance from Mr. Bridling's passionate desire to be kept in touch with what was going on. Having arrived, it was difficult to see how she was going to acquire any information, since she never stopped talking and Annie Castell

140

never seemed to open her lips.

Be that as it may, she went on talking for a long time after she got home.

'Annie's got something on her mind, you can't get from it.' She beat a pillow vigorously and slipped it back under Mr. Bridling's head with the dexterity of long practice. 'It isn't what she says, but I didn't go to school with her for nothing, and there's something she's got on her mind. You wouldn't have known the pastry for hers, for one thing. I don't say it was heavy, and I don't say there isn't many a cook that wouldn't be glad if she could make it as well, but it wasn't her usual.'

Mr. Bridling observed in a rather perfunctory manner that he didn't hold with cooking on a Sunday – not if it wasn't a work of necessity and mercy like doing for an afflicted husband.

Rightly considering that this required no answer, Mrs. Bridling continued.

'Mr. Castell, he keeps talking about his dear Luke and where is he going to find his equal. I could have told him, but I kept myself. In prison, or in any other place where there's off-scourings is what I could have said, but I kept myself. Never said a word, and let him run on about his dear Luke, which if ever there was a good riddance – '

Mr. Bridling gave it as a considered opinion that it was a judgement. He was a plump old man with a nice colour and a soft purring voice. Successive hospitals had failed to find any reason why he should lie in bed and be waited on hand and foot, but he continued to do so. He spoke through the sheet which his wife had drawn up over his face whilst she straightened the blankets.

'How's the others taking it?'

'Old Mr. Jacob Taverner, he sits by the fire with the Sunday papers.'

Mr. Bridling said he didn't hold with papers on Sunday.

'And I'll thank you to turn down the sheet and let me get my breath. If I was to die choked – '

Mrs. Bridling turned it down, and went on talking.

'Looks like a sick monkey and don't fancy his food. Mrs. Duke, she doesn't fancy hers neither – sits and looks at it and

141

doesn't eat a thing. Another one that doesn't eat is that Lady Marian's husband. Makes up with what he drinks – had to be carried to bed last night, so I hear.'

'One of the drunkards of Ephraim,' said Mr. Bridling. Then, in a less lofty vein, 'Then it wasn't him that did it.'

'Seems it couldn't have been. Well, then there's Mr. Geoffrey Taverner – some kind of a traveller, they say he is, but quite the gentleman. He walks into Ledlington and gets the papers and comes back and reads them and does the crossword puzzle. I'll fetch it along for you to do tomorrow. And that Lady Marian and the other one, Miss Taverner, they say they've been up all night and go off to their rooms and have a good lay-down. I could have laughed. A lot they know about being up in the night! I could have told them a thing or two! It's not so much the up, it's the up-and-down that gets you.'

Mr. Bridling checked her by shutting his eyes and groaning.

'Are you throwing my affliction up at me, Emily?'

Mrs. Bridling was struck to the heart.

'I wouldn't do it, Ezra – you know I wouldn't. It was thinking of a sufferer like you.'

He said in a resigned voice, 'There may be those that suffer more. I'm not complaining.'

'Nobody can't ever say you do, Ezra.'

'The nights I never close my eyes,' said Mr. Bridling. 'And nothing the least bit of use – not hop pillows, nor cups of cocoa, nor hot bricks to the feet changed constant, nor my mother's fumitory drink, nor yet your grandmother's herbal tea. Have we tried them all night after night, or haven't we?'

'Indeed we have. And if there was anything else – there's nothing I wouldn't do.'

He gave a confirmatory groan.

'I don't complain. What about that Al Miller? Mrs. Cleeve looked in and said he'd run off. Seems Mrs. Wilton where he lodged is some sort of a cousin and they met at the Congregational. Mrs. Wilton told her it was a real good riddance. She supposed he'd come back and want them to take him on again, but Mr Wilton wouldn't have it. What with coming in late, and coming in drunk, and talking big about how he was going to be a rich man and show everyone how, she said they'd downright lost patience. And there's a very respectable young man, a brother of Mr. Wilton's sister's daughter-in-law, that would like the room, so they're letting him have it.'

Mrs. Bridling said, 'Well, I never!' And then, dropping her voice, 'Run off, has he? You don't suppose – '

Mr. Bridling shook his head regretfully.

'Seems it couldn't have been, because he come in drunk just before half past eleven – made an awful noise and used language. And Mr. Wilton, he gave him his notice – told him he could get out in the morning and stay out, and went down and took away the front door key so they'd be sure they got their money before he went. What time of night did you say it was when they all roused up and found Luke murdered?'

'One o'clock, Annie says. And the police come it might have been half an hour later.'

'And the blood still wet,' said Mr. Bridling with gusto. 'And Al Miller locked in in Thread Street a matter of three miles away, and the key under Mrs. Wilton's pillow. Don't seem possible Al Miller could have a hand in it. A back slider and a sinner he is if ever there was one. In my class at Sunday school, and brought up Band of Hope, and look what he's come to now – drinking, and all kind of carryings on! But seems he couldn't of murdered Luke White, not if he was locked into a house three miles away.'

'They both wanted Eily,' said Mrs. Bridling. 'Time a girl's married when it comes to too many men wanting her. It makes trouble.'

'Girls always make trouble,' said Mr. Bridling. 'What about the rest of them up at the Catherine-Wheel?'

'The little detective lady, she has a lay-down too. Seems nobody knew she was a detective when she come. And the gentleman that's staying at Sir John Challoner's, he's another – '

Mr. Bridling took her up sharply.

'Don't you demean yourself calling him a gentleman!'

'He's Sir John's cousin.'

143

Mr. Bridling stared.

'Then he did ought to be ashamed of himself. There aren't any real gentry left like there used to be.'

Mrs. Bridling was mixing cocoa in a cup and being very careful about it, because Mr. Bridling was most particular in the matter of lumps and grit, and if there was one thing that roused her, it was for him to tell her that she couldn't make cocoa like his mother did.

'That's right,' she said. 'Well, this Mr. Abbott – Inspector Abbott – he goes off, and the other Inspector. And Captain Taverner and Miss Heron, they go off in his car, and not back till just on seven. And that's the lot of them, except for Eily.'

'What about Eily?'

Mrs. Bridling began pouring boiling water very carefully and stirring all the time.

'By the look of her, she'd been crying her eyes out. "I can't leave Aunt Annie," she says. And John Higgins wanting her to marry him right away.'

Mr. Bridling had his eye on the cocoa.

'Marriages and murders don't agree,' he said sententiously. 'That's enough hot water, Emily. Don't drown it.'

Chapter 24

On Monday morning Jeremy drove Jane up to town. At half past nine she was going in at the side door of Clarissa Harlowe's dress shop. Jeremy was about to drive off again, when he noticed that his off-side front tyre was flatter than it ought to be. He discovered that he had picked up a nail, and set to work to change the wheel.

He had just about finished, when Clarissa Harlowe's side door opened again and Jane came out. She had a bright colour and she was walking fast. She got into the car, sat down, and said crisply, 'I've got the sack.'

144

Jeremy whistled and said, 'Why?'

Jane looked at him angrily.

'Murder is quite the wrong sort of publicity,' she said.

He whistled again.

'Why did you tell her?'

'There's going to be an inquest, isn't there, and I've got to go down for it – and there are newspapers and reporters and things. Of course I had to tell her. And for goodness' sake let's get away! I never want to see the place again!'

Jeremy got in, banged the door, and said cheerfully, 'Let's go round to the flat and get something to eat. You'll feel a lot better after a cup of something hot.'

This, though infuriating, was true. At the time it merely brightened Jane's eyes and made her colour rise alarmingly, but after her second cup of coffee she relaxed sufficiently to discuss the future.

'I'll take the week off and get through with this blasted inquest, and then I'll hunt another job. I did hold my tongue, so she may give me a reference.'

'She's bound to, isn't she?'

Jane looked coldly at him.

'There are references *and* references. How many jobs do you suppose I should get if she were to say "Jane Heron? Oh no, I've nothing *against* her. It's just rather a pity she got mixed up in that murder case"!'

'She wouldn't play a dirty trick like that.'

Jane laughed without amusement.

'Let's say, "I hope she *won't*." That's about as far as it will stretch.'

There was a pause. Then he said, 'I want to go back to the Catherine-Wheel.'

Her answer was unexpected.

'So do I.'

'All right then – we'll go.'

'There's the inquest, and Eily, and – well, it's horrid, but it's interesting.'

Jeremy laughed.

'You needn't give your reasons. I'm not giving mine.'

'Have you got any?'

'Oh, yes.'

'What are they?'

'I'm not giving them.'

Down at the Catherine-Wheel Inspector Crisp was acquainting Miss Silver with the police surgeon's report.

'You see he says that the man had taken a considerable quantity of alcohol. Now you had the opportunity of observing Luke White – he was in the lounge, wasn't he, most of the time that you were?'

They were in the office. A nice snug fire was burning, Frank Abbott, who had a way with fires, having coaxed it from a reluctant smoulder to its present cheerful state. That he had done so without in any way impairing his customary air of having just emerged from a glass case had an irritating effect upon Inspector Crisp. It sharpened his voice a little as he enquired, 'You were in the lounge with him for about an hour and a half. Did he appear to have been drinking then?'

Miss Silver gazed thoughtfully down at the wide blue flounce to which little Josephine's woolly dress had now been advanced. Another two inches, and she would be able to make the sharp decrease which would impart a gathered effect to the skirt before beginning upon the tight plain bodice. She might have been considering how many more rows it would take to finish the skirt, or she might not. She kept Inspector Crisp waiting long enough to start him tapping on the table with his pencil. Then she raised her eyes to his face and gave him a quiet, 'No.'

Crisp tapped. She could speak plenty when she liked. Now, when he could have done with a few more words, she seemed to have run out of them.

'He let you in, didn't he? Did he smell of drink then?'

Miss Silver repeated the irritating monosyllable.

'No.'

'When did you see him last?'

She seemed to consider this too.

'It would be just before half past ten, when I went up to my room.'

'He didn't seem to have been drinking then?'

Miss Silver produced another 'No'.

Crisp tapped.

'Well, some time between then and the time he was killed

he must have put away quite a lot. Castell ought to know something about that. We'll have him in.'

He went out through the door on the kitchen side.

Frank Abbott, who had been standing in a lounging attitude beside the fire looking down into it as if admiring his own handiwork, now shifted his cool gaze to Miss Silver and said, 'What are you up to?'

'My dear Frank!'

'Yes, I know, I know, but you can't put it across with me.'

Without attempting any further reproof she said very composedly, 'There are some interesting points about this case.'

'As what?'

'The attempt to implicate John Higgins.'

'Attempt?'

Miss Silver coughed.

'Do you believe that he returned nearly two hours after he had said good night to Eily, and that having drawn attention to himself by whistling his customary tune under Miss Heron's window he induced Eily to let him in, that he then deliberately selected a knife from the trophy in the dining room and killed Luke White in the most public place in the house?'

Frank's fair eyebrows rose.

'Is that how it strikes you?'

'Undoubtedly.'

He said, 'Well, well – ' And then, 'You said, *"under Miss Heron's* window." Did you mean anything by that?'

Her needles clicked.

'Oh, yes. The person who whistled under Miss Heron's window knew that Eily was there.'

'If you say that to Crisp, it will go down to John Higgins's account. He's pretty sure he did it, you know.'

'My dear Frank.'

'You're quite sure he didn't?'

She smiled.

'He was telling the truth.'

'Then – '

'Someone in the house must have known that Eily had left her own room and gone to Miss Heron's. If we can find

147

that person we shall, I think, have found the murderer – or, at the very least, someone deeply implicated in the murder.'

'And who, do you suppose, could have known that Eily was in Jane Heron's room?'

She said thoughtfully, 'Almost anyone. Her room, as you know, looks out at the back, and is on the opposite side of the house from Miss Heron's. It is, in fact, the corner room at the end of the opposite corridor. There is only one other bedroom opening on to the back from that corridor. It is next the landing, and is occupied by Mr. Jacob Taverner, the intervening space being taken up by the back stairs, linen-room, and lavatory. On the same corridor, looking to the front, are the rooms occupied by the Castells and Mr. Geoffrey Taverner. There is also a bathroom, and a large housemaid's cupboard. Mr. Taverner might possibly have overheard Eily's conversation with John Higgins if he had opened his window and leaned right out, but I do not regard this as at all likely. The linen-room has no window, and that which lights the back stairs is not conveniently accessible, but the lavatory window, which is next to Eily's room, would be very convenient indeed. Castell says in his statement that he did in fact hear someone come along the road and go round to the back, and that he went across to the lavatory and looked out of the window. He says he heard someone come along whistling Greenland's Icy Mountains, and that he then went back to bed because he knew it was only John Higgins come to have a few words with Eily. Castell was, I think, a little too anxious to inform the police that John Higgins had been out to the Catherine-Wheel that night. We have only his word for it that he went back to bed without listening to the conversation between him and Eily. He could very easily have done so. On the other hand, Mr. Jacob Taverner or Mr. Geoffrey Taverner might also have done so.'

Frank made a slight grimace.

'Not so very likely.'

'Perhaps not. But we really do not know enough to say what is likely or unlikely at present. On the other side of the landing, in my own corridor, either Lady Marian and her husband, or Mrs. Duke, Miss Taverner, or myself could have heard Eily go into Miss Heron's room, though we could not, of course, have heard the conversation which induced her to do so.'

Frank Abbott gave her a quizzical look.

'Are you by any chance the villain of the piece? Did you hear anything?'

'No, Frank,' After a pause she continued, 'If John Higgins did not return at one o'clock, then someone was being at pains to manufacture evidence against him by whistling that tune under Miss Heron's window. It would have to be someone who knew that Eily was there. So far as we know, the most likely person to have that knowledge was Castell.'

Frank gave a slight sarcastic laugh.

'And, as Crisp put it, I'm here to get something on Castell! "The innkeeper Framed!" You know, it's almost too much to hope that it is Castell. He's so beautifully obvious, isn't he?'

If Miss Silver was going to reply, the sound of approaching voices stopped her. The door by which Crisp had gone out was flung back, and there came in Castell in full spate, with the Inspector only occasionally managing to stem the flood.

'If I can be of any assistance – any assistance whatever! All murders are atrocious – that goes without saying! The sight of blood makes me incapable of digesting my food! All are, I say, atrocious, but this one is an outrage! In the middle of a festivity – in the middle of a family reunion! Depriving me of a friend as well as of a servant most valued! Leaving me short-handed with the house full!' He threw up his hands in a gesture of horror. 'And the consequences! You will pardon me, but – the police in the house! Mr. Jacob Taverner, my patron, is indisposed! I myself – I will not trouble you with how I suffer! My wife Annie whose cooking is unsurpassed – last night her hand fails her! I do not say that the pastry is heavy – it is impossible for Annie Castell to make heavy pastry – if I say that it is made by an ordinary chef, it is enough! Can you then doubt how eagerly I would help to unmask the assassin?'

149

Inspector Crisp used the most repressive tone at his command.

'Sit down, Mr. Castell, and stop talking! I want to ask you some questions.'

Fogarty Castell spread out his hands in an expansive gesture.

'Anything – anything!'

'It's about this man Luke White. The police surgeon says he'd had a lot of drink. When did he get it, and how?'

Fogarty brushed away a tear.

'My poor Luke! Yes, I will tell you. There was some champagne left, and I said to him, "Come, my friend, we will finish it." That was after everyone had gone up to bed, you understand. For me, I take one glass – two – I am the most abstemious of men – and my poor Luke, he finishes the rest.'

'How much?'

Castell hesitated. Then he said, 'There was a half bottle –'

'You're not going to tell me you had a couple of glasses or so, and Luke White got drunk on what was left!'

There was that gesture with the hands again.

'No, no, no – I will tell you! He had a weakness that poor Luke. In his working-time he takes nothing, but – how shall I say – when he is off duty he takes what he can get.'

'Are you telling me he was a heavy drinker, Mr. Castell?'

Fogarty's dark face glistened with feeling.

'Only when he is off duty. And for champagne he has a passion. He finishes the bottle, and then he says, "Come on, boss – the old boy won't miss it!" and he opens another. There – I have told you! Do not repeat it, I beg of you. I would not, of course, have put it on the bill.'

Frank's eye rested upon him with cool enjoyment. Crisp said sharply, 'That's nothing to do with us. You're telling me White was a heavy drinker?'

'Only when he was off duty,' said Fogarty Castell.

Chapter 25

'WELL,' said Crisp when the door had closed behind him, 'there you have it. The man was drunk when he was killed, and the way he got drunk was drinking Mr. Jacob Taverner's champagne along with his manager after everyone else had gone upstairs to bed. Nice work, I must say! Not put it on the bill, indeed!' He made a sound that was more like a snort than a laugh.

Miss Silver said mildly, 'What is your theory, Inspector, as to how Luke White came to be lying in the position in which he was found? There was not more than eighteen inches between his feet and the bottom step. To fall in such a position he must have been standing either on the step itself or just below it with his back to the stairs, and the murderer must have been on the step behind him.'

Crisp stared.

'You mean they were both coming down the stairs?'

Miss Silver knitted two, slipped one, and knitted two together. Little Josephine's skirt was being gathered in to the waist.

'Can you think of any other explanation?' She paused, decreased again, and added, 'If he was really killed where he was found.'

Crisp said impatiently, 'There isn't the slightest reason to suppose he wasn't. Coming downstairs – I wonder. Let's see – Eily lets John Higgins in, and they go upstairs together. Luke White hears something – comes after them. Higgins has the knife. He turns round with it. Luke sees it, takes fright, and makes off. Higgins catches him up on the bottom step and stabs him in the back.'

Miss Silver shook her head, but she did not speak. It was Frank Abbott who said, 'You say John Higgins has the knife. Why?'

Crisp shrugged his shoulders.

'He's jealous – he's angry over the girl – he's where he's

151

got no business to be, and he knows Luke White is an awkward customer – so awkward that it's not many hours since he had threatened to cut the heart out of any man that the girl took instead of him. Plenty of reasons for picking a knife off the dining-room wall before he went upstairs with her.'

Miss Silver shook her head again. Her lips were primmed together. She knitted in silence.

Frank Abbott said seriously, 'I don't think it happened like that. The girl isn't that sort of girl, and the man isn't that sort of man.'

Crisp stared angrily.

'Then how did it happen?'

Getting no answer but that conveyed by a lifted eyebrow, he produced a counter-attack.

'It's got to be Castell to satisfy you, hasn't it – or one of the Taverners? Well, there's not a shred of evidence to connect them with the crime, or a shred of a motive. Mr. Jacob Taverner says he was in bed before eleven and slept until he was roused by the commotion in the house. Mr. Geoffrey Taverner says he read till after twelve. He heard no unusual sounds, he went to sleep as soon as he put his light out, and was waked by the noise downstairs. Castell's statement amounts to very much the same thing. After hearing John Higgins come along whistling round about eleven he lay awake for a bit, and then dropped off, waking up like everyone else when the noise began. Mrs. Castell corroborates as far as to say that Castell was in bed when the house was roused. She is a heavy sleeper and can't say anything about the earlier part of the night. Well, you can't expect alibis when people are in bed and asleep. There's nothing to say that all those statements aren't correct. Same with the people on the other side of the house, the Thorpe-Enningtons, Miss Taverner, Miss Heron – and yourself, Miss Silver. There is nothing to connect any of them with Luke White, or to suggest that they had the slightest motive for murdering him.'

Miss Silver coughed in an exceedingly pointed manner, and Frank Abbott said, 'What about Mrs. Duke? You've rather left her out, haven't you? She was very much on the spot at the time of the murder – victim's blood on her hands and a pretty thin story to account for it.'

Miss Silver said in a meditative tone, 'True stories often appear to be regrettably thin. Fabrications are so much more carefully composed. We do not know of any motive in the case of Mrs. Duke.'

As the words left her lips, the door through which Castell had made his exit was opened in a tentative manner. Castell looked through the opening with what was obviously intended for an ingratiating smile.

'If I intrude, it is, if I may say, my eagerness to assist in the discovery of the assassin.'

Crisp said shortly, 'Come in, Mr. Castell!'

He came in sideways like a thick-bodied crab, rubbing his hands together and turning his eyes this way and that.

'You will pardon if I interrupt –'

'Sit down if you've got anything to say!'

Fogarty balanced himself on the edge of the chair which he had occupied before.

'It is not I – it is my wife. You are married, Inspector? Yes? . . . No? . . . Ah, but what a pity! There is no fortune in the world like a good wife. So when I find my wife in tears just now when I go out of this room – when I find her in such a great distress that she cannot give her mind to the art in which she excels – I take her hand, I speak to her tenderly, I say, "What is it?" And she says, "Is it true that the police are suspecting John Higgins? Is it true that they think he killed Luke White?" And I say, "How do I know? I am not in their confidence. It looks that way." Then she says, "It will break Eily's heart. John is a good man. He is my own nephew. He did not do it." And I say, "He was jealous about Eily, and Luke had threatened him. If it was not John Higgins, who was it? No one else had any reason." Then she cries and says, "That is not true. There is someone who might have a reason".'

Miss Silver's eyes were on his face. Frank Abbott put up a hand and smoothed back his hair.

Inspector Crisp said, 'What! in a voice like a barking terrier.

Fogarty looked from one to the other. His expression
153

seemed to say, 'See how clever I am – how acute – how discerning! You are a lot of clever people in the police, but it is Castell who puts the clue into your hands!' He gestured complacently.

'That is what I say too. "What!" I say. "Annie!" I say. "Tell me at once what you are talking about!" But she does not. She puts her head down on the kitchen table and cries. We have been married fifteen years, and I have never seen her cry like that. She says, "What shall I do, what shall I do?" And I say, "I am your husband – you will tell me".'

He looked round again, as if for approbation. 'So in the end she tells me.'

Crisp tapped impatiently.

'Well – well – what did she tell you?'

Castell's eyes gleamed. It was quite obvious that he was enjoying himself.

'She does not want to tell me, you understand. She cries and says she has always kept it to herself. And I say, "What has always been must at some time come to an end, and when there is a murder and the police in the house, that is the time for it to come to an end." And at the last she tells me.'

Crisp fairly banged on the table.

'Mr. Castell, will you come to the point and tell us what your wife said!'

Castell spread out his hands.

'And with what reluctance she says it! That is part of the evidence, her reluctance, is it not? She does not wish to suggest a motive, to accuse, to say anything at all. I say to her, "It is your duty," and she shakes her head. I say, "I am your husband and I command you!" She weeps. I say, "Have you no heart for John Higgins who is your nephew, and for Eily who looks already like an apparition from the tomb!" Then she tells me.'

Frank Abbott said in his languid voice, 'All right, Castell, we've got the *mise en scène*. Just tell us what she said.'

If Chief Inspector Lamb had been present he would at this point have had something to say. It was his considered opinion that the English language contained all the words required by any police officer who hadn't got wind in the head. French words in particular had a highly inflammatory effect on his temper and his complexion. In his absence Frank could indulge himself with impunity.

Castell became very animated indeed. He turned from one to the other, he waved his hands.

'My wife Annie Castell, she says a name.'

Crisp said sharply, 'What name?'

'I will not disguise it from you, Inspector – it is the name of Mrs. Duke.'

'What does she say about Mrs. Duke?'

'She weeps as she says it. If you could have seen her!'

'Never mind about that! What did she say!'

Castell spread out those fat hands.

'She weeps, and she tells me. It is before we are married, you will understand, and my wife she is chef at the White Lion at Lenton. Never has the hotel done so much business. From all over the county they come – to lunch, to dine, to give supper parties, because of her cooking. And my poor Luke, he is the barman. She has known him a little all her life, you understand, because he is some sort of a cousin – on the wrong side of the blanket, as you say. One day he says to her, "I am going to get married, Cousin Annie." He calls her that because it vexes her, and he can be malicious that poor Luke. So then she says who is it he is marrying, and he says, "You would be surprised." And when he tells her it is her own cousin Florence Duke – '

This time both Inspectors said, 'What!' together.

Castell smiled and nodded.

'When he tells her that – well, she is surprised like you have been.'

Frank Abbott said, 'Florence Duke was married to Luke White?'

'My wife says so. Florence, she was behind the bar at the George, which is the other hotel at Lenton. Annie knew she was there, and they had spoken once or twice, but they did not know each other well, as cousins should, because of the quarrel in the family. She was also young and gay. My wife Annie, you will understand, is very particular, very respectable.'

Frank Abbott said, 'Are you sure there was a marriage?'

Castell nodded.

'My wife Annie says so. She says it would be in '31 or '32 – in July – at the register office in Lenton. And after that they went away, the two of them, to take a job together, and she did not see Luke again' – he shrugged and gestured – 'not for many years. When he comes here she asks him, "What about your wife Forence?" and he laughs and says, "It didn't last long, and she has gone back to calling herself Florence Duke again".'

Crisp said, 'Is that all?'

Castell leaned forward, dropping his voice confidentially.

'Shall I tell you what I think? I think that when Florence comes here she does not know at all that Luke is here. I think it gives her a great shock. She looks very bad after she has seen him. I think she comes down in the night to have a meeting with him. She says she was in the kitchen. Pfft! His room is opposite – I think she was there. I think they quarrel. He is very inconstant with women that poor Luke. He fascinates them, and goes away and forgets. What is it in the proverb – "Hell hasn't got anything so furious like a woman who is scorned"? It is not my business to say anything, but we all saw the blood on her hands.' He pushed back his chair. 'That is all! I go to console my wife!'

When they could no longer hear his footsteps going down the passage Crisp growled, 'What do you make of that?'

Frank cocked an eyebrow.

'I think Annie Castell wouldn't stand for putting it on John Higgins.'

Chapter 26

INSPECTOR CRISP fussed off to use the telephone and set the Lenton registrar looking up July marriages in '31 and '32.

When he had gone Frank Abbott remained draped

against the fireplace. He contemplated Miss Silver, whose attention appeared to be absorbed by little Josephine's bright blue dress, the completed skirt of which now lay spread out upon her lap. The gathered effect was very satisfactory — really very satisfactory indeed. The tight plain bodice which she was about to begin would be becoming and quaint. She decided that the measurements were just what they should be, picked up her needles, and set them clicking.

The smile with which Frank was regarding her would not have been allowed to betray him if they had not been alone together. It expressed very faithfully the feelings with which she had now for many years inspired him. They were an odd mixture of affection, respect, amusement, and something very like reverence. It would have surprised a good many people to catch the expression which softened those cool blue eyes, though there was still a hint of sarcasm when he smiled. It was there as he said interrogatively, 'Well?'

She looked up at him with gravity.

'What is it that you want to know?'

'Your reaction to Castell's *volte face*. First he pushes John Higgins at us up hill, down dale, and across country; and then he bounds in all helpful-boy-scout, says his wife Annie forbids the banns, and offers us Florence Duke intead. What do you make of it?'

She was knitting steadily.

'What do you make of it yourself?'

'What I said to Crisp. I think the bright idea was to frame John Higgins, shift the interest away from the Catherine-Wheel — I believe that's fundamental — make a *crime passionel* of the murder. And Annie Castell wouldn't stand for it — cut up rough — maybe threatened to spill the beans. She may, or may not, have any to spill, but if she has, I think she's been threatening to spill them if Castell doesn't lay off John Higgins. He's her own nephew, and she may be fond of Eily.'

Miss Silver inclined her head.

'I think so.'

'The bit about Eily, or the whole lot?'

'I think the whole of it. But the scene described by Castell could not have occurred as he described it. There was not time for all that story about Luke White's marriage to have been discussed by him and his wife in the interval between his leaving this room and returning to it, escpecially if Mrs. Castell was in the state of distress upon which he insists.'

Frank said, 'Yes – I agree. They had probably had a series of scenes about Higgins. When he came away from seeing us she presented an ultimatum – if he didn't stop framing John, beans would be spilled. Castell got the wind up, came to terms, and bounded in to offer Florence Duke instead. What do you think about her?'

She said in a meditative manner, 'She had certainly had a shock.'

'Do you mean before the murder?'

'Oh, yes. I noticed her at once. I thought at first that she had had too much to drink, but I came to the conclusion that there was something more than that. When Miss Heron was telling me about all the Taverner cousins I asked her whether anything had happened to upset Mrs. Duke. She looked startled, and replied, "Yes, I think so, but I don't know what it was." She then told me that she had met Mrs. Duke on the stairs just before dinner. Mrs. Duke asked if she was looking all right, and added that she had had "a most awful turn". Jane Heron enquired whether there was anything she could do, and Mrs. Duke said nobody could do anything. She then used these words – "That's the way when you are in a fix – you get yourself in, and you've got to get yourself out".' Miss Silver paused and coughed. 'As a matter of fact Miss Heron reports her as putting it more strongly than that.'

Frank Abbott laughed.

'Let's have it!'

Miss Silver let him have it in a prim quoting voice.

' "You get yourself in, and you've damn well got to get yourself out – nobody can't do it for you." After which she said, "Oh gosh – why did I have to come!" I have questioned Miss Heron again about this scene, and she gave me exactly the same account of it. I should consider her a reliable witness.'

Frank whistled.

'Looks as if Castell was right, both as to the marriage and the supposition that Florence had no idea that she was going to encounter the fascinating Luke. It begins to look as if she might have had a brain-storm and done him in. There would be the Eily motive –'

Miss Silver coughed.

'There is no evidence to show that she was aware that Luke White was paying attentions to Eily.'

He frowned.

'There is no evidence to show that she wasn't aware of it. That sort of thing is supposed to be in the air, isn't it? She may have seen the man look at her. Wouldn't that be enough for a jealous woman? That's a very thin story she put up about going out to the back premises to have a look at the dear old family kitchen. I think she went to have a meeting with Luke, and if they met they'd be likely enough to quarrel. He may have taunted her with Eily. I suppose there would be plenty of ways in which a hot-blooded woman could be worked up to the point of doing murder.'

Miss Silver had been knitting placidly. She now gave a gentle cough.

'When did she take the knife? If it was on her way to his room, then she already meant to kill him. It seems to me that that would be a little sudden after fifteen years or so of separation. If, on the other hand, she first quarrelled with him in his room, and then after reaching a state of passionate anger went into the dining-room and took the knife, what was Luke White doing? Did he stand in the hall and wait for her? If so, he must have seen her come out of the dining-room with the knife in her hand. She was wearing a tight thin silk dress and could not possibly have concealed it. If he was killed where he was found, she must have been standing behind him on the bottom step. You will remember the medical evidence states that the thrust had a downward trend. If it was made by a woman, she must have been standing above him at the time. Can you imagine any circumstances which would have brought them into such relative positions – she on the bottom step with the knife in her hand, and he not more than eighteen inches away with his back to her.'

Frank said, 'They must have been coming down the stairs – there isn't any other way it could have happened. Look here, we don't have to take her story about going through to the back premises. Suppose she didn't go to his room at all – suppose he came to hers. They quarrel. She follows him down the stairs and stabs him from the bottom step.'

Miss Silver coughed.

'And when did she get the knife? Are you presupposing that she took it up to bed with her?'

He made a gesture of submission.

'Revered preceptress! I give it up – you'll have to tell me. What did happen?'

She gave him a glance of indulgent reproof and knitted thoughtfully for a few moments. Then she said, 'I am unable to believe that he was killed where he was found. As you say, it could only have happened if he had been coming downstairs with the murderer a step behind him. This would imply premeditation, for the murderer must have had the knife ready. But who would plan to murder a man in so public a spot? At the sound of a cry, or of the fall, it was to be expected that the house would be roused. It would be very difficult for the murderer to retreat without being seen. I really am quite unable to believe that Luke White was killed in the hall. Then, if he was killed elsewhere, could Florence Duke have dragged him single-handed to the place where he was found? To say nothing of the fact that such a proceeding would almost certainly have left a trail of blood, can you give me any single reason why it should have been attempted?'

Frank shook his head.

'No, I can't.'

Miss Silver pursued the theme.

'A jealous woman who has just stabbed a man in a fit of passion would be in no state to transfer the body from one place to another. Mrs. Duke is a strongly built woman – she might have been able to move the body. But what motive could she have for doing so? A woman in the frame of mind you have supposed would either have remained beside the body in a dazed state, or else got back to her room as quickly as possible.'

Frank nodded.

'Florence Duke was found beside the body in a dazed state,' he observed.

Miss Silver said sharply, 'She was not beside it when Eily came downstairs.'

'She heard the girl coming and slipped into the dining-room. When Eily went into the lounge she thought she could get away up the stairs, but there wasn't time. Eily came out again, and Florence was caught with the blood on her hands.'

Miss Silver said in a mild, obstinate voice, 'That still does not explain how he came to be in the place where he was found.'

Crisp snapped the door open, came in from the lounge, and snapped it shut again. He looked alert and pleased as he came up to the table.

'Well, Mrs. Castell was speaking the truth. Luke White married Florence Duke at Lenton register office on July 7th '31. So now we'll have her in and ask her what about it.'

Chapter 27

FLORENCE DUKE took the chair which faced Inspector Crisp and the cold light from the window. Frank Abbott's cool cynical gaze dwelt upon her. A big strongly built woman. He thought she could have shifted the corpse all right if she had wanted to. But Maudie was quite right – why should she want to? But she was set on it that someone had shifted Luke White, and for the matter of that, why should any-one want to? There could be only one answer to that – he had been killed in a place which would have implicated the murderer. Suppose that place was Florence Duke's room. The idea occurred, only to be rejected. Impossible to believe that she had dragged the corpse along the corridor and bumped it down the stairs without at least rousing Maudie who had cat's ears and slept with one eye open when she was on a case. He remembered that Mrs. Duke's room was next to hers, and the idea which had for the moment seemed quite bright went out like a quenched spark.

His attention returned to Florence Duke. Crisp was reading over the original statement she had made, and he had leisure to observe her. She must have been a handsome girl of the type which coarsens young. He supposed her to be in the early forties. Good hair, good eyes, good teeth. Odd fleeting likeness to the magnificent Lady Marian, who wouldn't have been at all pleased if her attention had been drawn to it. Colour in the cheeks probably a good strong red when things were going all right – a nasty bluish look about it now. Frightful clothes – too tight, too bright, too short, too everything. Short royal blue skirt, elaborate revealing knitted jumper which failed to match it by a couple of shades, a cheap paste brooch pinned on to the front of it.

Crisp laid down the paper from which he had been reading.

'That's your statement, Mrs. Duke.'

'What about it?'

The words came in that slow way she had. Frank could imagine the voice having its attractions – the voice, and that slow way of speaking, and the really fine eyes. Might have been quite an alluring figure behind the bar of the George in '31.'

Crisp tapped the table.

'You call yourself Mrs. Duke. Is that your real name?'

'It's what I was born with.'

'But you're a married woman, aren't you?'

'Not now.'

'Do you mean you are divorced?'

'No – we separated.'

'What is your legal name?'

'That's my business. He was a bad lot. I went back to my own name that I'd a right to.'

Crisp tapped vigorously.

'Is your legal name White?'

162

Her colour drained away, then rushed back alarmingly.

Crisp said sharply, 'Did you marry Luke White at the register office at Lenton on July 7th, 1931?'

There was sweat on her forehead. She was flushed to the very roots of her hair. The colour receded slowly, leaving a hard fixed patch on either cheek. She said, 'You've got it.'

'The murdered man was your husband?'

'We were married like you said. It didn't last above six months. He was a bad lot.'

Crisp frowned severely.

'Well, this alters the position – you can see that, can't you, Mrs. White?'

She said sharply, 'Don't call me that!'

He gave a slight shrug of the shoulders.

'You can call yourself what you please. The fact that Luke White was your husband puts you in a very different position from the one you were in when all the information we had was that you and he were strangers. You can see that, I suppose. If he was a stranger, you hadn't any motive for wanting him out of the way. If he was your husband, you might have quite a strong one. I'm going to take you over that statement of yours again, and I've got to tell you that your answers will be taken down and may be used in evidence.'

Frank Abbott left his place by the fire and came forward to drop into the chair at the end of the table. He produced pencil and notebook and sat waiting.

Miss Silver continued to knit, her hands low in her lap, her eyes on Florence Duke, who did not speak. The fine dark eyes looked at Inspector Crisp with something of defiance. Frank Abbott thought, 'She's got cold feet all right – but she'll put up a show.'

Crisp had the statement in his hand. He ran his eye down the page.

'Here we are. You say you hadn't undressed, and you give a number of reasons for why you hadn't. You got thinking about old times – you were accustomed to sitting up late – you didn't think you would sleep if you went to bed. Now wasn't it the real reason that you were waiting for the house to be quiet before going down to see your husband?'

She went on looking at him without speaking. He only gave her a moment.

'You needn't answer if you don't want to, but wasn't that the reason? You were the only person in the house who hadn't undressed – weren't you? Everyone else had been in bed and asleep – hadn't they? You hadn't undressed because you were waiting to come down and go along to your husband's room. That's right, isn't it? Perhaps you had an appointment with him – '

Her lips parted on the one slow word, 'No.'

Something like a smirk of satisfaction just touched Crisp's expression. She had spoken, and she had practically admitted that she had in fact come down to see Luke White. He proceeded to follow up the advantage.

'But you came down intending to see him?'

Quite suddenly she blazed.

'What's the harm if I did?'

'Oh, none – none. He was your husband, wasn't he? You waited till everyone was asleep, and you came down to see him. No harm in it at all. Only what you said in your statement was that you were looking for a drink and something to read. That wasn't true, was it?'

The deep angry voice said, 'I wanted the drink all right.'

'But you came down to see your husband.'

She cried out, 'Not so much of the husband! I was through with him! I came down to see Luke White!'

'I thought so! And then you quarrelled.'

She said flatly, 'That's a lie! He wasn't there!'

Crisp said, 'What!'

Florence nodded.

'Nice to think there's something you don't know. He wasn't there.'

He looked furiously at her. Before he could speak Miss Silver said, 'Pray, Mrs. Duke, how did you know which room to go to?'

She turned her head, and seemed for the first time to be aware of Miss Silver's presence. She said, with all the heat gone from her voice, 'I asked that girl Eily where he slept. Not just like that, you know – she'd have thought it funny. The way I put it was, how many bedrooms did they have,

164

and where had everyone been put.'

Frank Abbott's hand moved to and fro across the paper. Crisp tapped with his pencil. He said impatiently, 'That doesn't matter! You say you went to Luke White's room and he wasn't there.'

She shook her head,

'No, he wasn't there.'

'Sure you struck the right room?'

'Yes. There's only the one bedroom – opposite the kitchen.'

'How long were you there?'

'I don't know. I thought he'd be coming. I looked round a bit. Then I thought I'd wait in the kitchen. That was all what I said before. I went in the kitchen and had a look round and a couple of glasses of sherry like I said. There was a bottle on the dresser.'

'How soon did Luke White come along?'

She shook her head.

'He didn't come. I got tired of waiting and went through to the hall like I told you. He was laid there with the knife in him, and that girl coming out of the lounge. I went to see if he was dead, and got my hands all messed up. Then Eily screamed, and everyone came down.'

He went on asking his questions, but he got nothing more from her. She had come downstairs to see Luke White, but she hadn't seen him. She hadn't set eyes on him until she saw him lying dead in the hall. She hadn't laid hands on the knife or used it. She hadn't stabbed Luke White.

Crisp let her go in the end. He was at once complacent over what he had got, and irritated because he had got no more. He stabbed with his pencil at the blotter and broke the point as he said, 'She did it all right. It couldn't be anyone else.'

Frank Abbott looked up from his neat shorthand notes. He used the voice which Crisp stigmatised as B.B.C. to say, 'I don't know.'

The Inspector fetched a knife from his pocket, released the blade with a jerk, and attacked the damaged pencil. Between slashes he said, 'Of course she isn't Castell! It's got to be Castell, hasn't it?' He laughed harshly. 'No substitutes accepted!'

Miss Silver coughed in a hortatory manner.

'Pray, Inspector, is there no news of Albert Miller?'

Chapter 28

JEREMY and Jane drove down from London. It was one of those grey afternoons when the clouds are low and a seeping vapour comes out of the ground to meet them. It wasn't a fog yet, but there was no saying when it might take a turn that way. They ran through Cliff just after four, and out on the other side within sight and hearing of the sea. Jeremy was looking to his right, watching, as he had watched before, for the pair of tall stone pillars which marked the entrance to Cliff House. As they came in sight, weather-beaten and damaged, the one topped by an eagle, the other with the bird and half the capital gone, he slowed down.

'I'm taking you to tea with Jack Challoner.'

Jane said, 'Oh!' in rather a startled manner, and then, 'Why?'

'He's a pal of mine. I rang him up. He said, "Bring her along to tea," and I said, "Right you are!" – just like that.'

'Why didn't you tell me?'

'I don't know. I didn't want you to say no. Its a mouldy old place, but I'd rather like to see it. Jack's a good chap.'

'Isn't Inspector Abbott staying there?'

'Yes. He's some sort of cousin. I don't suppose he'll be there. Anyhow we're not suspects.'

They had passed between the pillars and were pursuing a long, neglected drive with a tangled shrubbery on either side, wind-swept and stunted. The house when they reached it was gaunt and forbidding – a square, bare eighteenth-century block with the same neglected look as the drive.

An old man admitted them to an icy cavern of a hall,

took them across it, and down a passage to a small room with a blazing fire, curtains already drawn, and two oil lamps giving out plenty of light, heat, and smell. A red-haired young man with rather a flat, freckled face heaved himself out of a shabby armchair and clapped Jeremy on the shoulder.

'Hullo, hullo! How do you do, Miss Heron?. It's frightfully good of you to come – it really is. I get the pip when I'm here by myself. Frank's out chasing murderers, and I don't suppose he'll be back for tea, so you and Jeremy are probably going to save my life. Do you like muffins? Matthews always keeps them going because he likes them himself. I say, these lamps do stink, don't they? That's me, I'm afraid. Matthews always tells me not to turn them up, and then I forget and they smell to heaven. Of course, what this place wants is about ten thousand pounds spent on it. Nothing's been done for donkeys' years. My great-great-grandfather ruined himself playing cards with the Prince Regent, and nobody's had a penny ever since. He married an heiress and got rid of every farthing she had. Fun whilst it lasted!'

He was pulling chairs round as he spoke. The one Jane got had a broken spring. The curtains were Victorian – maroon velvet gone the colour of old blood, with a ball fringe ripped and hanging in loops. The carpet looked unswept, but that may have been merely an effect of age and decay. Jane thought how grim it would be to be saddled with a house like this. Jack Challoner seemed to bear up, but she felt sorry for his wife when he married.

As if her thought reached him, he laughed and said, 'What we want is another heiress – only I'd have to keep her carefully away from the place till it's too late to draw back. No girl in her senses would take on a mouldy old ruin like this. I mean, she'd have to be frightfully in love, wouldn't she? And I'm not the sort that girls fall frightfully in love with. Look here, would you like to see how bad it is? Jeremy said he'd like to – I can't imagine why.'

Jeremy hadn't sat down. He was leaning against the mantelpiece looking down into the fire. He turned now and said, 'Tales of my grandfather. His mother used to tell him stories about your people. It was Sir Humphrey Challoner in her time – somewhere in the eighteen-forties. I'd like to see the family portraits, you know.'

'All right. But we'd better go now, or there won't be any light.' He turned to Jane. 'What about you? Wouldn't you rather stay by the fire? I say, I do call you Jane, don't I? I've known Jeremy for centuries.'

He was about the same age as Jeremy, but he seemed younger. He reminded Jane of a large friendly puppy.

They went back through the icy hall to a stark dining-room full of dreadful Victorian furniture. Above a massive sideboard hung the portrait of a gloomy gentleman in a stock and side-whiskers.

'That's old Humphrey,' said Jack Challoner. 'What sort of stories did your great-grandmamma hand down about him? He was my great-grandfather.'

Jeremy said slowly, 'He disinherited his son, didn't he?'

'Yes – his eldest son, Geoffrey. Nasty family scandal. Geoffrey took after *his* grandfather, the old boy who ruined us – went the pace – was mixed up in some smuggling affray and got himself bumped off. After which everyone breathed more freely, and my grandfather, John, came in for the title and the place.'

Jeremy said, 'My grandfather said his mother used to talk about Geoffrey.'

Jack Challoner laughed.

'I suppose she would! I'm afraid it was your Taverner lot that led him astray. By all accounts the Catherine-Wheel was a regular Smugglers' Arms. There's a portrait of Geoffrey upstairs. Like to see it?'

They went up the big stairway, Jack Challoner carrying a tall candelabrum with twisted arms and candles which must have been in it since before the war, they were so dusty and yellow. The silver had probably not been cleaned since then either. Jack tapped it with a laugh.

'Only Sheffield plate, or it would have gone up the spout long ago.'

Jane said quickly, 'It might still be worth quite a lot.' Then, catching herself up and colouring, 'My grandfather had an antique shop.'

She got a cheerful shake of the head.

'Drop in the bucket. It'll have to be the heiress.'

They went on up the stairs. There was still daylight of the sort which doesn't do very much to a dark corner. Geoffrey Challoner's portrait hung in a very dark corner indeed – the black sheep tidied away out of sight. Jane wondered in an odd fleeting way whether anyone had been used to come and look at it there. His mother might have, if she had been alive. She wondered.

Jack Challoner set the candelabrum on the floor, produced matches from a bulging pocket, lighted the five discoloured candles, and lifted it high.

'You can't see in this corner even in the morning. That's why I brought the contraption,' he said. 'Well, there's our black sheep. Painted before the scandal of course, when he was twenty-one. Coming of age of the heir, and all that.'

The candlelight fell on a young man in a shooting-jacket carrying a gun under his arm and holding a brace of pheasants. The birds were very well painted, the iridescent feathers still bright. Geoffrey Challoner looked out from the canvas, very much the proud, good-looking young man with the world before him. The chance shot in the dark which was to come as a relief to his family was still a couple of years away.

Jack Challoner said, 'If you're looking for a family likeness you won't find one. It was my grandmother who brought the red hair into the family, and we shall probably never be able to get rid of it. She had eight daughters, all carroty.'

'No,' said Jane, 'there isn't any likeness, is there?'

And as she said it she knew it wasn't true. There was a likeness, and a strong one, but it wasn't the likeness that it ought to have been. She looked at Jeremy, and looked away quickly. Lengthen his hair, give him those little side whiskers just coming down on to the cheeks, put him into those clothes, and he might have sat for the portrait. She was aware of something, some tension. She couldn't risk a second look.

Jack Challoner said, 'He's more like Jeremy than me, isn't he?'

They went downstairs and ate muffins out of a cracked

169

Worcester dish, and drank tea from a solid hideous Victorian teapot all curves and bulges. it had a silver strawberry on the lid, and had probably served the red-haired Lady Challoner and her eight carroty daughters.

When they had said good-bye and were going slowly down the long drive Jeremy said, 'Mouldy old place, isn't it?'

'Frightful! I'm sorry for Jack.'

Jeremy laughed.

'You needn't be. He's a cheerful soul, and he's only there once in a blue moon.'

Jane laughed too.

'Will he marry an heiress? He doesn't look the sort.'

'He will not. He's in love with a girl called Molly Pemberton, a tremendously good sort. She hasn't got a penny, and neither of them will give a damn. He's down here now because someone wants the place for a sanatorium, or an orphanage, or something. Sea air – ozone – dollops of it. He's seeing lawyers and trying to make up his mind to the wrench.'

He stopped the car just inside the two tall pillars.

'Jane, I want to talk. The Catherine-Wheel is crawling with constabulary and cousins, so I think we'll have it out here. When are you going to marry me?'

He had let go of the wheel and taken her hands. She didn't pull them away, but they were rigid and stubborn in his.

'I haven't ever said I'd marry you at all.'

'Does it want saying?'

'Yes, it does.'

'Then say it!'

'Jeremy, let go!'

'Say it! Jane – darling – say it!'

She had meant to let him hold her hands for as long as he liked in a perfectly calm and friendly manner, but she couldn't do it. His voice did things to her when it changed like that. Suddenly friendship was all gone. A horrid undermining flood of emotion had swept it away. In a split second it would sweep her into Jeremy's arms, and if he kissed her she would say anything he wanted her to say. She snatched her hands away and strained back into the corner.

'No – no!'

'Jane!'

She pushed him away.

'No – no – I won't!'

'Why?'

'Cousins oughtn't to marry.'

'I'm not your cousin.'

He spoke quite quietly, but it was like a thunder-clap. It stopped the giddy feeling. She blinked and said, '*What!*'

Jeremy said it again.

'I'm not your cousin.'

Jane produced another monosyllable. She didn't seem to have enough breath for anything else. She said, 'Why?'

'I'll tell you. I've been going to. There hasn't been much chance up to now. But we might as well be comfortable. Stop doing the "Unhand me!" act and relax.'

Jane relaxed. The flood of emotion had subsided. It seemed, as Jeremy had just said, comfortable to have his arm round her. This place behind the pillars was dark. The Cliff road was dark and empty. She said, 'Why aren't you my cousin?'

'Because I'm not a Taverner at all. My grandfather was Geoffrey Challoner's son. That's why I wanted to see the picture. Even I can see that I'm like him.'

'You're frightfully like him.'

He laughed.

'I ought to be Sir Jeremy Challoner, with that old ruin tied round my neck, you know. Geoffrey was the elder son.'

'Jeremy – how exciting!'

'It is rather. My grandfather told me. You remember he was one of the twins, John and Joanna. Well, old Jeremiah Taverner died in eighteen-eighty-eight. His wife, Ann, lived another three years. She never said a word while her husband was alive, but this is what she told my grandfather John before she died. Geoffrey Challoner used to come to the Catherine-Wheel a lot. He was wild and he was in debt, and he got mixed up in the smuggling trade, partly for the fun of the thing, and partly because he wanted to make enough money to run off with Mary Layburn. She was Sir John Layburn's daughter – same family John Higgins

171

works for – and they had been engaged, but old Challoner and Sir John fell out over politics and the engagement was broken off. That's what started Geoffrey running wild. The Layburns sent Mary away to a strict aunt in London, but Geoffrey followed her and they were secretly married. Ann Taverner was positive to my grandfather about the marriage. She said she had seen the certificate, but she couldn't remember the name of the church. "One of those grand London churches," she told him. Well, about six months after that Geoffrey had to skip over to France. A coast-guard had been hurt, and he had been recognised. They planned to let the thing blow over, and then for him to come back and get Mary. Unfortunately the man died – not at once, and not with any certainty from his injuries. But the Layburns pressed the matter. They wanted to keep Geoffrey out of the country, and a warrant was issued. That meant Geoffrey couldn't come back. And Mary Layburn was going to have a child. She came to Ann Taverner and told her she couldn't hide it any longer. She didn't dare tell her people she was married – fathers were fierce in the 'forties. She was a gentle, timid girl, and she said he'd kill her.'

'What happened? Go on – quickly!'

'Ann Taverner told Jeremiah, and he sent word over to Geoffrey in France. They used to run the cargoes pretty regularly when the moon was dark. Geoffrey sent word back that he'd come on the next run – that would be three weeks away – and he said Mary must manage till then. When the time came Ann was to let Mary know, and she was to slip out of her room when everyone was in bed and come out to the Catherine-Wheel. None of them seem to have thought it was anything to make a song and dance about, but I don't suppose the poor girl had ever been out by herself at night before. She arrived terrified and upset, and Ann was afraid of what might happen. It was awkward enough without that, she said, because she herself was expecting her sixth child at any moment. As it turned out, that child was born about midnight. The midwife was in the house – Ann Taverner's cousin, and a very discreet woman. At one o'clock there was a noise of fire-arms under the cliff. The run had been spotted or given away, and the

172

coastguards were there. Geoffrey Challoner was fatally wounded. Jeremiah and one of his men got him away into the Catherine-Wheel by the secret passage, and he died in Mary's arms. It finished her, poor girl. She had her baby before its time, and was dead by morning. With the mid-wife's help Ann Taverner passed the child off for a twin of her own child. Hers was a girl, Joanna. She was John Higgins' grandmother, and the Challoner baby was a boy – my grandfather John.'

Jane drew a quick excited breath.

'Did old Jeremiah know?'

Jeremy stared.

'Must have done.'

She shook her head.

'Oh, no – not if the women didn't want him to. Ann and the midwife, they could have managed if they'd wanted to. I wonder if they did.'

'I don't know. My grandfather didn't say. You've got to remember that Ann was very old when she told him – it was in her last illness. What she was out to impress on him was that Geoffrey Challoner and Mary Layburn were legally married, and that he was their legitimate son.'

'Why didn't they say so at the time? I mean, the baby was Sir Humphrey Challoner's heir – why didn't they hand it over to him?'

'Because it would have got them into a peck of trouble. Geoffrey was wanted for the coastguard's death. Though everybody in the neighbourhood must have known that Jeremiah Taverner was up to the neck in the smuggling trade, having it all come out at a coroner's court would have been quite another pair of shoes. Anyhow, whatever Jeremiah knew or didn't know about the baby, he wasn't for having an inquest on two sudden deaths on his licensed premises.'

'What did he do?'

'Well, I gather he was all for throwing the bodies into the sea, but Ann wouldn't have it. I don't know that she'd have got her way if it hadn't been for her final argument. "Two people dead like that and done out of their rights – the sea wouldn't keep them," she said. That's what she told my

173

grandfather, and it brought Jeremiah up with a round turn. It wouldn't have suited him at all to have those bodies come ashore.'

'What did they do with them?'

'Bricked them up in the secret passage together with the marriage certificate which Mary had brought along and a statement signed by Ann and the midwife. Ann put all the papers together and sealed them with Geoffrey's signet-ring. She kept that, and she gave it to my grandfather. I've got it now.'

'But, Jeremy, there wasn't any brickwork in that passage we went down – not any at all.'

Jeremy said in rather an odd voice, 'No, there wasn't, was there?' Then he put his hands on her shoulders and said, 'Never mind about that just now. I'm not your cousin – I'm not the farthest, most distant relation. We are in fact complete strangers. Are you going to marry me?'

Jane caught her breath and said, 'I suppose I am.'

Chapter 29

THE inquest was to be next day. It was understood that the police would offer merely formal evidence and ask for an adjournment. Inspector Crisp reported to his Chief Constable that he thought a good enough case could be made out against Florence Duke. On the face of it, Randal March was inclined to agree, but recommended caution and some further enquiries.

'Abbott now,' said Inspector Crisp – 'he's come down to work up a case against Castell. I'm not saying anything behind his back that I haven't said to his face, and that's about the size of it.'

March said with a kind of pleasant firmness, 'I know Abbott rather well. He wouldn't pull a case.'

Crisp looked injured.

'I'm not saying he would. He's down here on this dope-smuggling business, and it's likely enough Castell's up to his neck in it. But we've looked for evidence against him ourselves, and if we haven't found any, I don't see it's likely someone down from the Yard will have any better luck. Stands to reason the locals have the better chance, if there are chances going, which it doesn't look as if there were. What I mean to say, Abbott's got Castell in his mind and he can't see past him. But as far as he is concerned, the murder isn't his pigeon – it's only, as you might put it, incidental. It's natural he should see it linked up with the job he came down about, but they mightn't have anything to do with each other.'

'Or they might,' said Randal March.

'Not if it's Mrs. Duke, sir.'

'No, not if it's Mrs. Duke.'

'Or John Higgins. There's a strong jealousy motive there, and it's suspicious that girl Eily being downstairs in her dressing-gown. In the lounge too, with the window unlatched. I must say before all this Duke business came out it looked very much to me as if Eily Fogarty had let Higgins in, and was letting him out again after Luke White was stabbed. She admits having gone into the lounge, and there was a window there unlatched.'

The Chief Constable glanced down at the pile of papers in front of him.

'So I see.'

Crisp continued a thought morosely.

'Then there's this Miss Silver.'

March raised his eyebrows.

'You're not telling me she's a suspect?'

A good many years ago a delicate and insubordinate little boy of eight had shared his sisters' schoolroom, a schoolroom presided over by Miss Maud Silver. The respect she then inspired had never left him. It had been cemented by a very real affection. He had certainly on one occasion owed his life to her professional acumen. The case of the poisoned caterpillars was an old story now, but he never forgot it. Subsequent encounters of a professional nature had only served to increase his admiration for her powers of observation and deduction. There was, in fact, no one whose opinion he more valued, or to whom he would more willingly defer. Aware that she was unofficially concerned in this case, he had been wondering what Crisp's reactions would be. Enquiring whether Miss Silver was a suspect, he was, in fact, both indulging his humour and fishing to see what he would get.

Crisp sat up a little stiffly.

'I wish she was anything you could lay hold on. The Yard can do as they like, but I must say it all seems a bit irregular to me. I don't say anything about her being down there to get the gossip of the place – that's what she's supposed to have come down for, isn't it? But when it comes to Abbott treating her the way he does – well, she might be his superior. And mine.'

March leaned back in his chair. Crisp was ruffled, and Crisp must be soothed. He smiled slightly and said, 'I know. He's worked with her a good many times before. I've heard him say that when she comes in on a case the police come out of it in a blaze of glory. And you know, actually it's true. She's a remarkable person. Do you happen to know what she thinks about this case so far as it's gone?'

Crisp made an exasperated sound. But for the restraining influence of a superior officer it would undoubtedly have been more emphatic.

'I don't know what she thinks. I can tell you what she does. Sits there and knits, and keeps on asking every so often what about Al Miller.'

March shook his head.

'Albert – surely Albert –'

Crisp stared.

'Well, that's his name, I suppose. Everyone calls him Al.'

'I should be surprised if Miss Silver did. So she asks about the missing Albert, does she? Well, what about him?'

Crisp frowned.

'I made sure we'd have picked him up by now. Nobody seems to have seen him since he walked out of Ledlington station and said he wasn't coming back. That would be about seven-thirty Sunday morning. Of course there wouldn't be a lot about – people lie in Sundays. What I can't make out is why she thinks it matters. He couldn't have been mixed up in the murder, and that's flat.'

'Ask her.'

'I beg your pardon, sir?'

'Ask her why she thinks it matters. If she keeps wanting to know about him she'll have a reason, and it will be a good one. On the whole, I think we'd better find him.'

If it had been anyone but the Chief Constable, Crisp would have let fly. He restrained himself with an effort which brought the dark blood to his face and said with some emphasis, 'Look here, sir, he couldn't have had anything to do with it. He was out of the Catherine-Wheel by half past ten. We don't have to rely on Castell for that, because Captain Taverner watched him go. He was drunk, walking unsteadily, and singing bits of a song he'd been trying to sing earlier on in the lounge. Irish, I believe it is. Something about a girl called Eileen. It's in the statements.'

'Eileen alannah – yes.'

'That was just before half past ten. The Wiltons, where he lodged, say he was in before half past eleven. He made a shocking noise, singing this same song and stumbling on the stair. Mr. Wilton was fed up and told him he could clear out in the morning, and he went down and locked the door and took away the key so as Miller couldn't get away without paying his bill. There's St. James' church at the bottom of the street, and the chimes went for half past eleven as he was locking the door. Luke White was found dead a little before one – we had the telephone message at one a.m. The blood was still wet when we got there. The medical evidence is that he must certainly have been alive at half past ten. Dr. Crewe saw him at a quarter to two, and said he'd been dead something under an hour, 'Well, Al Miller couldn't have done it. Now could he?'

'Unless he got out of a window and went back to the Catherine-Wheel. I suppose he could have done that.'

'I put it to the Wiltons was there any way he could have got out of the house and back again, and they said they could swear to it he didn't. Seems his room was right over theirs, and he kept them awake the best part of the night – in and out of bed, to and fro in the room, groaning and carrying on. Now they're very respectable people, and they were properly worked up about it. Mrs. Wilton says she heard twelve o'clock strike, and one, and two, before she could get any sleep. They're properly worked up about Al Miller, and no reason to clear him, but as she says, right's right, and she's ready to swear he didn't leave the house all night. As you know, he was there all right in the morning. Paid his bill at the bedroom door and got the key to let himself out. It's my idea Miller walked out in a huff. He'd been on the edge of it for weeks. Well, he's gone, and he won't turn up again until he wants to. If he's heard about the murder that would be another reason for keeping out of the way. People disappear without half his reasons. He can't have had anything to do with murdering Luke White. And what Miss Silver wants, going on about it like she does, is more than I can say. Just waste of time, sir, if you ask me.'

Randal March hadn't asked him. He said in his pleasant voice, 'All the same, you know, Crisp, I think we'd better find him.'

Chapter 30

MISS SILVER sat in a corner of the lounge, to all appearance quite taken up with her knitting. Not very far away from her Marian Thorpe-Ennington engaged in conversation with Mildred Taverner. Occasional words and phrases were sufficiently audible to make it clear that she was imparting another instalment of that fascinating serial, her life story. Such phrases as, 'The very first time he saw me . . . swore, actually swore, that he would jump out of the aeroplane," and, most surprising of all, 'blood on the diamond wreath, and blood on the floor.'

Mildred Taverner was undoubtedly fascinated. Her Venetian beads clashed against her gold chain as she shuddered, her pale eyes remained fixed upon Lady Marian's beautiful face, her pale lips parted upon a hardly intermittent 'Oh!'

Miss Silver continued to knit in a very thoughtful manner. When the door was presently opened and Frank Abbott looked in she rose, picked up her knitting-bag, and advanced towards him.

'If you can spare the time, I should be glad of a few moments, Inspector.'

He held open the door into Castell's office.

'I shall be delighted.'

When he had shut it behind them she went across to the window and stood there looking at the room. There did not appear to be very much to look at, and with what there was she must by this time have surely been familiar, yet she continued to gaze in a rather abstracted manner until Frank Abbott said, 'I ought to know by now when you've got something up your sleeve. What is it?'

'My dear Frank!'

He returned her reproving glance with a smile.

'Come – out with it!'

She shook her head very slightly, came over to the low chair which she had occupied before, turned it round to the fire, and having seated herself, took up her knitting, observing, 'There is really a good deal that I would like to say, and if you can spare the time I should like to say it now.'

He pulled up another chair and stretched out his feet to the comfortable blaze.

' "Time spared is time saved," as the proverb says – and as you know I am very much at your service.'

Miss Silver's eyes dwelt upon him indulgently, her voice only mildly critical as she said, 'I do not recall any such proverb.'

'Perhaps not. It's an impromptu contribution of my own. After all, they have to be started by someone. I dedicate it – without permission – to you.'

'My dear Frank, when will you learn not to talk so much nonsense?'

His hands were deep in his pockets. He looked at her lazily through his fair lashes.

'I don't know. But I'm finished for now. What did you

want to talk to me about?'

Her needles clicked briskly.

'Our own particular connection with this case, and to what extent it is linked with the murder of Luke White.'

'Interesting thesis. Go on.'

She said, 'We came down here to investigate certain vague rumours with regard to the Catherine-Wheel. These involved the possibility that it was being used as a place of call by smugglers, by persons engaged in the illicit drug trade, or by jewel thieves. Chief Inspector Lamb pointed out that this family reunion organised by Mr. Jacob Taverner might be intended to cover some special activity connected with one of these illegal pursuits. As you know, a murder took place during the night following our arrival. It is of course possible, in theory, that the murdered has no connection with these illegal practices – in fact they have not yet been proved to exist. The whole matter has advanced very little from its original realm of suspicion and conjecture. In spite of which I must tell you that I am quite unable to dissociate the murder of Luke White from what I may perhaps term our case.'

Frank nodded.

'That means that you reject the case against John Higgins. His motive would be a strictly private one – jealousy over Eily Fogarty.'

She inclined her head.

'It was not John Higgins who murdered Luke White.'

The light eyebrows were raised.

'Sure as all that? All right, exit John. What about Florence Duke? Her motive would be a private one too – unless Crisp digs up evidence to connect her with the dope trade or any of these jewel thefts, in which case she might have fallen out with Luke over a division of the swag.'

Miss Silver gave a hortatory cough.

'My dear Frank, pray recall the undisputed evidence of the position of the body and the position of the wound. If Luke White was killed where he was found, the murderer was immediately behind him on the bottom step. No one has yet supplied any theory which makes this intelligible if Florence Duke is supposed to have committed the murder.

180

On the other hand, if he was not killed where he was found, what possible motive could she have for dragging him there? It could not have been done by one person without making enough noise to run the risk of bringing someone down to investigate. We have been over all this before, and I do not see my way to supporting a case against Florence Duke.'

'Well, what do you support?'

Her needles clicked.

'I have come to certain conclusions. They are these. The murder greatly deepens the suspicions attaching to the inn. Mr. Jacob Taverner's party and the circumstances leading up to it also deepen those suspicions. We will come back to this later. I believe that those suspicions are justified, and that the death of Luke White is linked with the circumstances which gave rise to them. It is my opinion that at least two people were engaged in the murder, and that it certainly did not take place in the hall.'

He looked at her keenly.

'Two people?'

'It would have required two people to carry the body to the place where it was found, if this was to be accomplished without risk.'

Frank was regarding her with a slightly quizzical air.

'Is that all?'

'I have reached no definite conclusions beyond these. But I have some observations to offer on the subject of Mr. Jacob Taverner and his party.'

'What are they?'

'These, Frank. I have had opportunities of conversing with several of the Taverner cousins. All of them have been extremely communicative. They are, Captain Jeremy Taverner and Miss Jane Heron — friendly likeable young people — Lady Marian Thorpe-Ennington, and Miss Mildred Taverner. Lady Marian has the habit of talking about herself and can easily be induced to do so. Miss Taverner is nervously apprehensive. She has led a very narrow life, and the murder has alarmed her very much. Her brother represses her. She is frightened of being alone, and has been glad of my company. From these four people I have learned

181

that Mr. Jacob Taverner has made a point of pressing each of them as to what they may have heard about the Catherine-Wheel from their grandparents, with whom there was in each case a rather particularly close association. Looked at in the light of what has since happened, those questions would seem to refer to the existence of some concealed passage from the house to the shore. Miss Taverner gave me the best information on this point. Jane Heron really knew nothing. Captain Taverner said his grandfather had mentioned such a passage, but he had no idea where it was, and so he had told Mr. Jacob. Lady Marian talked a great deal, but I really did not discover that she knew anything. Florence Duke denied any knowledge, but admitted to having been questioned by Mr. Jacob Taverner. She has not been inclined for conversation, but when I put the question to her directly she answered me. I am, however, very strongly of the opinion that she was holding something back. I did not question Mr. Geoffrey Taverner. His manner to me has been discourteous, and I did not think I should gain anything by doing so.'

Frank Abbott drew up his legs, leaned forward, and put a log upon the fire. He knew his Miss Silver tolerably well, and it wasn't like her to flog a dead horse. He said, 'But Jacob Taverner knew all about the passage to the shore. He took the whole party through it on the Saturday night as soon as they had finished dinner. He showed it to us without any hesitation, and we've been through it with the proverbial tooth-comb. No contraband, no corpses. Not the least, furthest smell of a clue.'

The fire blazed up. Miss Silver's needles caught the glow and flashed it back. She said very composedly, 'I refer, of course, to the other passage.'

There was a brief electric silence. Frank Abbott got to his feet gracefully and without hurry. Standing against the mantelpiece and looking down at her, he said with some accentuation of his usual manner.

'Would you mind saying that again?'

'My dear Frank, you heard me perfectly.

'It was the mind that boggled, not the ear.'

'Pray bring your mind to bear upon the evidence. Since

Jacob Taverner was already aware of the passage leading from the cellars to the shore, his questions cannot be taken as referring to it. But he did, either directly or by implication, question four or five of the Taverner cousins as to their knowledge of a secret passage. I believe he questioned them all, but there is no evidence in the cases of Mr. Geoffrey Taverner, John Higgins, or Albert Miller. These questions cannot be taken to apply to the passage leading out of the cellars.'

'He might have wanted to find out if they knew about it.'

Miss Silver coughed.

'I believe not. The impression left upon my mind after hearing what these people have to say, and especially after listening to Miss Mildred Taverner, is that the entrance to this second passage is somewhere upstairs. Miss Taverner's grandfather – he was Matthew, the second son of old Jeremiah Taverner – told her that when he was a very little boy he woke up frightened because he heard a noise. He went to see what it was, and he saw a light coming out of a hole in the wall. He was dreadfully frightened, and he ran away back to his bed and pulled the blankets over his head.'

'Is that all?'

'That is all she could tell me.'

'He may have dreamed the whole thing.'

'It is, of course, possible, but I do not think so. It is the kind of thing that a child would remember.'

Frank looked down meditatively into the fire.

'Interesting theory,' he said. 'Not of any immediate practical value perhaps.' He bent down and carefully added another log. Then, as he straightened up again, 'And what, after all this, are your views on Jacob Taverner?'

She stopped knitting for a moment and looked at him very seriously indeed.

'I am unable to make up my mind. There are, of course, two possibilities. His father was old Jeremiah Taverner's eldest son, a second Jeremiah. After his father's death he came in for the whole of the family property, but he is said almost immediately to have severed his connection with the Catherine-Wheel. I gather there was an impression that a sale had taken place. But this was not the case. The inn was leased.'

'Yes – March handed that on. There were two generations of Smiths, father and son, and when the last one died the place reverted to Jacob Taverner. Castell was already manager and he kept him on. The question of course is, had the Taverner connection with the Catherine-Wheel ever really ceased – did the smuggling trade still go on, with part of the profits going to Jeremiah the second, and afterwards to his son Jacob – have they continued during the last five years – and is Jacob an active partner? That's what we're here to find out, isn't it?'

Miss Silver was knitting again. She said, 'Precisely.'

'Well, that brings us back to what do you think of Jacob Taverner?'

Miss Silver coughed.

'I have seen very little of him. Yesterday, as you know, he kept to his room. Today he came down to lunch. He complains of the cold, and is said to be suffering from a chill. He appears to me to have had a shock, but so have we all. He may be implicated in the smuggling, but not in the murder.'

'You think that?'

'No. I have not enough information to draw any conclusions. It is merely a hypothesis which would account for the known facts. If he were implicated in the smuggling, it would explain his desire to find out whether his Taverner cousins were in a position to give away any secrets. If there were two passages, one of which was very much more important than the other, he might consider it well worth while to sacrifice one of them by making it public property, and thus protect the secrecy of the other. He would hope that any stories or rumours, whether current locally or preserved by the family, would thus be laid to rest. This would account for his getting the family together and making a feature of displaying the passage from the cellars to the shore. It will, of course, occur to you that Luke White may have been murdered in order to preserve the secret of the other passage. If he knew of it, and was using his knowledge to blackmail his associates, there would be no need to look any further for

184

a motive. I may say that I consider this far more likely than the motive of jealousy insisted on by Inspector Crisp.'

'It might be.'

'It is not possible at present to say whether Mr. Jacob Taverner is implicated or not. He may be merely what he appears to be, an elderly man with a great deal of money, no ties, and the desire to promote a family reunion, perhaps with the intention of deciding upon the terms of his will. He might have a financial interest in the Catherine-Wheel, without any knowledge of its smuggling activities, if indeed these exist. There is, of course, no proof that they do, only a good deal of suspicion, and the suggestion that where there is smoke one would expect to discover a fire.'

Frank stood up straight.

'In fact Jacob may be innocent, and so may the Catherine-Wheel. We've got nasty suspicious minds, and we are apt to see what we are looking for – as per my esteemed colleague Crisp. Well, we shall see.'

Miss Silver was folding up her knitting and putting it away. She now rose to her feet.

'Just one moment, Frank. I would like you to have this carpet washed.'

'My dear Miss Silver!'

'Very carefully, of course. I should not, perhaps, have said washed. I should like it to be examined very carefully, with a view to ascertaining whether there are any blood-stains.'

'Bloodstains?'

'Recent ones, of course. The colour of the carpet and its dirty condition would conceal them.'

He gazed at the floor. The square of carpet which covered it to within a foot of the walls must originally have been of a deep brownish red with a small all-over pattern now almost entirely lost in the general gloom. He said slowly, 'Just what do you expect to find?'

Miss Silver coughed.

'Evidence that Luke White was killed in this room,' she said.

Chapter 31

Jeremy and Jane, returning to the Catherine-Wheel in a state of mind blissfully superior to murder, were encountered by Miss Silver as they opened the front door. She had, in fact, been listening for the sound of the car.

'Just one moment, Captain Taverner,' she said.

They stood where they were, the door still open, until Miss Silver stepped outside and shut it between them and the inn. It was then that Jane came down to earth sufficiently to realise that Miss Silver was attired for the road. She wore the black cloth coat, the elderly tippet, the black felt hat, and the woollen gloves.

Without any delay she came to the point.

'Captain Taverner, I am going to ask you a favour. Will you be so kind as to drive me in to Ledlington?'

Jeremy said, 'Of course.'

Miss Silver coughed.

'It is very good of you. I should prefer to start immediately if it would be quite convenient. There is someone with whom I should like to have a short conversation. I think I can undertake not to keep you waiting more than twenty minutes. It might be less, but I think I can promise that it will not be more.'

Jeremy laughed.

'Jane will hold my hand!'

Miss Silver sat at the back and smiled indulgently at the two young people in front. She had, of course, been offered the seat beside the driver, but her refusal had been definite.

'I should really greatly prefer to be behind. I find the headlights disturbing.'

She sat in the dark and watched them go by. Not so very many after all. It hardly needed the sudden flashing light to inform her that Jeremy and Jane were sitting very close together, and that they were in a state of extreme happiness. Neither of them would really mind if her conversation with

186

Mrs. Wilton were to last more than twenty minutes.

They drew up in Thread Street, with the old church of St. James looming dark at the corner. Measuring the distance to No. 6 with her eye, Miss Silver could well understand that the Wiltons need never be in doubt as to the time. As she pressed the bell, the clock in the church tower gave two chiming strokes for the half hour. Once you were accustomed to the sound it would no longer rouse you, but if you were lying awake in the night you would hardly fail to hear it.

The door was opened a little way. A dimly lighted passage appeared, and, blocking most of the view, someone very tall and broad.

'Mrs. Wilton?'

'Yes.' The voice was firm and pleasant.

Miss Silver moved so that what light there was might fall reassuringly upon her own face and figure.

'My name is Silver – Miss Maud Silver. You will not know it. I wonder if I might have a very short conversation with you.'

Mrs. Wilton hesitated.

'If it's about a subscription – ' she began.

'Oh, no – nothing of that sort, I assure you.'

The passage light enabled Mrs. Wilton to observe the smile which had won so many confidences.

'It is just that I should be very grateful if you would allow me to talk to you for a little about Albert Miller.'

For a moment the thing hung in the balance. If it hadn't been for Miss Silver's smile, the scales would have gone down with a bang on the wrong side and the door would have been shut. The momentary pause allowed a variety of considerations to present themselves. Mrs. Wilton had her share of curiosity, but if she had been expecting Mr. Wilton home to his tea she would not have allowed it to interrupt her preparations. But Mr. Wilton was working overtime and would not be home until eight o'clock. She wouldn't mind a bit of a sit-down and a bit of a gossip. She opened the door and asked Miss Silver in.

The room into which she showed her smelled of furniture-polish and moth-ball. Except on occasions of state the Wiltons used their warm and comfortable kitchen. The sitting-room existed as the shrine of their respectability. It housed in unblemished splendour the suite bought thirty years ago out of Mrs. Wilton's own earnings on the occasion of her marriage. It consisted of a sofa and two chairs – lady's easy and gent's ditto. The springs were intact, the bright blue plush as bright and blue as on the day when she had proudly paid the bill. Moth had been kept at bay by the cunning insertion of moth-balls in every crevice – hence the smell. The carpet, contributed by Mr. Wilton, matched the suite in colour and had been just as carefully kept. There was a white woolly mat in front of the cold hearth, where a fan of pink crinkled paper faintly simulated an absent flame. There were two blue vases on the mantelpiece, and a gilt clock which had at one time been a source of strife in an otherwise harmonious married life, Mrs. Wilton having bought it cheap at an auction because it took her fancy, and Mr. Wilton having used it as the text for a good many heavy-handed sermons when he discovered that it had no works. Everything in the room was spotlessly clean, and anything that could be polished had been polished until you could see your face in it. There were pink curtains at the bow window, and a gas-bracket with a pink glass shade on either side of the mantelpiece. At the application of a match to the nearest bracket all this colour and polish sprang into view.

Miss Silver, who shared Mrs. Wilton's partiality for pink and blue, and had no objection to seeing them mixed, was able to exclaim with genuine admiration, 'But what a charming room! So comfortable, so tasteful!'

Mrs. Wilton swelled with pride. She would at once have detected a feigned appreciation, but this was the genuine thing. She was not one to show her feelings, but she warmed to the visitor.

They sat down, Miss Silver in the lady's easy, and Mrs. Wilton in the gent's ditto. Under the pink shaded gaslight she appeared as a massively built woman with a fine head of grey hair. She had on a flowered overall which allowed glimpses of a brown stuff dress. Her whole appearance was that of a person who respected herself and expected others to respect her. Miss Silver surveyed her thoughtfully. Not the woman to gossip easily, or perhaps at all. She said, 'It is very good of you to let me talk to you about Albert Miller, Mrs. Wilton.'

There was a slight perceptible stiffening.

'If it's anything to do with his wanting the room again it isn't a bit of good. I wouldn't have him back, nor I wouldn't ask my husband. We put up with it long enough – too long, if it comes to the. And I wouldn't have done it if it hadn't been for knowing his mother, poor thing.'

'Is she alive?'

Mrs. Wilton shook her head.

'Dead these ten years. She'd a bad husband that she couldn't stand up to nor yet leave like I'd have done. And 'twas for her sake I took Albert in when he come out of the army, and put up with him when by rights I shouldn't have done. But we've had too much of him, Mr. Wilton and me, and we're not taking him back. Getting too big for his boots and talking about what a lot of money he was going to have – and where it was coming from, dear knows, for he wasn't going to keep his job the way he was carrying on, and Millers never had anything that I heard tell about.'

'He must have been a very trying lodger.'

Mrs. Wilton looked majestic.

'Coming in all hours,' she said. 'And the Worse. And no thought to wipe his boots on the mat.'

Miss Silver said, 'Dear me! How extremely inconsiderate!'

'We're not taking him back,' said Mrs. Wilton with gloomy finality.

Miss Silver coughed.

'No one could possibly expect you to do so. I can assure you that I am not here to question your decision. As I said before, he must have been a most trying inmate, but since you knew his mother and have spoken of her so kindly you would not wish any harm to come to him – would you?'

Mrs. Wilton bridled.

'I'm sure I'm not one to wish harm to come to anyone,' she said.

'Then I may tell you that I am seriously concerned about Albert Miller. It would help me very much if you would tell me just what happened on the Saturday night before he left you.'

For the moment there was no reply. Mrs. Wilton produced a rather portentous frown. She let the best part of a minute go by before she said, 'I'm not one to beat about the bush. I'm going to ask you right out what it's got to do with you.'

Miss Silver smiled.

'I did not know Albert Miller, but I know some of his relations. I am concerned as to what may have happened to him. I should like to know his present whereabouts, and I should like to ask him a few questions. That is all. Now will you tell me about Saturday night?'

Mrs. Wilton said slowly, 'There's nothing to tell.'

'Then it would be soon told, and you could do no harm by telling it.'

There was another frowning pause. Then Mrs. Wilton said, 'What do you want to know?'

'I should like you to tell me just what happened from the time he came home on Saturday night till the time he left on Sunday morning.'

Mrs. Wilton pursed her lips.

'Well, there's no harm in that, and it's soon told, as you say. He come home just before half past eleven, and he was the worse for drink, banging on the door and singing a song about that girl Eily he's been running after – out at the Catherine-Wheel. Never heard such a noise in my life. We were in bed, but Mr. Wilton wouldn't go to sleep till he heard him come in. He needn't have troubled – there was enough noise to wake the dead.'

'Did Mr. Wilton go down to let him in?'

The massive head was shaken.

'We'd left the door, but after Al got upstairs Mr. Wilton went down and locked it. We were both properly fed up, and we'd made up our minds about giving him his notice. What with him coming in like that and the noise that was going on overhead, we'd had enough. Mr. Wilton called up the stair to tell him so. And the language he got back! I had to put my fingers in my ears! Mr. Wilton come back into the room and said, "That's the last of him. Says I didn't need to give him notice, because he was getting out anyhow –

and getting out of the place." And then he went down and locked the front door and brought away the key because Al owed us a week's money and it wouldn't be right to let him go off without paying it.'

Miss Silver interrupted with her slight cough.

'Would there be any light in the hall, or on the stairs?'

Mrs. Wilton pursed her lips.

'We've lived thirty years in this house. Mr. Wilton don't need any light to go up and down.'

'But Albert Miller – he would not know the house so well as Mr. Wilton.'

'Uses a torch!' said Mrs. Wilton contemptuously. 'Nasty flickering things – I can't abide them!'

'Did your husband see him when he went upstairs?'

Mrs. Wilton stared.

'Saw him, and heard him – shouting about this Eily, and shining his torch into Mr. Wilton's eyes till he was pretty near blinded!'

Miss Silver said,

'Most inconsiderate and disagreeable.'

Mrs. Wilton achieved a magnificent toss of the head.

'*And* kept me awake best part of the night, bumping, and groaning, and making the bed creak.'

'Dear me!'

'And first thing in the morning down he comes and bangs on the door. Mr. Wilton calls out to him he won't get the key till he pays up what he owes us. Al says he's got it ready, and he won't be coming back, and Mr. Wilton says, "Not much you won't!" So then he lights the candle and goes over to the bedroom door and opens it just enough to take the money me being still in bed. And he counts it, and it's all right. And Al says he's giving the railway the sack and he'll send for his things when he gets another job. So then Mr. Wilton gives him the key to let himself out. And that's the last we saw of him.'

Miss Silver coughed.

'When you say *saw*, Mrs. Wilton – it would be quite dark in the passage?'

Mrs. Wilton nodded.

'He'd got his torch,' she said, 'Swinging it about like I

191

told you. Put Mr. Wilton's back up properly.'

'Did Mr. Wilton take the candle over to the door?'

Mrs. Wilton stared.

'He hadn't any call to. Took the money and brought it across to me to count, and then back with the key. He'd no call to take the candle, nor to stand at the door with the draught blowing in and that nasty torch in his eyes.'

Chapter 32

MISS SILVER sat silent in the back of the car until they had passed through Cliff. Then she leaned forward and spoke.

'Captain Taverner, would it be trespassing too much on your kindness if I were to ask you to take me up to Cliff House? I would like to speak to Inspector Abbott.'

Jeremy said, 'Of course.' And then, 'We had tea with Jack Challoner, you know. Abbott wasn't there then, but of course he may have come in since.'

Frank Abbott had not come in. Matthews stood there waiting. Miss Silver addressed herself to Jeremy.

'Sir John Challoner is a friend of yours. Do you think he would allow me to use the telephone? I would rather not use the instrument at the inn.'

Jeremy went into the house and came out again with a large red-headed young man, whom he introduced. Miss Silver was inducted to the study and left there with the telephone and the only fire, whilst the others shivered in the hall and Jeremy brightened the proceedings by announcing that he and Jane were engaged.

The number called by Miss Silver was Ledlington police station. A hearty male voice responded. Yes, Inspector Abbott was there. He was in conference with Inspector Crisp and the Superintendent. He didn't know –

Miss Silver said in a peremptory manner, 'Would you tell him that Miss Silver would like to speak to him.'

At the other end of the line Frank Abbott was not sorry to exchange his present society for that of Miss Silver. He found that a little of Crisp went a long way, and had most regrettably summed up the Superintendent as a pompous bullfrog. It was not in his nature to suffer pomposity with resignation.

Just behind in the adjoining room Crisp and Superintendent Johnson heard him say, 'Hullo!' and then, 'Yes, it's me. What can I do for you?'

Following on this he said at irregular intervals, 'Florence Duke – yes, I could. . . . Well as you say – I shouldn't think there would be any difficulty. . . . No, I shouldn't think so. . . . Well, I'll put it to him. . . . All right. Goodbye.'

Miss Silver rang off, thanked her temporary host in the most gracious manner, and again relapsed into silence at the back of the car.

As she stepped into the narrow entrance of the Catherine-Wheel, someone had just set foot upon the stairs. She had the impression that this person had come from the direction of the dining-room, but so newly from the dark, and with the lamplight in her eyes, she could not be certain. She thought that there had been a movement from left to right across the hall, but she could not be certain. By the time her eyes were really serving her clearly the person whom she had seen had mounted to the third or fourth step.

Miss Silver came out into the hall and recognised Florence Duke. A most vexatious theory which would explain Mrs. Duke's presence in the dining-room presented itself. She had particularly asked – she had made it quite plain – it really would be very vexatious indeed.

She mounted the stairs with more than her usual brisk-ness and came up with Florence Duke on the landing. With a slight preliminary cough she observed that she had been out and had rather forgotten the time.

'I hope that I am not late. I should be glad to change my dress before dinner.'

In the light of the wall-lamp Florence Duke turned a ghastly face. Fear sat naked in her eyes. Almost involuntarily Miss Silver took her by the arm.

'Mrs. Duke – are you not well? I am afraid you have had a shock.'

The pale lips twitched. A sound like an echo came from them.

'A shock – '

'Were you talking on the telephone?'

Florence stared with the wide, blank eyes of a sleep-walker. The echo came again.

'The telephone – '

Miss Silver said firmly, 'You are unwell. Let me help you to your room.'

This was no conversation to hold on the open landing for anyone to hear. She got Florence Duke into her room and shut the door.

'What is it? Can I help you?'

The big woman went across to the washstand, tipped half a jug of cold water into the basin, and stooped down to plunge her face into it. She came up gasping, to do it again, and yet again. Then she took the rough bath-towel and scrubbed herself dry. Cold water, rubbing, and time to catch at her self-control – between them they worked wonders. The dreadful bluish look was gone from her face and some of the natural colour had come back. She said in something very like her ordinary voice, 'Just one of my turns – I have them sometimes. I'll be all right now.' Then, after a good long breath, 'We haven't got too much time if we're going to change.'

'You feel able to come down?'

'I'm going to.' She laughed without merriment. 'Do you suppose the old man will stand us champagne? I could do with it.'

Ten minutes later Miss Silver descended the stairs. She had changed into her last summer's dress, which like the one she had been wearing every day, was of a dark olive-green in colour but distressingly patterned in a kind of morse code of orange dots and dashes. There were hints of other colours too, but on the whole the orange had it. Nothing could have been less becoming. The bog-oak brooch re-posed upon her bosom. She also wore an extremely ancient black velvet coatee – most warm and comfortable – without which she never ventured upon a country visit. In her experience country houses, especially old country houses, were apt to be cold and draughty in the extreme. The gong having sounded when she was halfway down the stairs, she joined the rest of the party on their way to the dining-room.

They were all seated before Florence Duke appeared, looking very much as she had looked all that day and the day before. She could not have known how closely she was being observed. If she had, it would perhaps have made no difference, since she was already making the maximum effort at self-control. On three separate occasions when she discovered her hand to be shaking she dropped it quickly to her lap. Miss Silver, facing her across the table, missed nothing of this. There was, in fact, very little that she did miss in the behaviour of any one of the Taverners.

Jacob was in his place. He had an old, frustrated look. The likeness to a sick monkey was painful. He had Marian Thorpe-Ennington on his right and Mildred Taverner on his left. Lady Marian talked uninterruptedly from one end of the meal to the other, and everyone was grateful to her for doing so. She told them all about her French mother-in-law who was, to put it mildly, eccentric.

'Absolutely *nothing* but high-heeled slippers with pink feather trimming and a diamond hair-band which used to belong to Josephine – really too embarrassing. And one never knew where one was going to meet her – it was such a rambling old château – oubliettes and all that sort of thing. Of course the servants were trained to look the other way.'

Florence Duke stopped crumbling a piece of bread and said in a voice louder than she meant it to be, 'What is an oubliette?'

Marian Thorpe-Ennington was only too pleased to explain.

'All those old places had them. There was a story about one at Rathlea, but we never found it. The one at René's place was quite horrid. You pulled out a bolt, and a bit of the floor gave way and let your enemy down into a frightful sort of cesspool. Of course it's been drained and all that – and I believe there were quite a lot of bones. But I don't think the French are very thorough about that sort of thing, and I never really fancied living there, what with Eglantine being quite mad and there being no money to keep anything up, so perhaps it is a good thing we didn't have any children. Though of course it was a frightful tragedy when René crashed, and I thought I should never get over it.'

She looked down the table and kissed her fingertips to Freddy Thorpe-Ennington.

'Freddy, my sweet, do you remeber how absolutely crushed I was? I know I never thought I should marry again. But perhaps it was all for the best, if it hadn't been for Freddy's father's pickle factory crashing too.'

Jacob surveyed her with just a hint of his old sardonic amusement.

'What you want is someone to leave you a fortune, isn't it?'

She could not have agreed in a more whole-hearted manner.

'Of course my first husband ought to have left me his, but most of it went to his secretary, a perfect frump. Shattering – wasn't it?'

Mildred Tavener was fingering her Venetian beads. She said in a low hurried voice, more as if she was talking to herself than to anyone else, 'Oubliette – *oublier* – that's French for forget – at least I think it is – I never was good at languages, and my French is very rusty. I suppose it means they went down that hole and were forgotten – ' She gave a sharp involuntary shiver. 'Oh, that's horrid! I hope I shan't dream about it.'

Marian Thorpe-Ennington glided into the full history of Freddy's courtship.

When everyone had left the dining-room Miss Silver watched her opportunity for a word with Eily. She managed to intercept her coming through with the coffee-tray.

'Eily, is there an extension to the telephone?'

'In the pantry there is – for my uncle to use.'

'Is he in there now?'

Eily looked surprised.

'A moment ago he was – putting away the silver. But you could telephone in the dining-room, Miss Silver. There's nobody there.'

Miss Silver returned to the lounge. Presently, when she saw Castell come in, she slipped across to the dining-room and called up Cliff House. Matthews, answering the call, was requested to deliver a message to Mr. Abbott — Miss Silver would like to speak to him

Mr. Abbott was produced. The first tones of Miss Silver's voice informed him that she had reason to suppose that caution was necessary. The fact that she was ringing up at all made it clear that she had something important to say. It became immediately apparent that she required answers to two questions.

'I have something to ask you — two things in fact. The request I made of you before you left the hotel this afternoon — have you done anything about it?'

'Well, there was a bit of obstruction, now overcome by my well-known tact. I'll get on with it bright and early tomorrow. That all?'

Miss Silver coughed.

'By no means. I made a second request to you later. Was that acceded to?'

'Yes.'

'I requested that no communication should be made till the morning, but I have reason to believe — '

'I know. But I couldn't stop him. I'm sorry.'

She said, 'It was a mistake. I hope — '

As she said this last word she heard a faint unmistakable click. The receiver on the extension had been lifted. She continued quite smoothly and with no perceptible pause, 'You will give my love when you write, and say I always take the greatest interest? Goodbye.'

Frank Abbott had also heard the click, and was able to applaud his Miss Silver's presence of mind.

As he rang off at his end he considered the points which she had raised. Crisp had been very sticky about the carpet — sticky and fussy. He didn't want a row, and he didn't want to do the job himself without a witness. It occurred to him that Crisp would hate to have his neat presentment of the case upset. The inquest was set for eleven-thirty. If they were going to find bloodstains on the carpet in Castell's study, the case to be served up wouldn't be neat at all but highly complicated. Because if Luke White hadn't been killed where he was found, all the bits of evidence about Eily and Florence Duke coming down and finding him would go by the board. Instead of the murder being a sudden affair of passion it would become a carefully premeditated crime almost certainly involving more than one person. No, Crisp wouldn't be a bit keen on those bloodstains. He wasn't really keen on them himself, but they would have to be looked for, and before the inquest opened. As to Miss Silver's second question, he had done his best to prevent Crisp ringing the Duke woman up. His best hadn't been good enough, and that was that.

He dwelt for some time on the implications of this second question. The affaire Duke had its possibilities. He went on considering them.

Chapter 33

COMING back into the lounge, Miss Silver took particular note of the occupants. All the Taverner cousins were there, but Mr. Castell was not. She took a chair and got out her knitting. Little Josephine's dress was now a complete skirt and bodice, and she was halfway down the left sleeve. She had chosen a chair beside Florence Duke. After a moment or two she remarked, 'It's for my niece, Mrs. Burkett's little girl. She had three boys already, so they were of course delighted when Josephine was born. Such a pretty child, and so good.'

Florence Duke had been staring in front of her. She shifted her gaze now and focused it upon the bright blue dress.

'I like kids — I'd have liked to have some. But you never know you luck — I expect it's as well I didn't. He wasn't any sort of father to have in the house with children, and he wouldn't have changed. Bad all through, Luke was.

198

There aren't many you can say that about, but it's true about Luke.'

Miss Silver went on knitting. She said very kindly, 'Marriage can be a most unhappy state. It is very hard on the woman when it turns out that way.'

There was a sombre spark in the big dark eyes.

'I'll say it is – ' She made a heavy pause, and then brought out more words in the slow, deliberate way she had. 'The worst is you can't get rid of it. There was a gentleman I used to know when I was at the George – partner in a firm of solicitors – I came across him again after Luke went off. He wanted me to see about a divorce, but I wouldn't. "I've had enough of being married," I told him, "and I won't want to do it again. And as far as it goes for *him*, I'm not letting him loose to marry some other poor girl." He said, "You'll think better of it, Floss," but I said, "No," and I haven't.' She gave herself a sort of jerk. 'I don't know why I'm talking to you like this.'

Miss Silver's needles clicked.

'If you keep everything to yourself, things come to weigh too heavily,' she said.

Florence Duke nodded.

'That's right – like a ton weight, till you don't feel you can get your breath. Seems you've got to get some of it off your chest.'

There was a short silence. Then the slow speech began again.

'There's things you can't forget – you'd like to, but you can't – they come back on you.' She gave another of those jerks and got up. 'I'm talking too much. I don't know what's got into me. What do you say we have some more coffee? I'll take your cup and see what's left.'

She went across to the coffee-table, and as she did so, Geoffrey Taverner came strolling over with his cup in his hand. He took the chair upon Miss Silver's other side and said in his pleasantest voice, 'May I come and talk to you for a little? I should like to think you for being so kind to my sister.'

Miss Silver could have been justified in showing some surprise. As she had informed Frank Abbott, Mr. Taverner's manner had not hitherto commended itself, or him. It had, indeed, conveyed the opinion that she was a negligible dowdy person and a meddler. Now quite suddenly all was changed – she was being addressed with courtesy and deference. She replied with rather more than her usual sobriety.

'You need not thank me, Mr. Taverner.'

He was looking at her in an earnest way.

'Oh, but I do. Mildred is so very highly strung. She has not, if I may speak frankly – well, she has not a very stable mentality.'

Miss Silver said, 'Dear me!'

Geoffrey became explanatory.

'You mustn't think – I didn't mean to imply – I'm afraid what I said might give you a wrong impression. I really didn't intend to convey more than that she is highly strung and not well fitted to undergo a strain. To be in the house where a murder is committed is naturally a shock. I have noticed that you have a calming and reassuring effect upon my sister, and I want you to know that I am grateful.'

Miss Silver coughed.

'Thank you, Mr. Taverner.'

He finished the coffee in his cup and set it down.

'Mildred has always been nervous,' he said. 'Fortunately the friend who lives with her is a cheerful, sensible woman. I may say that I was not at all anxious for this invitation to be accepted, but she has always been fanciful about the old place – from a child she would make up stories and act them – and when I advised her to stay quietly at home she became so excited that I thought it would really be best to let her come. In fact I do not think that I could have prevented her. Like all nervous people she can be extremely obstinate.' He heaved an exasperated sigh. 'It is a combination which can be very difficult to deal with.'

Miss Silver agreed with him.

He sighed again in a resigned manner.

'Oh, well, I suppose we shall all be allowed to go home tomorrow as soon as the inquest is over. Do you happen to know whether that is so?'

Miss Silver turned the bright blue knitting in her lap.

'I really do not know, but I should think there would be no objection. Neither you nor Miss Taverner are in a position to do more than corroborate what other witnesses have said.'

He gazed at her earnestly.

'My sister is not likely to be called as a witness, Inspector Crisp tells me, but he said she had better attend. If you would add to your kindness by sitting with her – ' He met her thoughtful gaze with a quick attractive smile. For a moment his rather priggish manner gave way sufficiently to permit some genuine feeling to appear. 'If I may say so, she has come to – well, rely on you.'

Miss Silver said, 'I shall be pleased to do what I can. But there is surely no need for Miss Taverner to be nervous.'

Geoffrey shook his head.

'No – no – of course not. But a person of her temperament doesn't need a reason for being nervous, and you undoubtedly have a calming effect. I just thought that I would like to express my gratitude, and to ask whether you would sit with her tomorrow. It will relieve her mind very much if I can tell her that you will do so.'

'By all means, Mr Taverner.'

She watched him go over to his sister and take the vacant seat beside her. Knitting as she did in the continental manner, it was possible for her to make rapid progress with little Josephine's left sleeve whilst continuing her observation of what was going on in the room. She saw Mildred Taverner look uneasily at her brother as he approached and then brighten up and send a glance in her own direction, after which only an occasional remark appeared to pass between them. Miss Taverner, she considered, would have been the better for a piece of good plain knitting to occupy her hands. It was, of course, indicative of her nervous state that she seemed unable to keep them still. They plucked at the stuff of her dress, they twitched, they jerked, they fidgeted with those unbecoming bright blue beads, with the old-fashioned gold chain. They were not still for a moment.

After some half dozen remarks at widely spaced intervals Geoffrey got up and drifted over to the fire, where he presently engaged in conversation with Jacob Taverner, who was doing a cross-word puzzle. In a short time they appeared to be doing it together.

As Florence Duke came back with fresh hot coffee, Mildred got up and came to join them, fluttering and uncertain.

'Would you mind. . . . Oh, that is very kind of you! It makes one feel so nervous sitting alone. Not you, of course, because you are not like that. Oh, no – no coffee, thanks. I'm afraid it might keep me awake.' She addressed Florence Duke. 'You don't find it does?'

Florence Duke looked at her as if she were seeing something else. She said with a sort of slow finality, 'It isn't coffee that would keep me awake.'

At ten o'clock they went upstairs together. Their rooms were next to each other along the right-hand passage, Miss Silver nearest the stairs, then Florence Duke, and beyond her Mildred Taverner.

Florence went straight into her room, but Mildred lingered, her door half open, the knob in her hand, as if she could not make up her mind to go in.

'Perhaps this is our last night here. Oh, I do hope so – don't you?' And then, 'You are so very kind – I wonder if you would just stand at the door whilst I look in the cupboard and under the bed. I always do it at home – not that I think there will be anyone, but it just gives me a more comfortable feeling. And my friend comes with me, because of course if there should be anyone there, or – or anything, I don't really know what I should do.' She drew a long breath. 'There was a very large spider once, and I have never been any good about spiders.' Her head poked and her long nose twitched.

Miss Silver came briskly to the door and opened it wide.

'I do not suppose for a moment that there will be any spiders,' she said with her slight dry cough.

There was neither a spider nor a cockroach, there was not even a concealed miscreant. With a sigh of relief Mildred Taverner said goodnight all over again and locked the door on the inside.

Miss Silver went into her own room, where she took off her watch, which she wound, and her bog-oak brooch. She then stood for a few moments in thought, and had just begun to cross the room in the direction of the door, when there was a light tap upon it. In response to her 'Come in!' Eily appeared, carrying four hot-water bottles.

Miss Silver was so used to her own that she took it from Eily without having any thoughts about it at all, but she felt that she could at once allocate the other three to their respective owners. Very fine white rubber in a white satin bag with pale green quilting could not possibly belong to anyone but Lady Marian. Bright blue with no cover at all would, she thought, be Jane Heron's. But the last one? There were two more ladies and only one bottle, a rather battered specimen with a washed-out flannel cover. It might belong either to Florence Duke, or to Mildred Taverner. It took her only a moment to decide. Florence Duke might have owned one as shabby, but both it and its cover would have started life in some gayer shade. With hardly any perceptible pause she was asking Eily.

'Does Mrs. Duke not have a bottle?'

'Oh, yes, Miss Silver. But I saw her go over to the bathroom, so I thought I'd slip it in and get rid of it. It's a red one. Fortunately they're all different. Sometimes it's a job not to get them mixed – and that's a thing nobody likes.'

'No – I suppose not.'

Miss Silver had placed her own bottle inside the turned-down bed. She now went over to the door and closed it.

Eily watched, three bottles in her arms and a look of surprise on her face. She was to be still more surprised. Miss Silver said, 'Where are you sleeping, Eily?'

'In my own room.'

'I think it would be better if you were to sleep with Miss Heron tonight.'

The dark blue eyes were fixed on her in a look between wonder and fear.

'But, Miss Silver – '

'I think it would be best. I advise you very strongly to ask Miss Heron to let you share her room.'

Eily shook her head.

'My uncle wouldn't like it.'

'I do not see why he should know.'

There was an odd fleeting look before the lashes fell.

'There isn't much my uncle doesn't get to know.' Then, more quickly, 'And what's the need? It was Luke I was afraid of – and he's gone.'

'Eily – '

She shook her head again.

'My uncle wouldn't like it at all. If you please, Miss Silver – the bottles will be getting cold.'

Miss Silver moved away from the door. She was satisfied upon one point, but seriously uneasy upon another. She saw Eily go out of the room, and waited with her door ajar for Florence Duke to return from the bathroom.

As soon as she heard what she was listening for she looked out into the passage.

'Mrs. Duke – if I might have just a word with you – '

Florence came across with a slow, unwilling step. She had taken off her dress and was wearing her outdoor coat in place of a dressing-gown. Her face, stripped bare of make-up, had a sagged, unhappy look, the lines from nose to mouth accentuated, the colour in cheeks and lips dull and lifeless. She said heavily, 'I just want to get into bed and sleep.'

Miss Silver shut the door.

'I will not keep you. There are one or two things I could not say downstairs, where there was a risk that we might be overheard. Inspector Crisp rang you up this evening, did he not?'

'What if he did?'

'He asked you to give evidence at the inquest tomorrow?'

Florence said heavily, 'What if he did?'

'Mrs. Duke, is there no one in this house who might be concerned to prevent you from giving that evidence?'

'Why should they?'

'Do you not know of a reason?'

She stared down at the bath-towel she was carrying. It hung on her right arm, but she had slipped her left hand under it too. It hid both her hands. She stared at it with hidden eyes. A moment passed before she said, 'I don't know what you mean.'

'Do you not?'

The eyes were lifted. They were angry now.

'Let me alone, can't you! What has it got to do with you?'

Miss Silver said very quietly and steadily, 'I am concerned for your safety, Mrs. Duke. Will you please listen to me for a moment?'

The anger flickered and died down.

'What do you want?'

Miss Silver said, 'You have been asked to give certain evidence. I do not know what that evidence will be, but I can think of circumstances in which it might prove dangerous to people who have already shown that they will stick at nothing. I would like you to consider whether you might not be in danger, and whether it would not be safer for you to spend the night elsewhere.'

Florence Duke looked past her.

'I don't know what you mean.'

As if she had not spoken, Miss Silver continued.

'I would like to ask Captain Taverner to take you to Cliff House, where Inspector Abbott is staying. He would, I am sure, arrange for you to be accommodated.'

Florence Duke gave a sudden laugh as far removed from merriment as it well could be.

'Cliff House? Me – at this time of the night? I suppose you think I haven't got a character to lose – going to stay with two young men, and one of them in the police! No, thank you!'

'Mrs. Duke – '

Florence put a hand on her shoulder.

'Look here, you mean well, I grant you that, but this isn't your business. And I don't know what you're talking about neither, and if I did I wouldn't care. Get that – I wouldn't care! If someone was to bring me a good glass of poison this minute, I'd just as soon drink it and be done with everything! So you can stop your hinting about my being in danger! I don't care if I am! Do you get that? I don't give a damn!'

Miss Silver looked at her with compassion. There was a moment when their eyes met, a moment when things hung in the balance. The hand on Miss Silver's shoulder weighed heavily. It shook a little, and then it was withdrawn. Florence

205

Duke said with a catch in her voice, 'Oh, well, it'll be all the same a hundred years hence.'

Then she turned and went out of the room and into her own, and shut the door.

Chapter 34

MISS SILVER waited for what she was hoping to hear, the sound of a key being turned in the lock of the door which was next to her own. It was turned roughly and with no attempt at concealment. To all whom it might concern, Florence Duke had locked herself in for the night. Miss Silver experienced a decided feeling of relief. She had no desire to sit up all night, but if that door had not been locked, she might have felt herself obliged to do so. As it was, she felt quite sure that by setting her door ajar she would at once become aware of any attempt to tamper with the lock of Mrs. Duke's room. The mere fact that her own door was ajar would act as a deterrent.

She undressed, put on her dressing-gown, and went across to the bathroom to wash, taking her towel with her. There was a faint pleasant scent in the passage. The light from a small wall-lamp disclosed the fact that powder had been spilled upon the carpet. The scent was agreeable and not too insistent. It suggested an expensive beauty-shop and Lady Marian. The bathroom smelled of it too. It required no great powers of deduction to assume that Marian Thorpe-Ennington had taken a bath and had spilled some of her powder as she came or went.

Her ablutions over, Miss Silver crossed the passage again, drew a blue crochet shawl about her shoulders, and sitting up in bed, reached for her old shabby Bible. It was her custom to read a portion of Scripture before she slept. As she opened the book, the yellow candlelight fell upon the psalm in which David prays to be delivered from Saul and Doeg:

'The proud have laid a snare for me and cords; they have spread a net by the wayside; they have set gins for me.'

The words appeared to her to be almost too appropriate. She turned the leaves in search of a more consoling passage.

She did not put out her light for quite a long time. With her door some six inches open, sounds came to her from the other rooms, from the well of the stairs. Footsteps crossed the landing, entered the passage on the farther side, and passed out of hearing. The murmur of voices from the Thorpe-Enningtons' room died away. Midnight and silence were in the house. She blew out her candle and fell into a light sleep. The smallest sound would have roused her. Even without being aware of such a sound she was never far from consciousness. When the old wall-clock downstairs struck each of the hours between twelve and seven she was at once fully awake and, waking, was aware only of sleep in the house and the silence gathering.

At seven the footsteps came again, a long way off in the passage on the other side of the landing – doors opening, the distant sound of voices. Eily and the Castells were up. Miss Silver got up too. She went over to the bathroom to wash, as she had done the night before, and was pleased to find that the water was still warm.

Before she came back into her own room she very gently tried the handle of Florence Duke's door. It was still locked. She completed her dressing with a feeling of satisfaction. The night was safely over, and within the next few hours the inquest would be over too and Florence Duke's evidence would have been placed on record. Alone in her room, she admitted to herself that it would be very pleasant indeed to get back to her comfortable flat, and to the ministrations of her devoted Hannah.

By eight o'clock others were stirring. There was some competition for the bathroom. Jane Heron came out of her room looking fresh and blooming. She ran downstairs humming a tune, and Jeremy joined her. Mildred Taverner appeared next, pale, nervous, and not sure whether she ought to wear her blue beads to an inquest. Miss Silver's door being half open, she knocked upon it and came in to invite an opinion.

'I shall have my coat on and a scarf, so I don't suppose they will show, but if it should be very hot – at the inquest, I mean – I should want to open my coat – I always do get hot when I'm nervous – and perhaps take the scarf off too, and then the beads would show. Of course the scarf is a coloured one, but I haven't any black, and I couldn't be expected to know that anyone was going to be murdered.' The tip of her long, pale nose became quite pink with agitation. 'It really is so difficult, because I shouldn't like anyone to think I was heartless, and in a sort of way I suppose you might say he was a cousin.'

Miss Silver said in a kind, firm voice, 'I am sure no one would think that you were heartless, but if it made you feel any more comfortable, you could leave the beads in a drawer and put them on again after the inquest is over.'

Mildred Taverner's nose became a much deeper pink. Her agitation was sensibly increased.

'Oh, but I wear them always. I shouldn't like to leave them here, not with things like murders happening. I really couldn't bear it if – you see, they were given to me by such a very dear friend – such a *very* dear friend – and he is dead, and I have always worn them. We weren't exactly engaged, but he gave me the beads.'

Miss Silver said briskly, 'Then I should wear them.'

The door was still open to the passage. It really was a relief that Lady Marian should come out of her room at this moment, since, without some interruption, it seemed quite possible that Mildred Taverner might continue to discuss her qualms indefinitely. Unfortunately the sight of Lady Marian in a beautifully cut black town suit had anything but a calming effect. She gazed at the white crepe blouse, the two rows of pearls, the small black hat, and the slimming elegance of the coat and skirt with a feeling akin to despair. So smart, so suitable, so completely beyond her reach. She resigned herself, but the feeling of inferiority sank deep and added to the chronic uncertainty with which she contemplated the problem of living.

Lady Marian was in excellent looks and spirits. She had

208

enjoyed nearly ten hours of refreshing sleep, and by lunch-time the Catherine-Wheel and its unpleasant happenings would have gone to join all those other past events which served her as an inexhaustible source of anecdote. Even the fact that Freddy with another painful business meeting before him was in a state of suicidal depression raised no more than a ripple upon the surface of her mind. She showed, in fact, some zest in explaining how low he was. 'But, as I said to him, "Something always does turn up, and as to being ruined, well, who isn't? And I can't see it makes any difference whether the creditors have your money, because it all goes in income tax anyhow, and when you haven't got any more they do have to stop, so we shan't have to go on filling up any more of those dreadful forms." '

Miss Silver, who was nearest to the door, had not been attending very closely to these remarks. From where she stood she could see the landing and the top of the stairs.

At this moment Eily came round the corner carrying three or four pairs of shoes newly cleaned. She put Jane Heron's inside her room, Lady Marian's and Freddy Thorpe-Ennington's beside their door, and then crossed over with the remaining pair in her hand – shabby patent leather with bulging toes and exaggerated heels. She had put them down at Florence Duke's door and was straightening up again, when Miss Silver stepped into the passage and addressed her.

'Just knock on the door, Eily, and see whether Mrs. Duke is up.'

Eily tapped on the panel, waited for a moment, and tapped again. When there was no reply she looked round at Miss Silver in a hesitating manner.

'Do you think she is asleep?'

Miss Silver stepped forward, put her hand on the knob of the door, and turned it gently. The door was locked, as it had been when she tried it last. She knocked herself this time, so loudly that Mildred Taverner and Marian Thorpe-Ennington came out into the passage to see what was going on. But from behind that locked door there was neither voice nor answer.

Miss Silver turned from it, her face grave.

'I am afraid that there must be something wrong. I think,

Eily, that you had better fetch Mr. Castell.'

Eily looked scared.

'Should I just take a look through the keyhole?'

Miss Silver coughed.

'They key will be in the lock – '

But Eily was already stooping down.

'But it isn't,' she said. 'I can see right over to the bed. . . ■
Oh, Miss Silver, she isn't there – it's not been slept in!'

'Can you see any sign of Mrs. Duke?'

'Oh, no, I can't! There's the bed turned down – like I
left it – '

Miss Silver said in a quiet voice, 'Go and fetch your uncle.'

As they stood waiting, Geoffrey Taverner came along the
opposite passage from his room and crossed the landing to
join them.

'Is anything wrong, Miss Silver?'

'I am afraid that there may be. I think you had better
take your sister away.'

But Mildred refused to go – or at any rate no farther than
Miss Silver's room, where she sat trembling on the edge of
the bed and shed weak, forlorn tears. They dripped upon
the Venetian beads, and so down into her lap as she listened
whilst Castell enquired of all and sundry why heaven should
be thus afflicting him.

'My respectable house!' he groaned. 'Mrs. Duke – are
you there? If you are asleep, will you wake up and speak to
us! We are getting alarmed. I shall have to break in the
door if you do not answer.' He raised his voice to a bellow –
'*Mrs. Duke!*' then turned away with a gesture of despair.
'It is no good. She may be ill – she may have taken too much
of a sleeping draught – she does not hear – we shall have to
break the door – '

Jeremy and Jane had arrived to swell the crowd. Jacob
Taverner came across the landing wrapped in his great-
coat. Freddy Thorpe-Ennington, fully dressed but with his
fair hair wildly unbrushed, stared from the threshold of his
room. Jeremy said, 'Wait a bit – don't any of these other keys
fit?'

'Fool!' said Castell, smiting himself upon the breast. 'Idiot
– imbecile! Why did I not think of that? I tell you I am

out of my senses with all this trouble! The key of the cupboard at the end of the passage, perhaps that will fit – I do not know. It fits one of these rooms, but I have forgotten which. It may be this one, or it may be one of the others – I do not know any more. I have no memory left – the brain gives way – I am distracted!'

In this state of distraction he precipitated himself along the passage, wrenched the key from a cupboard door, rushed back with it, and forced it violently into the lock. It grated, creaked, and under the utmost pressure turned.

Castell jerked at the handle and threw the door wide open. Every inch of the rather dingy room was visible. One side of the curtains had been pulled back. The daylight which entered was not bright, but it was sufficient. It showed the bed as Eily had described it, stripped of its coverlet and turned down for the night. It showed the space beneath it quite empty. It showed a worn square of carpet on the floor, a chest of drawers, a washstand, and two chairs. It showed a hanging-cupboard with the door fallen open. Inside it hung the bright blue coat and skirt and the sheepskin coat in which Florence Duke had arrived. But of Florence Duke herself there was no sign whatever. Except for its ordinary furniture the room was empty.

Chapter 35

It was the police who found her getting on for an hour later. She had gone over the cliff at its highest point, about a hundred yards beyond the hotel. She had fallen upon the rocks, and must have been killed immediately. The body had not been in the water, since this heaped and tumbled mass of rocks was covered only at the highest tides. She was wearing what she had worn the night before, the brightly flowered dress of artificial silk, the silk stockings, and indoor shoes. One of the shoes had come off and had been caught up on a small straggling bush about half way down.

A little later in Castell's office Inspector Crisp was giving it as his opinion that it was a plain case of suicide, and that in the circumstances it was as good as a confession to the murder of Luke White.

'Clears the whole thing up, if you ask me. Can't see any reason for putting the other inquest off myself, but the Chief Constable seems to think it would be better.'

Frank Abbott nodded.

'Yes – I think so.'

'Well, I can't see it myself. But there, I'm not the Chief Constable – as I expect you were going to say.' He laughed quite good-humouredly.

Miss Silver, who had so far contributed nothing to the conversation, now gave a slight dry cough. Frank Abbott turned his head as if expecting her to speak, but she did not do so. For the moment her eyes were upon her knitting. The blue dress approached completion. He turned back to Crisp.

'You are satisfied that it was suicide?'

Crisp made a gesture.

'What else? She killed Luke White – jealousy over that girl Eily – and when I rang her up and told her she would have to identify the body she got the wind up. Wouldn't face it – went and chucked herself over the cliff.' He gazed complacently at the London man who couldn't see a simple solution when he'd got it right under his nose. 'Psychology,' he said – 'that's what you've got to bear in mind, especially when you're dealing with women. This Florence Duke – you've got to put yourself in her place, look at it from her point of view. She was jealous of Eily Fogarty. This Luke White, he'd got the name for being able to get round any woman, and by all accounts he got round a good few of them. He got round Florence Duke, married her, and left her. Then she comes here and finds him making love to this girl Eily. On her own admission she went down to meet him the night he was murdered, and she was found practically standing over the body with his blood on her hands. Well, a woman will stab a man she's been fond of if she's jealous enough. But this is where psychology comes in. She's

212

done the murder when she was all worked up, but when she's told she's got to come in cold blood and look at the corpse she just can't face it – she goes and chucks herself over the cliff. That's psychology.'

Miss Silver laid her knitting down in her lap and coughed again.

'That would be one explanation, Inspector, but it is not the only one.'

Crisp looked hard at her.

'Look here, Miss Silver, you were the last person to see Florence Duke or to have any conversation with her. Was she, or was she not, in a state of nervous depression?'

'I have already told you that she was.'

'She was nervous and depressed because she knew she had got to see her husband's body and give evidence at the inquest?'

'She was frightened and nervous about the identification. I would remind you, Inspector, that I had particularly desired she should not be told until this morning that she would have to identify the body.'

Crisp frowned.

'I thought it best to let her know. Now, Miss Silver – are you prepared to state that there was nothing in Mrs. Duke's conversation or behaviour to support the idea of suicide?'

Miss Silver looked at him in a candid manner and said, 'No.'

'Then I think I have a right to ask you what she did say.'

Miss Silver said gravely, 'She spoke of her married life. It was obviously very much on her mind. She spoke of there being things which she could not forget. When I warned her that she might be in danger and begged her to let Captain Taverner take her to a place of safety for the night –'

He interrupted forcibly.

'You did that?'

She inclined her head.

'I am thankful to be able to recall that I did. She would not listen to me. She said she did not care. She went so far as to say, "If someone was to bring me a good glass of poison this minute, I'd drink it".'

213

Crisp brought his fist down with a bang on the table.

'That's all I want, thank you, and that's all the jury will want! Short of someone seeing her go over the cliff it's all anyone could want!'

Miss Silver said, 'I wish to be perfectly fair, and I have told you what the poor woman said. But I did not believe at the time, nor do I believe now, that she had any serious intention of taking her own life. She was in the mood to wish herself dead as an alternative to the painful position in which she found herself, but I have to state that I do not believe she committed suicide. I believe that she was murdered.'

Crisp threw himself back in his chair.

'Come, come, Miss Silver, you can't expect us to swallow that! On your own showing Mrs. Duke locked herself into her room last night. You left your own door open, and you say that you are a very light sleeper and that the slightest noise in the passage would have waked you, yet you heard nothing. Are you going to ask us to believe that someone got into Mrs. Duke's room, overpowered her, got her downstairs, and threw her over the cliff, all without making any sound at all?'

'No, Inspector.'

He went on in a tone flavoured with contempt.

'To start with, according to you she had her key in the door, so no other key could have been used from the outside. To go on with, she walked down that passage on her own feet. There was powder spilt there, and she had walked through it – her stockings were full of the stuff. Look here, it's simple enough what she did. She knew you were watching her, and she meant to give you the slip. You say you went over to the bathroom to wash. Well, as soon as you'd gone she unlocked her door, locked it again on the outside in case you tried the handle, took her shoes in her hand, and went off along the passage and down the stairs in her stocking feet. That's how she picked up the powder. Castell found the back door unlocked this morning, so that's how she got out of the house. Then all she'd got to do was walk up the hill to the top of the cliff and throw herself over. And to cap it all, there's the missing key in her pocket. It's

214

as plain as a pikestaff.'

Miss Silver's expression remained mildly obstinate. Before she had time to speak the door opened and the Chief Constable came into the room.

Chapter 36

HALF an hour later Randal March sat looking across the table with something very like exasperation dominating his thought. He now possessed all the information with which a zealous and efficient subordinate could supply him. The medical evidence was not to hand, but as Crisp had put it, 'When a woman has broken her neck you can't get from it. And if she hadn't done it herself, it looks as if the law would have had to do it for her. A clear case of murder and suicide – and how anyone can make out anything else, well, it passes me.'

March was inclined to agree with him. But there sat Miss Maud Silver with that mild air of deferring to authority which, as he very well knew, could mask a quite incalculable degree of obstinacy. He had sent the estimable Crisp to take statements from other members of the party, and was now alone in the office with Frank Abbott propping the mantel-shelf and Miss Silver who sat with her hands folded in her lap upon little Josephine's completed dress. On his first entrance she had risen to go, but he had detained her. Crisp undeterred by her presence, had expressed himself quite vigorously on the subject of amateur detectives and their theories, to all of which Miss Silver had listened with un-ruffled calm. She had not, as a matter of fact, advanced any theories of her own. She had actually hardly opened her lips, but she undoubtedly conveyed an impression of uncom-promising disbelief in the theory advanced by Inspector Crisp. She sat there with folded hands and waited in very much the same way in which she had been used to wait when she was governess to the March family and Randal did not know his lesson. He was Chief Constable of the county now, and she was a little elderly person with no status at all, but the atmosphere of that schoolroom and its moral values persisted.

Randal March's exasperation proceeded from the fact that he found himself influenced by all this. Whatever his reason said, he could never quite rid himself of the old feeling of respect with which Miss Silver had managed to imbue a singularly disrespectful little boy of eight. There were reinforcements in the shape of all those subsequent times when Miss Silver had taken her own line in the face of other people's theories and earned a good deal of credit, not for herself but for the police.

Frank Abbott, watching the two of them, was being a good deal diverted. His affection and admiration for his Miss Silver did not at all stand in the way of his considering her entertainment value to be high. He was perfectly well aware of what she was waiting for, and could spare a rather sardonic sympathy for Randal March. With all the evidence on one side and Maudie on the other, he was certainly in for a bad time.

It was really only a minute or two before March said, 'You know, Miss Silver, Crisp is perfectly right – no jury in the world is going to hesitate about its verdict.'

Miss Silver looked at him mildly.

'I have not said anything, Randal.'

He gave a half-angry laugh.

'Not in words perhaps, but the amount of solid disapproval with which you have been filling the room – '

'My dear Randal!'

He laughed again.

'Are you going to tell me you don't disagree, disapprove, and thoroughly dissociate yourself from Crisp and all his works?'

She gave her prim little cough.

'No, I shall not say that.'

'Then what have you got to say? I would rather hear it, you know. There's the evidence – part of it resting on your own statement. You saw the woman with the murdered man's blood on her hands, and you heard her say that she didn't care if anything happened to her or not, and that if anyone offered her a glass of poison she'd be glad of it. On the top of that, don't you believe she murdered Luke White and then committed suicide?'

'No, Randal.'

'On what grounds? You must have reasons for refusing to accept all this evidence we've just been through. Do you expect me to disregard it?'

'No, Randal.'

'Then what do you expect me to do?'

She coughed reprovingly.

'It is not a case of expecting. It would, I think, be advisable – '

'Yes?'

'There are points upon which further evidence should be obtained.'

'Are you going to tell me what they are?'

She inclined her head.

'I have mentioned them before. I should like, if I may, to urge them very strongly now. There should be more evidence as to where the first murder was committed. I have repeatedly asserted my belief that it did not take place in the hall, where the body was found. I suggested yesterday that there should be a careful examination of the carpet in this room. I think it extremely probable that the crime was committed here, in which case traces of blood may still be found. That is my first point.'

Randal March looked at her gravely.

'Well, I have no objection. What else?'

Miss Silver met his look with one to the full as grave.

'Thank you, Randal. The second point concerns the identification of the body.'

Frank Abbott's colourless eyebrows rose perceptibly. There was a brief but startled pause before March said, 'Luke White's body was seen by everyone in the house. Castell has made the formal identification. Do you suggest that there is any doubt about the matter?'

'Yes, Randal, I do.'

'My dear Miss Silver!'

She said, 'You say that the body was seen by everyone. There were three, or at the most four, people present to whom Luke White was not a complete stranger. They were Castell, Eily, Florence Duke, and perhaps Mr. Jacob Taverner. As to the others – and I include myself – what they saw was a dead man lying face downwards dressed as they had all the previous evening seen Luke White dressed, in dark trousers and a grey linen coat. Let us now take the three or four people who really knew Luke White. Mr. Jacob Taverner did not go near the body. Eily was overcome with horror and half fainting. Castell identifies the dead man as Luke White, and it is his identification that is in question. Florence Duke actually handled the body. We have no means of knowing whether her subsequent condition of shock was due to the fact that she accepted it as that of her husband, or – ' She paused.

March said, 'Or what?'

'Or that she did not.'

'You suggest?'

'That the body was not that of Luke White. If she had realised this she would, I think, have known that her husband must be a party to the murder. She knew him to be a most unscrupulous man. She may have known more than that, but she had once cared for him very much, and she had suddenly to decide whether she would shield him or give him away. I think all her behaviour is accounted for if you accept the theory that she made up her mind to shield him.'

'But, my dear Miss Silver – ' March broke off. 'Are you suggesting that the murdered man was – '

'Albert Miller.'

Frank Abbott straightened up. March leaned forward.

'Albert Miller!'

'I think it possible.'

'But – was there any likeness?'

'Oh, yes, a very strong one. They were both grandsons of the disreputable Luke, old Jeremiah Taverner's fourth son. Luke White was the elder, and much the stronger character, but the resemblance was very decided. I was struck by it as soon as I saw them.'

'You did see them together?'

'They were practically side by side whilst we were having coffee in the lounge on Saturday night. Even the difference in dress and the fact that one man was drunk and the other sober could not disguise the likeness. I do not mean that I would have mistaken one for the other in life, because there was a very obvious divergence of character, but if I had been shown the dead body of one dressed in the clothes of the other, I cannot say whether I would have suspected anything.'

'Then what makes you suspect anything now?'

Miss Silver gazed at him thoughtfully.

'The fact that Albert Miller should have such a perfect alibi and then disappear completely. It struck me as so extremely odd that I was unable to believe it had no bearing upon the murder. Yesterday evening I saw Albert Miller's landlady and discovered the following facts. There was no light in the passage or on the stairs on Saturday night when her lodger came in, and both were still dark when he left in the morning. Mr. Wilton spoke to him at the bedroom door, but he was dazzled by the beam of a small torch which, as Mrs. Wilton put it, "that Albert kept flickering across his face." Mr. Wilton identified the man with the torch as Albert Miller because they were expecting Albert Miller and he was singing a song which they associated with Albert. I myself and everyone in the hotel had heard Albert singing snatches of this song, the well known Irish air "Eileen alannah".'

March said, 'Albert Miller may not have been seen by the Wiltons, but he was seen at Ledlington station.'

Miss Silver asked quietly, 'In what circumstances? From what Inspector Crisp said, the man supposed to be Albert Miller arrived at Ledlington station soon after seven o'clock, when it would still be dark. He was wearing Albert Miller's clothes, and had all the appearance of a person who has been drinking heavily and is not yet sober. He did not go on duty, but shouted out that he had had enough of his job and of Ledlington, and that he was not coming back. If this man was really Albert Miller, why did he go near the station at all? Why did he not simply leave the Wiltons' house and disappear? But if he was Luke White, his appearance at the

219

station was part of the plan to make it quite clear that Albert Miller had disappeared of his own free will.'

Frank Abbott said, 'If there was a plan to murder Albert Miller and cover it up in the way you suggest, Luke White would have to disappear – permanently. Well, there might be quite good reasons for that. Things were getting a bit hot for him at this end. He may have thought he'd be safer in France. I've always thought that if there was any funny business going on here, any backstairs traffic in dope and diamonds, that Luke would be in it up to his eyes.'

March turned in his chair.

'If the dead man was Luke, Albert Miller couldn't have killed him. But the alibi works both ways. If it was Albert who was murdered, you can't pin it on Luke. Whichever of them it was who was keeping Mrs. Wilton awake by tossing and turning overhead whilst she heard the church clock strike twelve, and one, and two, he wasn't murdering the other somewhere between half past twelve and half past one at the Catherine-Wheel.' He turned back to Miss Silver. 'This is a very interesting theory, you know, but where is the motive? If the murdered man was Luke White, there is a very strong jealousy motive both for John Higgins and for Florence Duke, and the bare possibility of a blow struck in self-defence by the girl Eily. But what motive would there be for the murder of Albert Miller?'

'A very strong one, Randal. I cannot offer any proof of it, but I suspect that he was engaged in a highly dangerous attempt at blackmail. He threw out hints to Mrs. Wilton that he might soon be rich. I think he knew too much, and was attempting to use his knowledge.'

'What could he have known?'

'My dear Randal, from first to last in this case there has cropped up the question of a secret passage or a secret room. That it was not the passage between the cellars and the shore is proved by the fact that Mr. Jacob Taverner not only knew all about this passage but was quite willing to display it to his guests and to the police, whereas he continually plied the Taverner cousins with carefully contrived questions as to what they might have heard from the grandparents with whom each had been rather closely associated.

These questions strongly suggest a second passage, or perhaps merely a secret chamber, the existence of which was known to Mr. Jacob Taverner, but of whose whereabouts he was ignorant. I have thought all along that this second passage might prove to be of immense importance in the case. I think most of the Taverner cousins know something about it. Florence Duke may have passed her knowledge on to her husband, and so may Annie Castell. If these two men were making money out of their knowledge, and Albert Miller was using what he knew to blackmail them, you have a motive which would account for the events of the last few days.'

There was a hint of humour in March's eyes, but he said quite gravely, 'Since you know everything, are you going to tell us who killed Al Miller?'

Miss Silver shook her head.

'I am afraid I do not know.'

Frank Abbott allowed himself a short laugh.

'Not Castell?'

'Possibly. But there was more than one person concerned. I am quite sure that the murder was not committed where the body was found. Albert Miller was more than half drunk when I saw him in the lounge. He became very noisy, and was hustled through into this room by Luke White and Castell. I do not think he ever left it alive. It would have been easy to complete the process of making him drunk, to give him a wound on the back of the hand corresponding to that which Luke White had received when he tried to kiss Eily and she picked up Jane Heron's scissors to defend herself, and then, when the right time had arrived, to inflict the fatal stab and convey the body to the hall. As I have said before, I think that two people must have been involved in this. There is no one in the house of sufficiently powerful physique to make sure of moving a dead body from this room to the hall without noise.'

Randal March said, 'I agree to that. But all the rest is, if you will let me say so – well, pure hypothesis.'

Miss Silver smiled.

'I only ask that you should put it to the test. I suggest that Mrs. Wilton should be approached. She was a friend of Mrs. Miller's, and must therefore have known Albert from a child. She might be aware of some distinguishing mark. Then, as to the scene of the murder, the carpet may provide you with evidence.'

She put little Josephine's dress into her workbag and rose to her feet.

'I feel sure that I can leave the matter in your hands. But with regard to Florence Duke there is a point which deserves your attention. If she committed suicide shortly after I had seen her lock herself in her room, can you tell me why she did not just walk to the edge of the cliff behind the house and throw herself over? The tide was high and she would have fallen into the water. Do you think it possible that any woman would climb in the dark to the top of the cliff and throw herself down upon rocks?'

'She might not have known –'

'My dear Randal, we had all been out walking along those cliffs. There had been talk about the tides. It had been mentioned that those rocks were only covered by a spring tide. I think it an incredible place for a suicide. But if it was murder, there would be a strong reason for choosing it. It would be necessary that Florence Duke's body should be found, because it was intended that she should appear to have killed herself out of remorse for the murder of her husband. There must be immediate proof that she was dead. She could not just disappear. There are very strong currents here, I believe, and a body might be carried out to sea and never washed up.'

Frank Abbott said in his most casual voice, 'Well, about the only thing you haven't told us is how Florence was spirited out of her locked room. Crisp made a point there, you know. She walked along the passage in her stocking feet, as he said, probably carrying her shoes. Why?'

Miss Silver looked at him gravely and compassionately.

'I think, Frank, that the poor woman went to meet her husband, and that this time Luke White will have no alibi.'

Chapter 37

THE Thorpe Enningtons departed to town for the day, Freddy to his business meeting, Lady Marian to a fitting, a hairdresser, a lunch engagement. It was understood that they would return in the evening 'Though I am sure I don't know what we can do, and as far as the inquests go, I'm thankful to say we didn't see anything. But of course we shouldn't like to feel we were running away, should we, Freddy my sweet?' Freddy having made some mournfully inarticulate response, they got into their expensive car and slid away in the direction of London with Marian Thorpe-Ennington at the wheel.

Geoffrey Taverner had gone off in his small cheap car an hour earlier. As he explained to Inspector Crisp, he could do a day's business and be back by seven o'clock – 'Quite a number of contacts to make in the Lenton direction, so I shan't be far away.' Jacob Taverner gave the Thorpe-Enningtons half an hour's start, after which he also took the London road. Miss Silver wondered if he was really fit to drive.

Randal March and Inspector Crisp departed somewhat later, leaving Inspector Abbott and a young man called Willis, who was a plain-clothes detective, shut up in Castell's office.

Miss Silver, after a few words with Jane Heron, descended to the lounge, where she cast on the requisite number of stitches for a pair of bright blue knickers to match little Josephine's woolly frock. She had chosen a chair quite close to where Mildred Taverner sat nervously turning the pages of an old *Picture Post*. After looking at her sideways once or twice Miss Taverner edged her chair a little nearer.

'Oh, Miss Silver, when do you think we shall get away?'

She got a kind reassuring smile.

'I am afraid it is impossible to say.'

Mildred's hand went up to her blue Venetian beads.

'It's all so dreadful, isn't it? Having to pass that poor thing's door every time I go up to my room. Do you believe in haunted houses and ghosts – ' She broke off with a little gasp.

Miss Silver knitted placidly.

'What makes you ask that, Miss Taverner?'

Mildred Taverner shuddered.

'I was thinking how dreadful it would be if the door were to swing open when I was going past – her door, I mean – and *something* – were to come out.'

Miss Silver counted briskly.

'Sixteen – eighteeen – twenty – twenty-four – yes, I think that will be about right. No, I think you should put aside these unhealthy fancies. There is nothing in the least supernatural about what has been happening in this house. Now I wonder whether you can tell me whether Mr. and Mrs. Castell are occupying the bedroom which used to belong to your great-grandfather old Jeremiah Taverner and his wife. Family tradition is an interesting thing, and it occurred to me – '

'Oh, yes – ' Mildred Taverner was quite brightly interested – 'it's the same room. The landlord has always slept there. The windows look out in front, and when the coaches came down from London the postillions used to blow their horns at the top of the hill so that he could hear them and be ready to come down. My grandfather said he could remember hearing the horns, though of course his window looked the other way. He and his brother Jeremiah, and Mark, and Luke, they all slept in the corner room. Eily has it now. It looks out at the back, and you can see the sea from the window, but he said he could hear the horns quite late at night. Of course travelling by coach was really over, because the railway had been built, but they had these coach parties just the same. People used to come from quite a long way off – and gentlemen riding, and in their dog-carts and all. I think, from what he said, there was a lot of gambling and high play. You know, one doesn't like to say it, but I can't help feeling that it wasn't really a very respectable house. My grandfather didn't say so of course. He left home when he was quite young, and he had the highest

– oh, the very highest character himself. But I think a lot of people in those old times weren't exactly what we would call respectable now, and I can't help thinking that Jacob Taverner is making a mistake in trying to rake things up. Geoffrey doesn't like it, and – and I don't either.' She gazed at Miss Silver from under damp pink eyelids. 'I mean, we're all respectable now, so why not leave it alone?'

Miss Silver opined that there were incidents in the histories of most families which might very well be forgotten. Mildred Taverner said, 'Oh *yes*!'

It was shortly after this that Frank Abbott walked through the lounge. Since he could have left the office without doing so, Miss Silver's eyes followed him. As he went out into the hall he turned and gave her a brief nod before he closed the door. Mildred Taverner was well away with the story of a haunted house in Hampstead. Having received Frank's nod, Miss Silver gave this narrative all the attention she could spare.

At a quarter to one John Higgins arrived. The news of Florence Duke's death had reached him, and he announced that he had come to take Eily away. He could not, of course, have chosen a more tactless moment. Lunch was imminent, Annie Castell was up to her eyes, and Eily and Jane were laying the table.

John said, 'I'm sorry, Aunt Annie,' and walked through the kitchen, passing Castell as if he wasn't there. He pushed the baize door and went through, letting it fall back in the angry landlord's face.

Eily looked up as he came round the varnished screen at the dining-room door. He didn't see Jane Heron – he didn't see anyone but Eily. He had just one thing to say, and he said it.

'I've come to fetch you away.'

Eily flared up. It is wonderful what a little anger will do for a failing courage. Ever since the horrid moment when they had all stood looking into an empty room and seen that Florence Duke wasn't there Eily had had a little clear picture in her mind. It was the picture of herself running down the road to Cliff – running like the wind, beating in John Higgins's door, and throwing herself into his open arms. This

picture was at once a source of alarm and of solace. A source
of alarm because it admitted to some dreadful danger from
which she could only save herself by headlong flight. A solace
because it pointed the way to safety. And now here was John
in the middle of their all being busy over lunch, talking to
her as short and sharp as if she was something he could
order about. Well, what would any girl feel like? Fear
ceased to operate, because of course, with John here, there
wasn't anything to be afraid about. Anger took its place.
Her dark blue eyes gave him a spirited denial. She said, 'I
won't go?'

'Eily!'

Eily stamped her foot.

'I'm in the middle of getting lunch!'

'I'll wait for you.'

'Now look here, John –'

'Eily –'

The foot stamped again.

'I'm not leaving Aunt Annie, and that's flat!'

And with that Castell came round the screen, magnificent
in dignity and control – no gesticulation, no spluttering
rage. He was the respectable host, under his own respectable
roof. It had been hard of achievement, but he had achieved
it. Self-satisfaction exuded from every pore. He took a
striking pose and pointed to the door.

'You will leave. At once. We do not desire your presence.
We do not invite it. I will not serve you. If you were not the
nephew of my wife Annie, I would have more to say. I
control myself. I do not say it. I say only this – "Go – and
immediately!" '

John didn't even look at him. He went up to Eily and
took her hand.

'Come away with me, my dear. This is a bad house.
Come away out of it.'

She jerked her hand from his. She wanted to throw herself
into his arms, but a host of little things held her back. Uncle
– she'd always been afraid of him, she didn't quite know
why – lunch to serve – Aunt Annie and the washing up –
She jerked her hand away.

'Oh, for goodness sake, John, get along out of here and let

226

me get on with my work!'

He stood for a moment, and then turned and went out without another word. The minute he was gone Eily had that picture in her mind again, small and bright like something seen through a peephole – the road to Cliff and herself running down it. But this time John was there too, walking away ahead of her and never turning back, and run as she would she couldn't catch up with him. She came back with a start to Castell's hand on her shoulder.

'Come, come, come – get on with your work! You did that very well, but there's no time to stand here dreaming.'

Jane Heron ran after John Higgins and came up with him by the baize door. Her breath hurried and her colour came and went, not because she had run that little way, but because she had a sense of urgency and she couldn't find the right words. She caught at his sleeve, and he turned and looked at her with grave blue eyes. Under the gravity there was distress. Jane knew right away that it was not for himself, but for Eily. She said, 'Don't worry about her – I'm with her nearly all the time. Miss Silver asked me –'

'Why?'

'She said Eily had had a shock and had better not be left by herself. She slept with me last night. She told Miss Silver she wouldn't, but she did after all, and I'll get her to do it again.'

He said, 'There's a lot of badness in this house. It isn't fit for her.'

Jane nodded.

'I'll talk to her. She just doesn't want to be rushed, and she's fond of Cousin Annie. Don't worry. I'll see she's all right.'

Chapter 38

Miss Silver spent the greater part of the afternoon in the lounge teaching Mildred Taverner to knit. In reply to the complaint that she knew it was very stupid but she never could help dropping her stitches Miss Silver instructed her firmly that if the needles were held in the continental manner, it was practically impossible for this to happen. She was not a quick learner, and the effort involved so engaged her attention that she had none to spare for what her preceptress had previously described as unhealthy fancies, and was able to partake of her tea with a very good appetite.

The evening dusk closed down. After some windy days there was a light mist and a mild, still air. The tide was coming up and could be heard lapping against the cove behind the hotel. There was sand there between the rocks – quite a wide half-moon of it when the sea was out. In summer the bathing would be pleasant and safe.

Jeremy and Jane went out after tea and walked up and down watching the tide come in and the last light fade. Eily would be washing up the tea-things in the pantry with Annie Castell. It couldn't be selfish to snatch half an hour for themselves.

It must have been just short of half past five when Miss Silver pushed the baize door and went along a rather dark passage to the kitchen. It was in her mind that she would like to talk to Annie Castell. Not about anything in particular, but just to talk to her and see what kind of a woman she was. There were a good many possibilities about Annie Castell. Even quite a short conversation might eliminate some of them. But when she came to the bright streak which showed the position of the kitchen door she knew that she would not be able to have her conversation with Annie. Fogarty Castell was there, and even the thick old door could not disguise the fact that he was angry. He was, in fact, shouting at the top of his voice.

Miss Silver took hold of the door-knob and turned it gently until the catch released itself, after which she drew in her hand until the door stood a finger's breadth from the jamb. As a gentlewoman, eavesdropping was naturally repugnant, but as a detective she was prepared to engage in it without flinching. She now heard Castell shout, 'Leave me? You would leave me?'

A string of words in the French language followed.

Miss Silver had never heard any of them before, and she had no difficulty in concluding that in this case ignorance was scarcely to be deplored. She hoped that Annie Castell did not understand them either. But Castell's voice, expression, and manner required no translating. An angry man who is swearing at his wife sounds very much the same in any language. Miss Silver could not see into the kitchen, but she could hear well enough. She could hear Annie Castell take a long breath and steady it when Castell stopped swearing, and she heard her say, 'I can't stand anything more.'

Castell stamped his feet, first one and then the other.

'You will stand what I tell you to stand, and you will do what I tell you to do! Are you not my wife?'

She said, 'Not any more. I'll cook the dinner tonight, and I'll cook breakfast tomorrow, and then I'll take Eily and go.'

'Go? Where will you go?'

'I can get a place – any day – at once.'

Castell roared at her suddenly – a French word culled from the Marseilles slums where he had played as a child. And then, like someone checked in a spring, his voice dropped to a horrid whisper.

'The door – who opened the door?'

Miss Silver did not wait for anyone to answer that question. She was light on her feet, and she could move very quickly indeed when she wanted to. She moved so quickly now that by the time Fogarty Castell looked out in the passage the faint lamplight showed it empty. She had not risked trying to reach the baize door, but had taken the cross passage and gone quickly through the office to the lounge. When presently the door opened and Castell looked in, she was making good progress with little Josephine's knickers and encouraging Mildred Taverner in what, it must be confessed, was a sadly bungling effort.

At six o'clock Frank Abbott returned and once more walked through the lounge, but this time in a reverse direction. He left the door of Castell's office ajar, and Miss Silver immediately joined him there. As she came in and shut the door behind her, he was turning up the old-fashioned wall lamp. The light struck upon his face and showed him with rather more than the usual dash of sarcasm in his expression. At her sober, 'Well, Frank, you have something to tell me?' he smiled provokingly.

'Have I? I wonder. You see, you always know the answers already.'

'My dear Frank!'

He laughed again.

'Oh, you were quite right of course! You always are!'

She shook her head in a reproving manner.

'Exaggeration is a bad fault in a detective. An attempt to improve upon facts may be fatal.'

As she spoke she seated herself and resumed her knitting. With a brief murmur of 'Facts!' Frank took a chair and stretched out his long legs.

'Mrs. Wilton delivered the goods,' he said. 'She had bathed Albert when a baby and nursed him with a broken collarbone. She deposes to a large mole on the left shoulder-blade, and has identified the corpse in the mortuary as that of Albert Miller. That being that, the police are naturally anxious to interview Luke White. Alibi or no alibi, the changeover must have been with his consent. Of course he may have been bumped off since.'

Miss Silver said, 'I do not think so.' After a slight pause she continued. 'You will, perhaps, agree that he would have a strong motive for preventing Florence Duke from seeing the body which Castell had identified.'

Frank said, 'He and Castell would both have a motive.'

'Yes. That was why I made such a particular point of her not being told until just before the inquest that she would have to identify the body. As soon as Inspector Crisp rang her up I knew that she would be in danger, and I did my best to persuade her to place herself under your protection at Cliff House. Captain Taverner would have driven her there, but she would not hear of it. There is no doubt that someone was listening to that call on the extension. Did it never strike you as peculiar that the extension should have been in the butler's pantry, and not in this room which was in use as an office? There could be but one reason for so odd an arrangement, and that was the greater privacy of the pantry. No one could approach it without being seen by Annie Castell. But this room, with its two doors, one opening upon a passage and the other on the lounge – '

Frank nodded.

'Yes, I agree. Well, that's that – so much for the identity question. You were right about the other thing too. Willis and I got to work on the carpet in here, and there's been blood spilt on it. Wiped off the surface, but some of it had soaked through. It wasn't quite dry. Miller was killed in this room, just as you said.'

'Yes, I was sure of it.'

'Crisp is a bit shaken, but still clinging to the idea that Florence Duke committed suicide.'

Miss Silver shook her head.

'Oh, no, she didn't do that. When it was known that she would be asked to identify the body it became too dangerous to let her live. I do not think that the substitution had ever taken her in. I think she knew very well that the body in the hall was not that of Luke White. I think she lifted it sufficiently to see the face – she was a strongly built woman – and that she was not deceived. She must, therefore, have known that her husband was implicated in the murder, and she had to decide at once what she should do. She decided to screen him. A very disastrous decision, but it is hard to blame a wife for shielding her husband. But the people who had murdered Albert Miller would not know whether she had recognised him or not. They would not dare to take the risk of her being confronted with the body and asked to make a formal identification. We have no means of knowing whether it was then and there decided to remove her in such a manner as to make it appear that she had committed suicide, or whether there was an intermediate stage during which they or Luke White entered into negotiations with her. As I said, we shall probably never know, but I incline to the belief that she received some kind of communication. It may have been something directly from her husband, or something purporting to furnish her with information about him. Whatever it was, it decided her to leave her room and meet her murderer.'

Frank nodded.

'I expect you're right. But we shan't be able to prove anything – unless somebody turns King's evidence.'

It was at this moment that there was the sound of running feet. They came from the direction of the lounge. The communicating door was thrown open and Jane Heron appeared, her eyes startled, her colour coming and going. She checked on the threshold with an 'Oh, Miss Silver!' and then came out with, 'I can't find Eily!'

Chapter 39

MISS SILVER knew then what she had been afraid of. She rose to her feet and put her knitting down upon the table.

Jeremy had come up behind Jane. Mildred Taverner was straying towards them across the lounge. There was a horrid similarity to the scene before the door of Florence Duke's room that very morning. Mildred said in a trembling whisper, 'Things always happen in threes – first Luke, and then Florence, and now Eily. Oh, why did I come to this horrible house!'

Miss Silver said, 'Hush!' And then, to Jane. 'Was she not with you?'

'We went out just for a little – really only up and down on the cliff. Eily said she was going to help Cousin Annie. When we came in she wasn't there. She isn't anywhere – we've been all over the house.'

'You do not think that she has gone to meet John Higgins?'

'No – he's just been up asking for her. He's outside now. He didn't want to come in. That is why I was looking for Eily.'

Miss Silver acted with decision.

'Please go and fetch him. Miss Taverner, will you go back to the lounge.'

She shut the door upon herself and Frank Abbott.

'Frank, this may be serious. Inspector Crisp should be here, and enough men to take charge. There are dangerous criminals involved. If Eily has really disappeared, it means that one of them has played his own hand and is risking the safety of the others. I don't need to tell you just how dangerous that may be.'

'Crisp should have been here by now. He may be here at any minute.'

She said in as grave a voice as he had ever heard her use.

'We have no minutes to spare. That man Luke White is not sane about Eily. If, as I have suspected, he has the secret of the other passage and is somewhere in the house – '

'You think he has carried her off? But the risk – '

'My dear Frank, when did the thought of risk deter a man with a crazy passion?'

The door on to the passage was thrown open and John Higgins came in, Jane and Jeremy a little way behind. It was clear that he had run and outstripped them.

'Where's Eily?' he said.

Miss Silver went up to him and put her hand on his arm.

'We will find her, Mr. Higgins, but everyone must help.'

'Help?' He gave a sob. 'What do you mean?'

She said, 'I will tell you,' and at the same moment Frank Abbott touched her.

'There's Crisp. What do you want – the Castells rounded up?'

'Everyone rounded up. I think one of the Mr. Taverners has returned. I thought someone came in while we were talking. I want everyone together, and at once. There must be no delay. It is extremely urgent.'

He said, 'All right – everyone in the lounge,' and went out that way.

Miss Silver spoke to the three who remained.

'Mr. Higgins – Captain Taverner – Miss Heron – if any one of you know anything at all about this house, you must disclose it now. Mr. Jacob Taverner showed you a passage between the cellars and the shore. I think that it was shown to you as a blind. It may have been shown to him in the same way – I do not know. But I am sure that there is another passage, or at the very least a secret room, perhaps communicating with that passage to the shore. If Eily has disappeared she will be in this room, and the entrance must be found without delay. It was Albert Miller who was murdered on Saturday night. Luke White is alive. This is the first time since Saturday that the moon and the tide would be favourable to his being put across the Channel. Eily's disappearance looks as if the attempt was to be made tonight and he was making a crazy bid to take her with him. Now if one of you knows any single thing that will help us to discover the entrance to this second passage or room, you will see that you must not hold it back.'

A few minutes later she was saying this all over again to a larger audience. There were present Inspector Crisp, the plain-clothes detective Willis, a constable at either door of the lounge, Castell, and, of the Taverner connection, Annie Castell, Jane, Jeremy, Mildred Taverner, and her brother Geoffrey looking as neat as she was dishevelled and a good deal concerned.

'Most unfortunate – there must be some mistake. Surely the girl may have gone out to meet a friend – I really can't imagine – '

Most of these sentences were addressed to Jane, who merely received them with a shake of the head, upon which they petered out and led to nothing.

Inspector Crisp rapped upon the table at which he had seated himself and said, 'Eily Fogarty has disappeared. She is not in the hotel. Her outdoor coat and shoes are not missing, and it seems improbable that she would have gone out without them. Miss Silver has something which she wishes to say. I don't take any responsibility for it, but I am willing to give her the opportunity of saying it. Miss Silver – '

Miss Silver rose to her feet and looked about her. Mildred Taverner was sniffing into a damp handkerchief. Her brother Geoffrey had a bewildered air. Annie Castell sat large and shapeless upon a chair which disappeared from view beneath her bulk. Her face was pale and without any expression, the eyelids faintly rimmed with pink. Her hands lay one on either knee. Every now and then the thumbs twitched. Castell, beside her, bobbed up like a jack-in-the-box.

'What a lot of nonsense is this? Eily is not in the house? Eily is out? Does a young girl never go out? Am I a slave-driver that I always keep her in? Does she not have a boy friend – a lover? Does John Higgins think he is the only one she meets? If he does, I tell him he can have another think coming!' He gave an angry laugh. 'That she even runs away, how do I know? There has been a murder – there has been a suicide – she has a crisis of the nerves – and she goes off – with this one, that one – how do I know?'

Crisp said sharply, 'Sit down and hold your tongue, Castell!'

Miss Silver said what she had already said to John Higgins and to Jeremy and Jane.

When she had finished there was a silence which was broken by Jeremy.

'You are right about there being another passage. My grandfather told me enough to make me feel sure of that And I think the entrance is on the bedroom floor, because a wounded man was brought up through it and died in the room which Eily has now.'

Frank Abbott said, 'How do you know that?'

'It was a corner room at the back. The younger children slept there to be near their parents, but on that occasion they had been turned out. My grandfather told me what his mother had told him. The whole thing was very hush-hush – I don't think they could have risked carrying that wounded man through the house. That's all I can tell you.'

Castell snapped his fingers.

'What you call an old wives' tale!'

235

Miss Silver said reprovingly, 'It agrees with what Miss Taverner's grandfather told her about being frightened at seeing a light coming out of a hole in the wall when he was a little boy. He was one of the children who slept in what is now Eily's room. But it is clear that he had left the room before he saw this light. It is impossible to believe that he went down to the cellar.'

John Higgins said heavily, 'I don't know where it is, but there is a room. My grandmother told my father, and he told me. I've never spoken of it till now. I don't know where it is.'

Miss Silver said, 'Miss Taverner?'

Mildred sobbed and sniffed.

'Oh, I don't know anything – I don't really. I only thought – he wouldn't have gone very far – a little boy like that. It must have been somewhere near his room – he said he ran back to it.'

'Mr. Taverner?'

Geoffrey's eyebrows drew together.

'Quite frankly, I have always thought my grandfather made the whole thing up – or dreamt it. He became very childish in his last illness, and I am afraid that my sister is credulous. There certainly is a passage which we have all seen, but as to anything more – well – ' He shrugged his shoulders.

'Mrs. Castell?'

Annie Castell did not move. Miss Silver addressed her again.

'Mrs. Castell, what do you know about this secret room or passage?'

She did speak then, with the least possible movement of pale, flabby lips.

'Nothing.'

'Are you sure?'

The single word was not repeated. This time she shook her head.

Miss Silver rose to her feet.

'Then I think we must go and look for ourselves. There is certainly no time to be lost.

Chapter 40

EILY came back to consciousness. She had lost herself and all the world she knew when the door she was passing had opened slowly upon the dim passage and showed her a dead man standing there. Luke White was dead, but he stood there looking at her, and she fell from him down into fainting depths. Now she was coming back, but not to any place she knew. The ground was hard under her and she could not move. At first she did not know why. Consciousness ebbed and flowed. Then it came to her that her ankles were tied together, and her wrists, and that there was something stuffed into her mouth. It was difficult to breathe, and she couldn't call out or speak. The thing in her mouth was a handkerchief, she could feel the stuff against her tongue, and there was a bandage which covered her mouth.

She made an instinctive movement with her bound hands, and from somewhere behind her Luke White said, 'Don't do that!'

Her eyes had been shut, but she opened them now. She was in a small narrow place, and Luke White was coming into view with a candle in his hand. He set the candle on the ground, kneeled down beside her, and took both her hands in one of his. His touch was warm and strong, and at that the worst of the fear went out of Eily, because it wasn't a dead man's hand which lay on hers. As if he knew her thought, he gave her the kind of careless caress he might have given to a dog or a child, a mere flick of the fingers as he said, 'No call to look like that. I'm not a ghost, as you'll very soon find out. It was a good trick, wasn't it? And it took everybody in, just as it was meant to. They'd all seen me in my waiter's jacket, and when they saw that jacket on a dead man they didn't look past it – not close enough anyhow to see that it was Al Miller who was wearing it for a change. It was a very clever trick, and you're going to have a very clever husband.'

With one fear gone, another began to take its place. This was not a dead man. It was Luke, most dangerously alive. She pulled to get her hands away, but he held them fast.

'Now, now – what's the good of that? I'll marry you safe enough when we get over to France. Floss is dead, and it can all be quite proper and legal. They're coming for me to-night. There's no moon till two, and the tide's high at eleven. All you've got to do is to be good and quiet till then. We'll be in France before morning along with as sweet a cargo as we've ever run, and we'll be married just as soon as I can fix it.'

She moved her head in a frantic gesture of denial. Her tongue pushed against the gag and tried to make words, but nothing came except small muffled sounds without meaning or any power to reach him – or anyone.

His teeth showed white against the dark face as he smiled. 'Save the love words,' he said – 'they'll keep.' He touched her lightly on the cheek again. 'Best try and sleep – it'll be some hours yet.' And with that he went past her and out of sight, and took the candle with him.

Time went by.

Inspector Crisp led the way up the stairs, but when they came to the landing he stood aside, and it was Miss Silver who turned to the left-hand passage. To left and right were the rooms occupied by Jacob and Geoffrey Taverner. Beyond Geoffrey a large housemaid's cupboard, a bathroom, and the room occupied by the Castells. Beyond Jacob Taverner a back stair, the linen-room, a lavatory, and Eily's room.

Miss Silver turned to John Higgins.

'Mr. Higgins, you are a carpenter. If there is a concealed room here, what would you take to be the most likely place?'

'He looked at her, frowning and intent.

'Round about the chimney or the stair it would be.'

'The stair is an old one?'

'Yes, ma'am.'

'But the lavatory – that wouldn't be so old. There must have been work done here when the plumbing was put in. The passage would be older than that. They wouldn't have risked the secret by having work done too near the hidden place. It won't be that side. But I have thought the linen-room would guard such an entrance very well. It would be quite natural to keep it locked. It seems to me that the entrance may very well be somewhere between the linen-room and the back stair. It might even be that the treads of the stair were utilised.'

Castell flung up his arms.

'But this is madness! Are you going to pull my house down over my head because Eily has taken a fright and run away?'

There was a delay over the key of the linen-cupboard.

'I tell you, Eily will have it! She is in charge of the linen. She has to change the sheet, the pillow-case, the towel. Do you think she comes running every time to me? Have I nothing else to do?'

Miss Silver turned to Annie Castell.

'There will be a duplicate key. I think you have it. Will you get it? Or must I ask Mr. Higgins to force the lock?'

Annie's lips moved without sound. But before it was possible to know what she would do her husband stepped between.

'This is folly! You cannot break my doors!'

Miss Silver coughed quite gently.

'There will be no need to do so if you will give me the key, Mr. Castell.'

He flung out his hands.

'You insult me! But I have nothing to hide. If there is another key, you shall have it. You shall see that there is nothing.' He turned upon his wife with a gesture of command. 'Annie!'

She went across the passage then, into their room. After a lagging minute she came back with a key in her hand. Castell took it from her, fitted it in the lock, flung the door open with a flourish, and stood aside.

'There – you can see for yourself! There are no girls shut up, no corpses – there is only the linen of the house! On the middle shelf there is a candle – take it, light it, and look for yourselves! And when you have found nothing except my sheets and my pillow-cases, perhaps you will apologise for this insult that you make me!'

The linen-room had no window, but in every other respect it really was a small room. Shelves ran from floor to ceiling. The candlelight played upon orderly piles of linen. There was a shelf devoted to pillows, another to the old-fashioned honeycomb bedspreads which are now hardly more than a memory. There was a smell of lavender and a just perceptible trace of something else.

Miss Silver went first into the room. She found the trace quite definite. As she struck a match and lighted the candle, it was for the moment overlaid by the smell of sulphur. But when the sulphur trace was gone the other was still there – a faint, light trail of cigarette smoke. None of the party was smoking, and there had been no hint of tobacco until Miss Silver stepped across the threshold of the linen-room and met it there.

She set down the lighted candle upon one of the shelves and came back to the doorway. She was looking for John Higgins, but when she saw him she waited for a moment before speaking his name. He stood back against the passage wall behind all those who had crowded forward to look into the linen-room. His hands were clenched at his sides, his eyes were closed, and his lips moved. There was sweat on his brow. The old-fashioned phrase, 'wrestling in prayer,' came into Miss Silver's mind. After a momentary hesitation she stepped forward, the others making way for her, and went to him.

'Mr. Higgins – '

As her touch fell on his arm, his eyes opened. They had a bewildered look, as if he had been a long way off and suddenly called back.

'Mr. Higgins, I think that you can help me. Will you come?'

He came after her then into the candlelight and the smell of lavender and that something else. As soon as they were there he said, speaking low so that only she could hear, 'I'd clean forgot, but the Lord has brought it to my mind – something my grandfather said, but I didn't rightly know what he meant – not till now. It was some carpenter's work he'd done up here, working with his father when he was a lad. That's how he came to court my grandmother, Joanna

240

Taverner.' He was down on his knees as he spoke, feeling along under the bottom shelf. 'He rambled a bit when he was old, and talked about his courting days, and about the work he'd done at the Catherine-Wheel with his grandfather. "A handle made clever to look like a strut," that's what he said. And he picked himself up and said, "And I took my Bible oath I'd never tell a living soul, so you take and forget it, my lad." And it went clean out of my head till the Lord brought it back. Just give me that candle, ma'am. . . . I think I've got it. There's a strut here where there's no call for one to be.'

Miss Silver gave the candle into his hand and stepped to the door. Her eye met Frank Abbott's. She noted with approval that he and Inspector Crisp stood side by side between the rest of the party and the back stair, and that Willis had cropped up again and was on the other side of the group. Mildred Taverner was sobbing audibly. Jane had her hand on Jeremy's arm. Geoffrey Taverner was leaning forward to see what was happening inside the linen-room, his expression one of vexation and surprise. The Castells stood side by side, he for the moment silent, she with her hands at her apron, pinching the stuff into pleats and letting it go – the same action mechanically repeated over and over again. There was no expression on her face, but the pale skin glistened with sweat.

As Miss Silver turned back to the linen-room, something very strange was happening. John Higgins had set the candle down upon the floor. He was using both his hands to move something under the left-hand bottom shelf, and as he pulled on it it did move, and the whole shelf with it, pivoting round so that one end of the shelf with a double pile of pillow-cases stuck out across the door and the other end went back and disappeared into the wall. There was left a gap some three feet wide and just over two feet high.

John Higgins reached for the candle and crawled forward through the gap. Miss Silver nodded to Jeremy Taverner and stood back to let him pass.

Outside in the passage Castell gave a roar like a bull and plunged for the stairs, to come down with a crash as Frank Abbott tripped him. During the ensuing struggle Annie

Castell did not turn her head. She looked down at her apron and pleated it – four pleats and let it go, and four pleats and let it go again.

Mildred Taverner screamed when the shelf swung in. She said, 'Oh, that's what he saw! Oh, no wonder it frightened him, poor little boy – the hole in the wall and the light coming out of it! Oh –'

Geoffrey said, 'Be quiet!' He leaned forward and listened. The light was receding now. The sound of footsteps was receding, going down an unseen stair which followed the line of the one which they could see.

Castell was handcuffed. He lay cursing vociferously. Crisp left him, ran to the linen-room, and so down after the others. When Frank Abbott was about to follow him, Miss Silver shook her head.

At the sound of those feet upon the stair Eily opened her eyes again. She could see nothing except the rough plastered roof and walls of the place where she lay. And then Luke White came into view, bending to pick her up. She tried again, most horribly, to scream. The effort sent the blood against her ear-drums, deafening them. She felt that she was dropped, her head bruised against the floor. And then her hearing came back, and there were voices – Luke White's – 'Fight for her then!' and John's, cursing him. At least it sounded like a curse, and even at that moment it surprised her a good deal. She heard them clash somewhere behind her just out of sight, and the sound of a fall, and more running steps and voices, and quite a lot more cursing, only this time it wasn't John.

And then John was undoing the bandage and taking the gag out of her mouth, and her tongue was sore and bruised, and she began to cry.

Chapter 41

Miss Silver stood waiting. The footsteps had gone away out of sound. She had heard them fall heavy on the secret stair and die away. An indeterminate sound came up, quite vague and indistinguishable. And then, what seemed a long time afterwards, there were footsteps again. She stood inside the linen-room. Someone had provided another candle and set it down upon one of the upper shelves. Beneath the bottom shelf the gap yawned wide to the secret stair. Outside in the passage everyone stood and listened, except Castell sitting handcuffed against the wall drawing long sobbing breaths, and his wife who took no notice of him. Or of anyone or anything. Mildred Taverner had stopped crying. She shook and trembled, her hand at her beads, her head poked forward, listening with the rest.

Then up through the gap in the linen-room wall came the voice of John Higgins:

'Can you manage it, Eily?'

It was only Miss Silver who could be sure of the faint murmur of assent. The sound was one of the most welcome she had ever heard.

The next moment Eily was crawling out of the gap and being helped to her feet. John followed her, to say briefly, 'They've got him. They're bringing him up.'

And then he and Eily and Jane went into Eily's room and shut the door.

There came out next Inspector Crisp, and then Luke White, propelled from behind by Jeremy. Miss Silver stepped into the passage to make way for them. Crisp put a whistle to his mouth and blew. As the sound of heavy feet fell on the stairs, he turned his head to say, 'Keep him inside there till we get the handcuffs on him, Captain Taverner.' Then, to Frank Abbott, 'It's Luke White all right. Higgins and the girl identified him. He can be charged with abduction, and as an accessory to the murder of Albert Miller.'

But behind him Luke White laughed.

'I never laid a finger on Al, and you can't prove I did! Let them swing for him that did him in! Castell, you fat pig, get up on your feet and tell them I wasn't anywhere near the place!'

Castell glared at him.

'You are drunk – you are mad ! Hold your tongue! What do I know about Al Miller – what does anyone know? It is a conspiracy against me!' He went spluttering and cursing into the Marseilles patois of his youth.

Two police constables came up the back stairs. Frank Abbott looked across at Miss Silver and found her face intent. She was listening, and in a moment he heard what she was hearing. Someone was coming up the main stairway. In another moment Jacob Taverner was in view. He crossed the landing, walking slowly like a tired man. But when he came to the group in the passage beyond his room he straightened up. His voice was harsh as he said, 'What's going on?'

From just inside the linen-room Luke White tipped him an impudent nod. There was enough drink in him to give him a kind of swaggering bravado.

'What's going on? Why me, when I ought to be dead! Shakes you up a bit, doesn't it? Here today and gone tomorrow and back again before anyone wants you!'

Castell erupted suddenly into English again.

'Why hadn't you the sense to leave Eily alone? There are ten thousand girls – what does it matter which one you have?'

Jacob Taverner came into the group of people and looked from one to the other – at Castell on the floor jerking at his handcuffed wrists – at Annie Castell, at Mildred and Geoffrey Taverner – at Miss Silver, Frank Abbott, Luke White with Jeremy Taverner gripping his elbows from behind. He saw the open linen-room door, the candle burning on the shelf, the gap in the wall. He said in a curious quiet voice, 'So you've found it. That's what I came down here to look for.' Then, on a rising tone, 'Who knew about it? This man of course, and Castell. But they wouldn't give it away. Who else?' His small bright eyes went from one to the other, came to rest upon Mildred and Geoffrey. 'Was it one of you – or perhaps both? Matthew's grandchildren. He came next to my father, and he was a builder too. I always thought he'd be the most likely to know. Why didn't you tell me? I'd have seen you didn't lose by it. Why did you wait until you'd brought the police into it?'

Miss Silver coughed. She looked at Geoffrey and said, 'Yes, why, Mr. Taverner?'

The words were clear and emphatic. If they had been stones thrown in Luke White's face they could not have had a more startling effect. He gave a kind of shout in which the only word distinguishable was Geoffrey Taverner's name.

'Him – *him*!' now the words came pouring out. 'You, Mr. blank Geoffrey Taverner! Give us away, would you – call in the police on us and save your skin? But you'll not get away with it – not while I've a tongue in my head! If anyone's turning King's evidence, it's going to be me, not you, and you can put that in your pipe and smoke it! And if anyone's going to swing for Al Miller, it's going to be you, not me – do you hear? I never laid a finger on him, and no one can prove I did!'

Geoffrey Taverner stood his ground with some courage.

'The man's mad,' he said. 'I don't know what he's talking about.'

With a sudden wrench Luke White had twisted free. He came at Geoffrey with a spring and took him by the throat. The two went down together, with Mildred Taverner screaming and the police rushing in.

Pulled off and handcuffed, with Geoffrey getting up greenish pale and holding his throat, Luke White was aware of two voices coming through the buzz of talk about him. Castell was cursing him for a fool, and Mildred Taverner was weeping on a high, shrill note and saying over and over again, 'But it wasn't Geoffrey who told them – he never told them anything! You didn't, did you, Geoffrey? It was Miss Silver – Miss Silver – *Miss Silver*!'

Luke White fell to cursing too.

Chapter 42

Much later that evening Frank Abbott came in to the lounge and found Miss Silver alone there. Castell and Luke White had been removed under arrest. Geoffrey Taverner had been taken to Ledlington police station for questioning. Mildred had gone to bed with a hot-water bottle, and when last visited had been found to be sleeping. Mrs. Bridling was with Annie Castell, and John Higgins with Eily. Jacob Taverner had made a statement to the police and had retired to his room. Jeremy and Jane were no doubt somewhere together. There were two stalwart police constables on the premises. There really seemed to be no further grounds for anxiety.

Frank took a chair and stretched himself out comfortably.

'Well, I suppose you want to know all about everything?'

Miss Silver coughed.

'Undoubtedly.'

His smile had a spice of malice.

'If there's anything you don't already know.'

'My dear Frank!'

She sat there very alert and composed, knitting briskly. Little Josephine's knickers were approaching completion.

'Well, we've done our job all right. The Chief will be pleased, and I shall get some of his best Advice to Rising Police Officers on the Importance of not getting Wind in the Head."

He received a benignant smile.

'It will not do you any harm.'

He laughed.

'I suppose not. Now, for your information. The stair runs down beside the open one and comes into the shore passage not a dozen feet from the other cellar entrance. It's all very ingenious, and of course a lot older than the linen-cupboard entrance. They used a dummy chimney-flue for part of the way, and just before you go through into the shore passage there's a concealed cellar full of stuff. That's where Luke White had Eily, and that's where they stored their contraband. There's a lot of stuff that looks like heroin and other assorted drugs which have been smuggled in and not distributed. And, all ready to go over, there was as pretty a collection of jewelry as anyone could wish for. They've identified the Laleham stuff and the haul from the smash-and-grab raid in Bond Street, but there's still a lot to go through. There's no doubt this has been a main clearing-house, and I don't mind betting my boots that Geoffrey Taverner was in it up to his neck. A commercial traveller's job could be a very convenient screen.'

Miss Silver gazed at him enquiringly.

'Geoffrey Taverner *was* in it?' she said, repeating his words with some additional emphasis.

He nodded.

'You're too quick. He had cyanide on him – he was dead before we got him to the station.'

Miss Silver sighed. 'It will be a terrible shock to his sister.'

'Not so great a shock as seeing him stand his trial for murder and be hanged at the end of it. Castell swears it was Geoffrey who planned and carried out Al Miller's murder. You were right about the motive. Albert knew about the passage and was threatening to go to the police if he didn't get a handsome rake-off. Castell says Geoffrey stabbed him. Luke White says he changed clothes with Albert and impersonated him – not because he knew anything about a plot to bump him off – how could we think that he would be a party to anything like that? All he thought was Albert was going to be shipped off out of harm's way for a nice little holiday in France. And after he had made his way back here, of course he had to be in hiding and nobody told him anything – only that the police were after the passage and he'd got to skip over to France with the next run. . . . Florence Duke? Oh, yes, they'd been married and separated, but he'd never set eyes on her from the time he walked out of the inn as Al Miller. It was very stupid of her to commit suicide, because, beyond telling him a bit about the passage years ago, she'd nothing to do with any of it, and it wasn't her business. That's going to be his line of defence, and he'll get a slick

247

lawyer to put it over for him. I'm afraid there isn't an earthly chance of pinning poor Florence Duke's murder on to him, but I shall be very much surprised if a jury doesn't find that he was up to his neck in the conspiracy to murder Al Miller, every detail of which must have been most carefully thought out and planned beforehand.'

Miss Silver said, 'I have no doubt of it.'

He nodded.

'Well, as I said, Castell swears Geoffrey Taverner did the actual stabbing, and if Geoffrey were alive, no doubt he would say it was Castell. Both of them were only just across the passage from that very convenient back stair which comes down on the far side of Castell's office. When last seen alive Al Miller was being bustled into that office through the door which opens from the lounge. He was then more than half drunk. This was about ten o'clock. At a guess I should say Castell kept him there, and kept him drunk. Remember, he said he had been drinking downstairs with Luke White till round about eleven. This, of course, wasn't true, because Luke was impersonating Albert at the Wiltons' in Thread Street, but I think it's pretty well certain that Castell was down in his office plying Albert with drink. He may have slipped upstairs about eleven and pretended to go to bed, in which case Geoffrey could have gone down and kept an eye on Albert. They had to give time for everyone in the house to be asleep, and they had to give time for Luke to establish his alibi. Then, right in the middle of their arrangements, John Higgins cropped up. He had heard from Mrs. Bridling of Eily's scene with Luke, and naturally enough he came out here hot-foot to try and get her to come away. As you know, they compromised on her going to sleep with Jane Heron. But meanwhile Castell had overheard their conversation, and it gave him a bright idea.'

Miss Silver said, 'I do not think that it was Castell's idea. We know very little about Geoffrey Taverner's part in the whole affair, but I am not inclined to minimise it.'

He looked at her sharply.

'Did you suspect him at all?'

Her needles clicked.

'I was beginning to do so.'

248

'On what grounds?'

'I thought him a little too calm and unruffled on the night of the first murder – a little too – no, I cannot get a word for it. But there was something, some discrepancy between his behaviour and the impression which it made upon me. It was all very slight, and people sometimes pose when there is no criminal motive. Then today, after Florence Duke had been found dead, he showed a definite change of manner towards myself. He had at first treated me in quite an off-hand way. This morning quite suddenly he changed, became confidential on the subject of his sister, and thanked me for my kindness to her. He had noticed that she was inclined to talk to me, and he was anxious to convey certain impressions with regard to her. He wished me to believe that she was nervous, fanciful, credulous, and more than a little unbalanced. Some of these things were true, but why should he desire to impress them upon a stranger? My answer to that was that he was afraid of what she might have told me and wished to discount it without delay. I naturally found this very suggestive. To begin with, Geoffrey Taverner and his sister were the grandchildren of Jeremiah's second son Matthew. Like his elder brother he was a builder. The older members of the family would have been the most likely to know the secrets of the house. A man who was a builder by trade would be apt to notice structural peculiarities. The eldest son obviously knew something which decided him to break off his connection with the Catherine-Wheel and strike out for himself. His son Jacob has shown an extreme interest in the matter. I discovered from Mildred Taverner that she had been the constant companion of her grandfather Matthew, the second son, and that he had told her he had been frightened by seeing a hole in the wall when he was a little boy. It occurred to me that he might have told Geoffrey a good deal more than that. The secret, if there was one, would be more likely to be handed down to a boy than to a nervous girl. These were some of the things which occurred to me.'

Frank nodded. 'Yes, I expect it was something like that. Well, to get back to Saturday night. I think we may assume Castell went and told Geoffrey that John Higgins had rolled up, and that one of them, probably Geoffrey, saw a way of making use of this. They waited until twelve or so, one of them in charge of Albert, and then they dressed him in Luke's clothes, bumped him off, and laid him out at the foot of the stairs to be found by the first person who came down. Then, I think, Geoffrey went out and whistled Greenland's Icy Mountains under Jane Heron's window. If nobody heard him, well, that was that. If anyone did, it would throw suspicion on John Higgins. Castell unlatched one of the lounge windows to help the good work along. Then they both went back to bed and waited for someone to give the alarm. It was a very ingenious plan, and if it hadn't been for you it might have come off.'

Miss Silver gave a modest cough.

'What about Mr. Jacob Taverner? He made a statement, did he not? What did he say?'

Frank's smile had a tinge of malice.

'He hasn't confided in you?'

'No.'

'How surprising! All the same, I'd like to know how he strikes you.'

She laid her knitting down for a moment and rested her hands upon it.

'Because a man has made a fortune in business it does not follow that his judgment in other matters is to be relied upon. I have thought that, having retired from active management, he has perhaps found time hang heavy upon his hands, and I think that he has always had some kind of romantic fancy about the Catherine-Wheel. Most men have a point on which they are not quite grown up. I think that with Mr. Jacob Taverner this point is the Catherine-Wheel. Like the rest of the family, he knew something, and I think at the back of his mind there was the idea that some day when he had time he would go into the matter and clear it up. The lease ran out, the property came back to him, he retired from business, and there was his opportunity. By assembling as many of Jeremiah Taverner's descendants as possible he hoped to piece together what they knew. I think he also may have had the idea of observing them with a view to the ultimate disposal of his fortune.'

'Well, well, you were looking over his shoulder, I suppose. Invisible, of course, because Crisp and I were there and we didn't see you.'

She smiled indulgently.

'Did his statement say anything like that?'

'Practically word for word – especially the bit about not being quite grown up. He said his father told him there was a secret room – *room* not passage – when he was a boy, and it took hold of him. He used to plan to go and find it, and to find it full of gold and silver. Rather an ironical way for a dream to come true! When he took the place over he pressed Castell about it. He didn't get anything at first, but after he had put in his advertisement and the relations began to roll up Castell showed him the passage between the cellar and the shore. He said Annie had only just told him about it. Jacob didn't believe him, and he still believed there was a secret room, because that's what his father had called it, and nobody would have called that passage between the cellar and the shore a room. So he went on fishing to see what he could get from the relations. He thought they all knew something, and if he got them all down here he'd be able to put the bits together and get what he wanted. Well, he got more than he bargained for. He's a bit shattered. Two murders and a criminal conspiracy – it's a little like going out with a shrimping-net and finding you've caught a shark!'

Miss Silver was casting off her stitches. She said gravely, 'It has been a very trying time, but it is over.'

Chapter 43

MRS. BRIDLING was very late in getting home. On any other day she would have felt some apprehension on the score of Mr. Bridling's temper, and would certainly have had to endure a prolonged dissertation on the duty of a wife, supported by quotations from the Scriptures, but tonight she had so much news to impart that she could count upon holding the floor. Mr. Bridling's curiosity, whetted by rumour and far from being appeased by the snatches of news which had come his way, was in a really rampant condition. Wat Cooling's aunt had rushed in with the bare statement that Geoffrey Taverner had committed suicide, and then rushed out again to give an irascible husband who was working overtime his belated supper. John Higgins hadn't been near him. He was, in fact, what Mrs. Bridling called 'all worked up'.

Mrs. Bridling found herself being listened to as never before, and she fairly let herself go.

'Seems there's been goodness knows what going on. Secret passages full of gold and diamonds and all sorts. And Mr. Castell taken up for murder – and Mr. Geoffrey Taverner too if he hadn't killed himself. And that Luke White not dead at all. Too bad to be killed easy is what I say!'

'Flourishing like the green bay tree,' said Mr. Bridling with a groan.

His wife gave an emphatic nod.

'You couldn't have put it better. You're a wonderful hand with texts, Ezra, and that I must say.'

Mr. Bridling groaned again, this time with impatience. 'Go on,' he said.

Emily Bridling went on with an extremely colourful narrative.

'It's poor Annie I'm sorry for,' she said at the end of it.

'She shouldn't have married a foreigner,' said Mr. Bridling.

Mrs. Bridling brought him his cup of cocoa.

'Someone's got to marry them.'

Mr. Bridling blew on the froth.

'Let them marry foreign,' he said. 'Annie Higgins was brought up chapel and she did ought to have known better.'

'She didn't know he was going to turn out the way he did. Ever such a way with him, and she was tired of cooking for other people – wanted a home of her own.'

Mr. Bridling sipped complacently.

'And look where it's brought her,' he said. 'Lucky for

her if she isn't took up too. There's no word of that, I suppose?'

Mrs. Bridling flushed.

'No, there isn't, nor there won't be if anyone's got a grain of sense. Poor Annie didn't know a thing. Nor they wouldn't tell her – why should they? A bit simple from a child, but that good-hearted, and such a hand for pastry as never was.'

Mr. Bridling sipped again.

'Ah, well,' he said, 'she's made her bed and she must lie on it.'

Up at the Catherine-Wheel Jane and Eily were talking in bed. Jane looked into the darkness and thought of all the things that had happened since Jeremy drove her down on Saturday evening. It was only Tuesday now, and by another Saturday she wouldn't be Jane Heron any more, because she was going to marry Jeremy. She had lost her job, she had got past feeling proud, they loved each other, he wanted to take care of her. There really didn't seem to be anything to wait for.

The last thought got itself into words.

'There doesn't seem to be anything to wait for.'

Eily made a rather indeterminate sound – a kind of murmur with a question in it. Then she said, 'John is in a terrible hurry.'

Jane said what she had said once before.

'He wants to look after you. You can't stay here.'

Eily shuddered. She put out a hand, and Jane held it.

'Don't you want to marry him?'

Eily didn't answer that. She said, 'He says there's room for Aunt Annie and she'll be welcome.'

'He's good. He'll look after you, Eily.'

Eily drew a long sighing breath.

'I shall have to go to chapel twice on a Sunday.'

THE END

The Watersplash

The country village of Greenings enjoyed a
year-round tranquillity which was only
occasionally broken by the rattle of cup on saucer
at vicarage tea-parties.

But underneath this surface atmosphere lurked a
tinder-dry passion which owed its origin to events
in the recent past. When the spark was applied –
albeit accidentally – the resultant blaze swept
hungrily through the village.

It was a situation in which Miss Silver quietly
revelled, and in the hunt for a bloodthirsty killer her
well-known astuteness in such matters was taxed to
the full.

"You can't go wrong with Miss Maud Silver"
The Observer

"Miss Silver is marvellous"   *Daily Mail*

Miss Silver Comes to Stay

Maud Silver was very pleased indeed to accept an invitation to stay with Cecilia Voycey, an old school-chum she hadn't seen in years. But instead of being a quiet sojourn in her friend's village, her holiday was destined to be something entirely different.

Incredible though it may seem, someone in Melling was a vicious blackmailer; someone else an embezzler; and someone else a murderer most foul. The local C.I.D. turned with some relief to the eminent lady detective, so providentially in their midst, and it would be wrong to say that Miss Silver resented this imposition on her leisure. The truth of the matter, of course, is that she enjoyed every imposing minute of it.

"Miss Silver is rapidly becoming one of my favourite detectives"   *Time and Tide*

"Maud Silver is a remarkable old lady" *Daily Mirror*

MISS SILVER THRILLERS
by Patricia Wentworth

All these books are available at your bookshop or newsagent, or can be ordered direct from the publisher. Just tick the titles you want and fill in the form below.

. . . .

CORONET BOOKS, Cash Sales Department, Kernick Industrial Estate, Penryn, Cornwall.

Please send cheque or postal order, no currency, and allow 7p per book (6p per book on orders of five copies and over) to cover the cost of postage and packing in U.K., 7p per copy overseas.

Name . . . .

Address . . . .

. . . .